MY FATHER,
HIS SON

D1112950

Also by Reidar Jönsson

MY LIFE AS A DOG

REIDAR JÖNSSON

MY FATHER, HIS SON

Translated from the Swedish by
MARIANNE RUUTH

Arcade Publishing • New York

Copyright © 1988 by Reidar Jönsson
English translation copyright © 1991 by Reidar Jönsson

All rights reserved. No part of this book may be reproduced in
any form or by any electronic or mechanical means, including
information storage and retrieval systems, without permission
in writing from the publisher, except by a reviewer who may quote
brief passages in a review.

First Arcade Paperback Edition 1993

The characters and events in this book are fictitious. Any similarity to real persons,
living or dead, is coincidental and not intended by the author.

Library of Congress Cataloging-in-Publication Data

Jönsson, Reidar, 1944–
    [En hund begraven. English]
    My father, his son / Reidar Jönsson ; translated from the Swedish by Marianne
Ruuth. — 1st English language ed.
        p.   cm.
    Translation of: En hund begraven.
    ISBN 1-55970-117-X (hc)
    ISBN 1-55970-201-X (pb)
    I. Title.
PT9876.2.03H813   1991
839.7′374 — dc20   91-11858

Published in the United States by Arcade Publishing, Inc.,
New York, by arrangement with Little, Brown and Company, Inc.
Distributed by Little, Brown and Company

10 9 8 7 6 5 4 3 2 1

RRD VA

Printed in the United States of America

MY FATHER,
HIS SON

ALGERIA
1976

What I remember best is the end. Or perhaps I ought to say the beginning of the end. This is how my downfall began. I was on the fifth day of a long journey from Stockholm to Algiers in our family's old Volvo. Between Stockholm and Marseilles I was in good spirits though somewhat flatulent since my stomach tends to act up during long drives. I did not sleep much, just short naps in the car, and then I spent the crossing from Marseilles to Algiers doubled up in pain. I ran around, trying desperately to find a toilet that was neither overflowing nor had turds all the way up on the bulkheads. In my distress, I recalled old sailors' tales about Arabs' relations to their own excrements, but these paled to prosaic catalogs of facts compared to the total collapse of the plumbing system on this modern passenger ship.

Goaded by a violent need, I finally crouched down furtively on the stern rail.

Here sits Ingemar Rutger, I mused. My last name is actually my second middle name. Earlier, my last name was Johansson. Ingemar Wallis Rutger Johansson. A rather noxious combination.

My wife, Louise, felt that I ought to change my name when we got married, which we did in 1968.

Everybody I know talks constantly about the year 1968. I do too, since I married Louise that year and took my middle name as my family name. It worked out all right for her. Louise Rutger sounds almost like high nobility, or at least I made it sound rather grandiloquent. But Ingemar Rutger only brings to mind someone who tries to fry snow. Or someone who forlornly roams aboard a passenger ship in the middle of the Mediterranean, searching for a toilet, and instead finds himself squatting on a stern railing. But not for long. I was overpowered by two able-bodied seamen who were of the serious opinion that life was worth living in spite of everything, even if one suffered from extreme hygienic hang-ups. They explained that my behavior was rather typical of the European double standard: clinically clean, white, and gleaming sanitary porcelain and tiles, but every country studded with nuclear plants. The whole Arab world turned topsy-turvy simply because we did not buy their oil. But a little shit does not hurt anyone, if one avoids looking at it.

The two guys were truly well read sailors.

They shared some lukewarm sweet muscatel with me.

The wine filled me with memories. We played cards and I tricked them out of a bottle, fell asleep, and dreamed that I was sixteen years old and in the process of killing myself somewhere in Valencia, Barcelona, or Lisbon. Or perhaps it was Ceuta or Tangier — or a Swedish town called Gävle. The last named is a place where a person could die from pure boredom.

With a pounding hangover, and still in dire need of a toilet, I arrived in Algiers and its three-hour lines to get to the ever-distrustful passport police.

Unshaven, wrinkled, and filthy, I explained in my rusty Mediterranean language — a little Spanish, a little French, a little Italian, and then some English to fill in the gaps — the reason for my visit. In their eyes, I must have seemed more than a bit mad, since I kept having fits of uncontrollable laughter. The passport police did not pronounce French at all as it was spoken on the tape I had listened to while I was driving. Then, somewhere around Hamburg, my *French in Ten Easy Lessons* was irretrievably chewed up by the tape deck. The last thing I heard was the polite question:

"Votre petit chien va bien?"

I found that hilarious. Imagine arriving in Algiers and asking the passport police how their little dog was doing?

My wife's address not only failed to amuse them, it increased their suspicions. Such a place simply did not exist. I agreed wholeheartedly. I had diligently studied whatever maps were available in Sweden, but nowhere had I been able to locate that tongue-twisting letter combination.

All of a sudden there she was, my wife, Louise, armed with the kind of authority needed to get me admitted into the country.

*   *   *

Thus I arrived in Algiers, a city that had once been familiar but had now become alien to me. Rather similar to my wife's welcome. Her excited words were slowly dripping into my inner being, like a familiar drug, while I was being directed along the noisy streets, round and round the block adjacent to the post office.

What her flood of words added up to was that she actually regretted having invited me. Moreover, there was no place for me to stay. Not in Algiers, not by the oasis, not even at some distance from their holy camp would I be allowed to pitch the tent I had lugged along. Louise had thoroughly pondered our relationship, which was how she, as a thoroughly modern woman, referred to our marriage. The problem was that she had to finish writing her thesis. With me around, that would be impossible. I was a danger to her mental health; and I had ruined her life. For that reason, she had made an irrevocable decision: We had to separate. As soon as she returned home, as soon as she was done with her work.

In what way her research plans had any bearing on our future divorce, I could not fathom. In contrast to her stupendous research, which never brought her anywhere, our separation meant two signatures and a moving van.

I should have pointed out such logistical errors, but instead I continued to stare at the dazzling white post office as we got stuck in traffic. And Louise got stuck, too. We were a couple of horses in the same harness. She insists that I only pretend to listen to her, while I contend that she always repeats the same thing at least twenty times. What is cause and what effect I don't know. Perhaps she was right. I wasn't even pretending to listen to her litany of complaints; actually I was dreaming of having a general delivery address. General delivery forever. I climb the steps of all the world's post offices: Calcutta, Singapore — why not Casablanca? Am I European? Am I American, Scandinavian, or perhaps Russian? No matter! I am the man without a home, I pick up my letters and answer them while enjoying tall, cool drinks at sidewalk cafés. My imagined heroic self-image serves as a filter that slowly expunges the main content of my wife's verbiage. The image is of a tenderhearted, wounded man who travels on forever in order to protect his feelings. Perhaps to Madrid's general delivery. There exists a post office designed for exquisite messages, including those so delicate they have to be put into double envelopes.

I dreamed away her words at a time when crystal-clear logic would have been essential. By the ninth round I wondered why she had sent the wire, asking me to come.

"But that was then!" cried Louise.

On such occasions I have developed a habit of recalling all her other double-edged and illogical answers. Whereupon she flies into a rage and repeats what I have heard many times before.

"But now I feel differently!"

Such immutable emotion sends me into a rage. Her ever-changing moods had driven me clear across Europe. The drive down here had put my life in danger. At any moment, I may die from flatulent dyspepsia in Algiers's most congested quarter, instead of registering at a hotel like any normal human being would. It was highly unreasonable to first say yes and then no to a reunion. Just another sign of how she was driving me mad. She was the dangerous one. Not me.

We were deep into our familiar arguments when we saw that three cars had surrounded us in a highly professional manner. One car in front, one behind, and one alongside. A perfect example of the paragraph in the police instruction booklet entitled "How to Nab Extremely Dangerous Persons in Automobile."

The self-assured display of small, pale pink police I.D. cards in front of our windshield confirmed the suspicion that they were indeed police officers. I attempted to explain that they must have made an unfortunate mistake as they had hailed and stopped the wrong car, but while I was still explaining two of the men were already in our car, waving their pistols.

Louise was dragged out of the front seat and thrown into the backseat. With her usual lack of logic, she screamed that I had done it again.

There was no time to answer. An unshaven, foul-smelling cop in jeans and sweater sat down beside me, his pistol pointed directly at my diaphragm. He shouted at me to drive on, follow the car in front. The car in front sped away, while I did my best to follow it. This in spite of the fact that the cop suddenly got it into his head that we should keep our hands above our heads. He probably got nervous when Louise, totally unfazed by the event, continued to say what she really thought of me. If only my French had been a tiny bit better, I could have asked him if by any chance he was related to my wife: The two of them seemed to share an impossible sense of drama. But the muzzle of the pistol pressing against my ribs clearly signaled that the man was in no mood for jokes and that he would only be too happy to send a bullet upward into my heart.

While I drove, and at the same time tried to steer with my hands up, I strove to give him the impression that I was a calm, secure, law-abiding Swede. So I decided to ask him how things were with his little dog.

"Votre petit chien va bien?"

That apparently only served to confuse him further. He probably assumed I was speaking in code. He shoved his gun into my gut and shouted that we should keep our mouths shut.

I couldn't begin explaining to the frightened cop that my wife always lit into me when she was afraid. Nothing to worry about, provided one understands the real reason for her fury. She is merely transferring her own fear to someone else. I tried to explain all this in French, using as an example the time I totaled our first car at an intersection. As luck would have it, Louise had come pedaling by on her bicycle only minutes later. She immediately concluded that the collision was her fault, since she had tried unsuccessfully to stop us from buying the car. The crumpled heap of metal before her proved without doubt that she had been right from the start. That I had nearly killed myself in the accident was a personal insult to her: I had tried to escape. She had stood there, banging on the window of the police car, screaming that everything was my fault from beginning to end, while I, as slowly as possible in order to remain detained inside the police car, answered the questions put to me by the amazed cops.

Of course, I bore the whole responsibility. But things could have been worse. If the police had really listened to Louise, I would have gone to prison for ten years.

For eight whole years I had been pondering my wife's complex emotional life without success. How then could I explain that emotional life to an Algerian cop who wasn't even courteous enough to answer my friendly question about his little dog? Besides, it was too late since at that exact moment we were driving into a black hole, ending up in a filthy, dark garage. There we were snatched out of the car along with our luggage. The method for both was identical: a quick yank and then being spread as much as possible on the greasy floor.

Louise disappeared in one direction. To judge from the male outbursts and her own haughty and icy voice, she was simultaneously kicking them and threatening them with Swedish justice, Swedish marines, the prime minister's personal intervention, which would mean immediate cessation of all aid and all interest-free loans, plus lodging a complaint to the United Nations about crimes against human rights.

As I was being jostled and hauled in the other direction, I couldn't help but admire her prowess in the French language. What a vocabulary! That line about human rights — and to be able to say it in an upright position and with all teeth still in place! Quite different from my own mushy mumblings and awkward attempts to bang on the slammed-shut iron door.

How did we end up in this mess?

Why did the Algerian police nab us with such force?

Had I driven the wrong way on a one-way street?

In my condition, that would be entirely possible.

I inspected the single windowless cell with all the Swedish disdain I could muster, but my mood turned to absolute bliss when I discovered the freshly scrubbed hole in the floor and the drippy faucet next to it.

After almost a week of painful nonproductivity, I finally had found a peaceful, secure place. Squatting down, I reflected that things could have been worse. That kind of philosophical musing is a habit of mine from childhood, beginning in my grandmother's meticulously clean-scrubbed outhouse. Many years have passed since my brother fell through the hole and got stuck, folded in two, whereupon I consoled him with the words "Things could be worse." He could have fallen headfirst, for instance.

Was it in Grandma's outhouse that I developed my personal view of the world? I remembered those whitewashed walls with ever-changing, delicate shadow patterns created by the door slats, chicken and rabbits clucking and scratching outside, and piles of old weekly magazines inside. How carefully I read about counts and barons in castles and country homes. The short but inspiring religious parables. And the romantic short stories. What a wonderful world right there in my grandmother's outhouse. . . .

Had Louise encountered a bedouin in the desert, a sheik with flashing black eyes and a white steed? Was that the explanation for her hostility? Infatuation is the elixir of life to her. She cannot live without being in love, as she confided to me the first time we met. I thought she meant me. What a fundamental mistake! I never learned to understand her peculiar need to fall constantly in love. But, according to her, I am not especially talented emotionally. That may be partly true. Are we both victims of some unfortunate mistake?

Before falling asleep on the hard bunk, I remembered a special day. Is it possible everything began then?

It was an early morning, and I remember in detail every color, every emotional pitch, every particularity in minute exactness.

SWEDEN
1975

Next to the third white birch is a pile of leaves. The air is moist and warm after last night's rain. Far away, the whistle of the train fades into silence. Bottom-heavy in our boots, Jonas and I walk across to turn over the leaves in the compost pile.

I am not one to rave about my strong feelings for nature, but when Jonas and I turn over the leaves with their deep, iridescent colors and the thick worms slip through his seven-year-old fingers and he emits small sounds of excitement — then the very air feels as if it had broadened and extended my senses a thousand times. The present time is registered without intention, without reflection, like a long, unbroken axis of time made up of rhythmic pulse beats in complete harmony.

Jonas's adventure in the present pulls me along. My enjoyment is intense.

Finally we have collected enough worms.

We walk along the pebbly lane. I am walking ahead, carrying the thick end of the bamboo fishing rod. Jonas is following, holding on to the thin end. Patches of light fog make it seem at times as if we were walking in two worlds, the bamboo rod constituting the link between us. It feels secure following the path, which descends in a lengthy, winding green tunnel toward the small stream and the old mill. I sneak a look back at Jonas's damp, expectant face. So many enigmatic moods travel over the open surface, as varied as the patterns the breeze creates in the water of the pond.

We work our way over to the edge of the stream. The wet ferns and the autumn-dry reeds barely reach my knees but for Jonas it must be like cutting his way through a rain forest.

He does not like putting the worm on the hook.

He does not want us to kill the first perch. He feels it should just swim around on the hook so he could pull it up again and again. Jonas insists it is possible to talk sense to the fish, to tell it that it doesn't hurt, that it likes to swim around with a hook in its mouth.

I remind him that one has to eat the fish. But this is his fishing adventure, after all. I let him be. We get along.

We concentrate on the float and our moment of happiness. Suddenly, I realize that the surface of the old millpond has turned black and forbidding. An unreasonable terror works its way up my throat, like an acrid odor of death and putrefaction. Jonas doesn't understand why I hug him tightly. It's my usual old fear of losing him.

Walking home, we are both proud. Stubbornly he insists on carrying the perch strung up on a forked branch. We pass the closed gas pump, cut through toward the building, walk across the lot where the old country store used to be, pass by the warehouse, and reach the front porch of my in-laws' house. As usual, I am amazed at the turns of fate. What but fate would place me as son-in-law to the grocer for the glassworks? The same glassworks where my uncle and aunt still live and where I came as a thirteen-year-old when my mother died. . . .

---

*　　*　　*

For almost a year I have been working with the union representatives of the glass factory as a researcher and sociologist. To them I am an active, compassionate, and helping hand; simultaneously I enter into my accounts every move in the enormous game of future structural changes. The owners have hinted at massive layoffs. The unions as usual set their hopes to their government representatives. And I? I live in a sort of symbiosis with the workers. They know me, they distrust me, but they also imagine they need me. To use my professional idiom, they are all investiture units. Whenever I hear that term, I always think of the insemination of cows. But then I am a bit perverse, according to Louise. I take nothing really seriously.

My in-laws' exceptional hospitality has saved me from the murderous boredom of hotel rooms. Instead the family has commuted between the province of Småland and the city of Stockholm in agreeable chaos. Jonas enjoys spending weekends with his grandparents. And Louise gets an extra burst of energy from our child-free weekends in Stockholm. She goes to the theater, movies, exhibitions, political meetings, occult séances, nostalgic jazz clubs, modern watering holes for pseudo-cultural derelicts, and new, obscenely expensive restaurants with a speed that makes me nauseous.

I am not like Louise. Due to her evangelistic background, she melts effortlessly into the intellectual and cultural world. A world she loves and I feel contempt for, as it is produced, directed, and owned by people who have never been in the proximity of physical labor, poverty, dire need, or real suffering. The exceptions simply confirm the rule. I am such an exception. Large parts of what Louise calls my lower-class brutality and lack of sensitivity stem from the fact that I am constantly being reminded of my background. These reminders produce hate. There is no return, no transformation formula, just a godforsaken hole behind me and an endless stretch of combative situations before me. He who crosses class boundaries is homeless. That is the eternal dilemma of the child from the working class and the autodidact.

Yet my career has been straight as an arrow even if I, like many others, have hit my head against society's economic ceiling. My future alternatives are determined by the possible death of the institution's professor. When that happens, even the weakest fowl will climb up one peg. The problem is, his imminent death is highly unlikely. Axel is only forty-five.

Such is my reality, despite the fact that I, at the age of thirteen, slammed the ordinary school door shut behind me forever. Since then I have muddled through every closed door and become something as unlikely as a social expert and researcher.

A remarkable twist of fate married me to Louise. It had to be fate that suddenly one day made me encounter Louise and fall in love with her before I even knew who she was.

I still remember her twelve-year-old body, a thin and tense bow that had a disturbing effect on me. Louise had straight, short hair then — it was much longer when I saw her again. But the eyebrows were the same. Totally straight and black, abrupt dashes above the serious, ice blue, burning eyes. Even at twelve, she spoke in endless, lecturing sentences, and had the ability to form a disdainful angle with those eyebrows. She remains a total enigma to me, despite our having lived together nearly eight years.

As Jonas and I walk toward the house, the cellar door is slammed closed. It has to be my father-in-law. He has probably stayed awake all night, thinking about the clogged sewage pipes. Yesterday he was supposed to start digging but all he did was pace around the house. There he comes, spade on shoulder. He congratulates Jonas on his fine catch and walks with determined steps toward the gigantic rowan. That tree must be more than a century old. When my father-in-law without a moment's hesitation puts spade to ground hardly three yards from the rowan, I understand his mission. It is all the tree's fault. The roots have no doubt penetrated the pipes to the old triple-chamber well.

It will be an enormous excavating job. My father-in-law can't know exactly where to dig. I walk over to him and ask for a thick piece of steel wire. After a few suspicious grunts, he directs me toward the cellar. In the cellar, I cut off a yard or so of galvanized wire and walk, holding it as a divining rod, from the house toward the rowan tree. The wire swings furiously at the very spot where he has begun to dig. Something in his hard, glassy brown eyes tells me that he is impressed by my proficiency as divining-rod master. I hand him the wire. Nothing happens. I put my hand over his and the wire begins to swing immediately.

"Weak current," I explain. "Some people have a strongly developed chemical weak current, which in this case functions as a magnetic pole in relation to water veins. Water has always —"

I fall silent. All of a sudden, he looks like a teddy bear with his hard, brown eyes. For some unfathomable reason I like him and understand that he doesn't care for any technical explanations.

From now on I am a master of the divining rod. That is enough.

We agree to work together. I return to the cellar to put back the wire and see something glimmer behind the boxes with nails. A bottle. A new bottle. Half full. My father-in-law is a strict teetotaler. But obviously he has begun to drink.

No wonder.

Seven years ago, his country store burned to the ground one night. That was the night before Father's Day, and that made Louise laugh hysterically over the telephone. As a child she had been terrified by her father's stinging belt and her mother's tales of the Day of Last Judgment. With great passion she can act out how she used to awaken in the grip of unspeakable terror, her body dripping with sweat and shaking uncontrollably. Was it now, this very second, the Day of Judgment?

The first five years after the fire, I was convinced that my father-in-law would recover. He did get the insurance money. But he had lost his spirit — it had burned itself out, too, that night. Or was it the dreadful laughter Louise had shouted into his ear over the telephone? It wasn't just the country store. He even stopped hunting and spent most of his time strolling in the yard. Now and then he sold a gallon of gas from the pump that remained standing there, or pulled himself together and poked about among the mysteries of the warehouse, where one could even find harnesses dating from the time of his father, the great businessman. My father-in-law used to sit among the shadows in the warehouse and shine up the bridles, just as he did as a child.

Now he has become a born-again teetotaler who stands in the cellar and imbibes alcohol in secret.

Jonas is playing near his grandfather.

I tiptoe upstairs to our bedroom. Louise arrived from Stockholm late last night. She was in a dark mood, fell onto the bed, and transformed herself into a sleeping rock as I made some unsuccessful groping sexual overtures. She is still asleep. I wash my hands in cold water in the small screened-off washroom, pull off my clothes, and crawl into bed with her. She pretends to sleep; her breathing betrays her. She turns her back to me, but now she has no excuse. Slowly I caress her behind. She is unwilling; she makes signals regarding my mother-in-law, who is busying herself making beds in the adjacent room. That excites me even more. Louise presses her legs together and arches her back toward me, but in the end we are soldered together anyhow. A long and breathlessly careful rocking ensues. We lie like two spoons against each other. I embrace her, holding on to her breasts. My right arm goes numb. When she begins to tremble convulsively, I interpret it at first as a huge orgasm and ejaculate rapidly in a few hard thrusts, not caring about the squeaking bed or my mother-in-law's movements on the other side of the thin wall.

But Louise is crying.

Through tears that drip all over my face, and while I hold her shivering body, she tells me in fractured sentences that Axel raped her in his office. She had gone to Stockholm to meet with him the week before the fall semester began at the university. They were planning the next step in her project. She was flattered by Axel's readiness to give up a week of vacation, intoxicated by the detailed work, the hours rushing by rapidly, and the keenness of his criticism. They dashed off to catch a bite to eat and hurried back to his office — where he underwent a sudden change, threw himself on her, tossed her on top of his big desk, and forced himself into her, having torn her panties to shreds.

In the middle of her stammered tale, she sits up. She seems cold as ice, dries the tears from her red-streaked face, and turns to me with a question.

"Do you understand? I was raped. Where is Jonas?"

So far as she is concerned, that is a perfectly normal and logical combination of questions. Whichever one I choose to answer, she will turn all her aggression toward me. I elect not to answer.

"Where does your father keep the ammunition?" I ask instead.

Louise responds automatically, unprepared but with a quick, blazing, satisfied glance.

"In his workroom. Why?"

"I'm going to shoot him."

"Shoot whom?" she cries out unnecessarily.

That's how she is. Always using correct grammar, always keeping subject and object in their place. Presumably one day she will mumble corrections from her own coffin if the poor minister puts his foot in the syntax.

I throw on some clothes and slam the door with such force that my mother-in-law frowns disapprovingly, her formidable eyebrows forming hard, black lines.

She ought to have put her hands together in prayer; she ought to have prayed for forgiveness for our sins.

ALGERIA
1976

Such were the thoughts whirling in my head as I was lying in the cell in the police station in Algiers. I fell asleep and awoke a number of times until I lost all sense of time. Since I had read many descriptions of prison life, I scratched the date and the year on the wall. We write 1976, January 20. I carved my name. Ingemar Rutger. It really sounded to me like a man trying to fry snow. I understand why Louise feels it is a fitting name for me. My soul is a Gemini, always pulling in two directions at once.

The same thing must have been true of the official from the Swedish Embassy. He kept chuckling all the time, probably because he had nothing to laugh about, as he tried to explain why I had ended up in prison. This past year the Algerian narcotics police had thrown the book at Scandinavians, who had been carrying great amounts of cannabis from Morocco via Algiers to Marseilles. The fact that I came from Marseilles, nervous as a bat in sunlight, had obviously made the police suspicious. Besides, I had tried to toss something overboard from the ferry. What was it?

He leaned forward, confidentially, to hear what I had to say. I threw knowing looks around the cell walls. Had this Swedish Embassy official never heard of hidden microphones? He chuckled. Evidently he had promised to cooperate with the Algerian narcs. Now he would hear the truth from a man with a sense of humor.

"In the hole," I whispered. "I flushed down the encapsulated list of every gang member."

He threw a rapid glance toward the hole in the floor and nodded eagerly. How absolutely brilliant, how expertly cold-blooded of me to think of such a solution, he whispered back and promised to get me set free without delay.

I appreciated his efforts, though I questioned his common sense. A telex inquiring about my person would have revealed me to be an unlikely drug smuggler. It was close to twenty years since I last smoked a pipe in Casablanca. While the papers giving me my freedom were being stamped, I hid a smile. I could see the whole picture — how the old-fashioned plumbing system in the cells would be ripped apart, piece by piece, how the Algerian narcs would turn into sewage divers, and how the Swedish Embassy, at some later date, would receive a note of reprimand — or perhaps a bill?

That I am an egoist is entirely possible.

That thought hit me with full force as I was hurriedly dispatched from the police station. My car was clinically free of any trace of marijuana and, I dared hope, correctly reassembled. The embassy official pressed a letter into my hand and advised me to leave the country as soon as possible. He disappeared, nervous chuckles and all, and I sat alone in the Volvo and stared at the windshield wipers. They were squeaking lazily over the windshield as a result of my pressing the turn signal to make a left turn from the police garage.

My beloved automobile had suffered a nervous breakdown at the hands of the police mechanics.

And worst of all: I had forgotten Louise. They had not let Louise go.

"Wait!" I yelled and pulled the hand brake to no avail.

I tried opening the car door but the lock had jammed. I rolled down the window and wriggled out of the car while it leisurely rolled into the heavy traffic. Too late. The garage door was closed and bolted. Not a sound, not a reaction to my kicking the door.

A young man in jeans and a rust-colored sweater smiled and recommended that I not be too persistent. It would be stupid to tempt fate a second time. Better to save the car.

He spoke excellent French — the kind one finds in books for five-year-olds. That suited me fine. We pushed the car against the edge of the sidewalk and let the long line of cars with exasperated drivers pass. It was late afternoon, the sun was high in the sky. I was hungry. I tried to explain to the helpful man that the police were probably having fun with my wife right at this moment. Good God! A Swedish blonde in an Arab prison!

And who was the helpful man? I asked.

"I'm Omar," he said.

"Thank God!" I replied.

Everybody called Omar in North Africa can fix anything, I soon learned. There is an Omar on every block, in every street where a European happens to put his inexperienced foot. Behind every small store, wherever there is the slightest possibility of making money from someone in trouble. An Omar is ready for any type of work. He will spend endless hours finding a solution that satisfies his clients. Omar is one of the most industrious human beings imaginable. He is intelligent, sensible, and ambitious. Why then, is such a man not a political leader? A bank president? Or a stockbroker? The answer is: He cannot read.

I really needed an Omar.

I couldn't even see the crumpled letter in my own hand. With gentle force, Omar brought it up in front of my eyes. We sat on the hood of the car, and I read aloud to him my wife's letter in Swedish. He with his sensible soul could probably understand the seriousness of Louise's letter from my tone of voice. She was writing that I ought to find myself. When I had calmed down, she would come to see me. She had gone off to her oasis. She did not want any more accidents. Why was I the way I was? And so on.

"Omar," I said. "She has disappeared."

I cried a little against his rust-colored sweater. In my condition I felt that Omar's brown eyes were pleasantly reminiscent of those of a female acquaintance of mine, a psychologist who works at a hospital in Stockholm. During some of our conversations she told me that it is every human being's duty to find himself or herself. I kept joking, as usual.

"What if I traveled as far as Africa to find myself — and then I'm not there! How can I find myself when I can't even find my wife?!"

I pictured myself standing on a sandy dune in the Sahara, gazing all around. It struck me as tremendously funny. And so unnecessary since the psychologist and I had found each other.

Oh well, that's another story. Of course, Omar had no idea of how Louise had changed overnight from a revolutionary and a comrade/lover to a castration expert.

"Omar," I said. "She wants me to find myself. How does one do that?"

Now the dog has bitten the turtle again. It's a mad dog. And the turtle ought to have learned not to thrust out its legs, or to pull in its head a good deal quicker. But no. There it lies, bleeding into the dust of the backyard. Such an ugly turtle. The shell is cracked. Here in Bordj El Kiffan a turtle is facing death because of my landlord's mad dog.

This time it is the left leg that bleeds.

I wind a piece of insulation tape around the leg a few times, the turtle pulls in the leg and the insulation tape stays on the outside as an extra, hollow leg. It's hopeless. It's easier to put the turtle in the dried-out pond and spend a few minutes scaring the dog.

Toward me that bastard is as ingratiating as usual.

He trembles and jerks his hind legs, slithers forward in the dust, wriggling, with evil looks and gaping jaws.

Yellow stumps of teeth bathe in running saliva. He thirsts for my throat but doesn't dare jump me. Poor dog. He has been beaten so much that his soul is split in two. He tries to behave as a friendly dog but hungers for revenge.

He is not alone. Cowering dogs are seen behind gates and fences everywhere. They are supposed to be watchdogs but are totally useless.

Of course it was Omar who found me a place to live in Bordj El Kiffan. I stay with a Frenchman who otherwise lives alone in his big house in the middle of the once-exclusive suburb. Now the large mansions shelter at least three Algerian families each. The old European upper-class district may be panting and whispering of its unjust history. Who knows? Like the whole country, this area has been liberated except for the home of my remarkable landlord. He has been a parachutist and took part in the colonial war. Now he works with pipes, presumably oil pipes.

One evening he showed me his most prized possession, a tenderly cared for old MAT 49. He was astonished and suitably impressed when I asked him to count as I, with my eyes closed, took apart and put together the machine gun. But he asked no questions, as if discretion were one of his professional habits. He just nodded in acknowledgment.

What kind of hold Omar has on him I don't understand; how he has been able to hang on to his house is a mystery.

He is an extremely quiet man, hard of hearing, who has a large model train layout in the living room. The bedroom walls are covered with pictures of nude women. There is an excellent stereo system. Every evening he plays Wagner at highest volume while fiddling with his miniature trains and smiling in big grimaces, as if I could understand that this constitutes the height of happiness.

But I am unable to share in his joy. My Volvo has been taken apart, reduced to its components by Omar. It was easy to unscrew it. Everything was already loose. The wheels wobbled when we drove to Monsieur Verdurin's house. Omar has promised to fix the car. I don't know if that lies within his ability, but what I do know is that until then I am stuck.

Consequently I sit here, trying to mend an old turtle and deciding to be nice to a mad dog while I wait for Louise. I have written her a letter and asked Omar to mail it to the strange oasis. Not even he knows where it is. Other than that I spend my time trying to find myself.

AUSTRALIA
1962

Every day the German fixed his pale eyes on mine and asked if I had spoken about Cape Town. And every day I told him that I had not. The same thing happened today. Again he did not believe me, spat into the dirty, yellowish water, and told me that, in his opinion, little turds like me would not be able to swim across the harbor basin, if one day I happened to lose my balance and fall into it.

I replied that I had actually qualified for the Sharks. Only two out of ten managed that at the swim club's first tests for seven-year-olds. The rest ended up with the Sticklebacks. That was an outright lie, but he couldn't know that. We were tramping a Swedish ship deck and nobody there had kept a written record of my pitiful Stickleback existence, shameful and long ago as it was. I was now seventeen years old, not seven. And Sweden existed somewhere on the other side of the globe. Furthermore, Cape Town would remain a secret between me and the German. We were not going past it anyhow. The trip home would be through the Suez Channel. So why did he keep nagging me about the past?

We had headed into Gulf St. Vincent and were safely moored in North Haven's outer harbor. Beyond the smoking, flat, tongue-shaped land, the dry brushwood, and the metal sheds smoldering in the heat lay Port Adelaide. Farther on, the city of Adelaide was supposed to exist. To me that was nothing but hearsay. Exactly as the rest of Australia's ports, by the way. Judging by North Haven, we had come to the end of the world. That was an opinion the captain shared loudly with the agent who delivered the message about a dockworkers' strike that had brought all work to a complete stand-still. In North Haven we would stop, and in North Haven we were stopped. A place where nobody came and nobody went voluntarily.

We were kept immobile by mooring gear at the quay, the gangway plank was down, but the city and the whole immense Australian continent turned their backs to us at the last minute. Everybody aboard, except me, was tired of the country and had counted on loading quickly, casting off, and slipping away over the meridians and on home. The crew sighed and whimpered hypocritically, as always. Everybody wanted to leave, get moving. Such is the sailor's lot and such desire burns like a poison in his blood. But Port Adelaide on Saturday night wasn't too shabby. Old Sweden could wait. Come sing me a song.

In front of us was the ugliest ship I have ever laid eyes on. It came from Jidda and was built to carry live sheep from Australia to the Muslims, who neither butchered sheep nor transported them frozen. Something to do with their religion. A short distance above the waterline, the ship looked like a gigantic open steel cage. Inside that cage were rows of smaller cages, filling deck after deck with tightly packed sheep. The animals couldn't move. They stank in the scorching heat and at times made such weird noises that many of us aboard at the approach to the port of call felt the chill of an alien horror sweep along the spine.

The strange dockworkers' strike that nobody could explain kept this sheep-filled ship tied up at the dock.

That is how things stood when the German came over to the bulwark and made his remark about my inability to swim across the basin. Defiantly, I had thrown one leg over the rail in order to jump into the water and swim clear across to the other side of the long, curved pier toward Gulf St. Vincent, when he tugged on my arm and pointed out toward the bluish ocean swells. A dead sheep was floating, so swollen it seemed almost alive. The head stuck up out of the water and nodded in the ground swells.

"One can trace that coffin all the way to Jidda. The sheep are already dying," said the German.

He grinned stiffly and spat toward the sheep.

"If it weren't for one thing. The sharks. Sooner or later the sharks come."

If he meant to scare me, he succeeded.

I understood clearly that I ought not to swim across the harbor inlet nor go out alone on deck in the dark. The German distrusted me and was prepared to throw me overboard. Less than two months ago, he had been like a father to me, checked to see if I had washed behind my ears, threw my underwear in a pail to soak, taught me ten German words a day, preached cleanliness, hard work, and everything in its place.

Leisure time had its place.

He also planned to teach me that. When we arrived in Cape Town.

Nothing turned out the way I had expected. There is nothing to tell. I had taken my punishment and expiated his crime — completely voluntarily, since it could not be overlooked that it was mine, too. As I had assured the German.

He, however, was a man who did not want to lose face, not even in front of a little stickleback like me. I recognized those strange drumbeats in my stomach. Thump thump. God, his pain only kept growing; he couldn't forget. But did he have to wish me dead because of that?

To him I was clearly of no more value than the sheep bobbing out there. I thought of something reassuring to say, something along the lines that we were in the same boat, but I didn't get further than a few staccato sounds because suddenly the water around the dead sheep foamed. The animal disappeared quicker than I could say "shark." Or perhaps I said "shock." And that with my mouth wide open! I stared and blinked in astonishment. No shark fin, no advance warning, just the boiling foam. I sat with one leg up and both hands grimly locked around the sun-warmed, salt-spattered railing. My right leg felt heavy as lead and melted down toward the surface of the water. The piece of steel I held on to was my most valued possession. The welder would have to pry me away from it.

"A big son of a bitch," said the German and left.

Help! I wanted to holler the word, but it sounded as if emitted by a wretched cat in a much too tall tree.

Why do I always feel compelled to make myself conspicuous? It's as if I have a magnetic ability to adhere to life's exaggerations. In only seventeen years of life, I had done enough to qualify for a rest home. As early as age twelve, I dreamed of being taken care of in an old folks' home. But even there I'd attract trouble. Probably wet the mattress until it would have to be thrown out. During this process, the one carrying the smelly evidence would stumble, fall down the stairs, and break his neck. To die weighed down with guilt seems to be my heritage.

I had to agree with the first mate: The population of Australia ought not to be burdened with the likes of me, even though I hungered for a glimpse of those black, small, quirky creatures who threw boomerangs against boxing kangaroos.

"Sure. You'll go ashore when kangaroos turn into camels," said the first mate.

A certain amount of bitterness and meanness mingled with my thoughts of the first mate. Then I had to laugh. He had been on a diet during the trip down here. His five-foot-five frame weighed around a hundred and forty-five pounds to begin with. Now he was down to a hundred and twenty-five. A vain, rather good-looking little dandy with American work gloves made of yellow pigskin. Blue eyes with an intense shine beneath inky black hair. A workaholic, generally doing things he had no business doing.

Whoever saw a first mate working with a rust hammer?

It made us sailors uncomfortable, and gave us the feeling that we ought to give him a hand. I believe that may be what is called moral superiority. He took one look at me and immediately put me in sail-sewing class during the watch. While the immense ocean mirrored the light of dawn, my fingertips were sore and bleeding. Now and then the first mate came out on the bridge wing to inspect. He tapped dots and dashes with his smoking pipe and urged me to learn the Morse code right away. That's how he was: It wasn't enough that I was stitching stiff, old, crumbled sailcloth, I should also learn the Morse code at the same time.

"Bon voyage," he tapped.

A really pleasant trip.

I and several of my shipmates suppressed hearty laughter when he climbed up the foremast to inspect. He inspected everything. In his short khaki pants, his yellow pigskin gloves, and his bone white uniform cap, he climbed upward, newly thin and quick as a small monkey. A few yards up, the wind took hold of his loose skin. See, there had been some skin left over. He looked as if he ran around inside himself. One bag of skin was close to blowing off. His monumental vanity did the rest when he saw his own fluttering upper body. With as much elegance as he could muster, he slid down. The inspection would have to wait.

I grinned. Others did too.

I let out an evil chuckle. Forty-five years of age meant that he was terribly debilitated. Why didn't he leave vanity to the young? For him it was too late, but we who were in our youths should love our bodies, I thought with steely fingers on the rail.

Besides — had I not just regained my life?

A life that nearly fell overboard when somebody bestowed a manly slap on my back.

Naturally the slapper was the first mate. He uttered brief, rapid orders about rust removal and painting of the ship's outside together with seaman Svenson on the raft. If I did a good job, I would get Sunday off. Otherwise there would be overtime. He would make me work so long and so hard that I wouldn't even be able to crawl ashore.

Gloomily I contemplated the raft, lying on the deck.

Was it sturdy enough to stop that giant shark lurking in the harbor?

A painting raft consists of a wooden platform and a framed structure of planks around four oil kegs. To give stability, the oil kegs are half filled with water. In order to work on the raft, one stands three inches from the water surface on old, worn planks, hammering and scraping away spots of rust, red-leading the surface, and then painting the enormous exterior with gray outdoor paint, pulling oneself forward by the long mooring lines. An endless job for two men, and nowhere to hide. The first mate was a guaranteed frequent visitor by the rail to inspect and tap his "bon voyage!"

For the moment, however, he had disappeared and left me with Svenson and the grinning German, who had already started up to the winches. There is an unwritten law that only able-bodied seamen, occasionally an ordinary seaman, crank the winch. Svenson and I fastened the hook with its clanking chain to the slings of the raft, pulled the bar over the rail and as far as possible over the raft. It's far from easy to handle a winch. Even experienced men can drop a sling on the dock, especially if it happens to be a case of Swedish export beer being unloaded right before lunch. Under such circumstances, a veteran longshoreman may easily have a little mishap.

So what could not a hostile seaman drop into the harbor basin, I thought with sinking heart as I stepped onto the raft to follow on down and undo the hook. Svenson was only a year older than I. That's why he took his position and duty as superior being totally seriously. He waved and directed the German's maneuvers with the winch so pompously that someone lacking experience would have thought he was the world's foremost hoisting supervisor. I myself saw his contradictory signals as yet another seal of fate. There was no doubt anymore: I was being prepared for a shark's supper.

The raft swung with dizzying speed over the rail. We broke toward the filthy, yellowish water while I hollered to Svenson to make the German slow down. But no, the raft hit the water with awesome force. I had no time to grab hold of the looped slings. Here goes the next sheep! I thought as I made contact with the water and swallowed enough of it to drown both my cries for help and Svenson's roaring laughter. To him it was an innocent joke on the part of the German. Meanwhile, I broke every speed record in crawling up on the raft. I lay on my stomach and coughed over the raft's edge, straight down into the eye of a shark. The shark rolled over, leisurely turning its belly toward me, and was gone without even touching the raft ever so slightly. An elegant exhibition put on before a hypnotized stickleback. I inched closer to the surface of the water and even dipped the tip of my nose into the water in order to see better. The visibility was a little over a yard. The shark was swimming toward me, again with the same gracious, rapid turn.

Or perhaps there were two sharks?

For the moment, I had to leave that question unanswered. Because it was not I who was inching closer to the water surface with the tip of my nose. The raft was about to tip over! And I slid down into the water again!

The German must have dozed off at the winch. The heavy hook with its chain cable kept flowing and pulled the raft along. I was back in the water but now underneath the raft and totally helpless, like a floundering morsel for a couple of ravenous sharks. Two immense shadows moved toward me at full speed while I hit my head against the raft and, from below, tried to claw my way right through the planks.

The sharks must have shared my confusion. Everything was total and absolute chaos. They glided past and took off, obviously not crazy about the idea of going under the raft. To get back up, I would have to let go, dive, and perhaps encounter the sharks during their next turn. My lungs were ready to explode, but I know that I hollered at the top of my voice underwater. Now or never. I pushed off and managed to complete the necessary arch below the water in order to heave myself back up on the raft.

The first sound bouncing against my eardrums was the first mate's voice, as he bellowed less than politely phrased questions about what I was doing. He thought me the only one who could do something so stupid as turning over a painting raft. I had neither time nor strength to defend myself. Completely spent, I happily counted the number of arms and legs. Miracle of miracles, everything was still there, exactly as before.

But this blissful math lesson did not last. I heard the first mate ordering us to bring the painting raft up on the deck. Such a maneuver would put me back into the water since the raft turned right-side up when the hook was raised. And this time the raft would continue through the air without me.

By now I was desperate enough to grab hold of the chain as it clattered by the edge of the raft. It burned and smarted the palms of my hands, but I clung to it, tightly, staying above the raft as it turned right-side up. I flew up in the air and didn't let go until we finally swung in over the rail. Wet and miserable, yes, but my lungs were strong enough to draw the crew's attention when I howled my news about the sharks.

Unfortunately for my credibility, those beasts had disappeared altogether.

Perhaps they had gulped down a can of red lead each and gone off to digest such potent soup. If so, they'd be rustproof for a long, long time. Of course, their reluctance to be seen translated unfavorably for me. They were thought to exist only in my imagination. Svenson had not seen any sharks and said that the German had not handled the winch according to given signals. The German just grinned menacingly.

"That's what happens when you take crybabies aboard," he muttered.

With my shipmates' laughter ringing in my ears, I was told to put the raft back in order and, together with seaman Svenson, begin our neglected chore, quick as lightning.

I swallowed. I'd get my revenge. But how?

In everybody's eyes I was nothing but a wet turd who had made a fool of himself one more time.

To change my clothes, a pair of cutoff jeans and a torn shirt, would be futile. Determinedly, I nailed a couple of extra planks below the raft to make it stronger. This way it had as good a deck on the bottom as on top. I also put cross planks along the sides, and would probably have continued to work with hammer and nails until this day, had there been enough planks.

My reinforcements made the raft float higher, as we discovered when we were lowered, amid loud cheers and stupid jokes about the preferred diet of sharks.

The raft wobbled with an unpleasant smacking sound every time we moved. It sounded slippery and ill-omened, but Svenson, who was all set to do Port Adelaide in the evening, joked and rocked the raft, pretending to keep an eager lookout for my imaginary sharks as he spoke glibly about women making the same smacking sound as the raft. But did I not see a glimmer of real caution and even fear in his round, slightly protruding eyes? Or was it just his regular pain flapping in there? Just a year older than I and already closely acquainted with alcohol, he had the kind of soft roundness that soon develops into flabby fat. In his eyes resided permanent spots of pain behind a dull grayness of disgust — as from a lighthouse before it breaks down and goes out completely. His sharks lived in his stomach. They would tear him to pieces one day; they were lying in wait.

Or could it be my own unnatural fear of alcohol that I read in his eyes?

When the sharks came toward me, I experienced paralyzing terror. When alcohol ran down the throats of human beings, I also felt a kind of terror. It began as a hollow, hopeless despair that grew into hate and disgust toward the slaves of the bottle.

Why? That's another story.

I kept my mouth shut and began the monotonous work with the rust hammer. Svenson followed me with scrape and red lead. The sun's heavy bolts beat on my neck. As the sun rose higher and higher, the rust-spotted gray metal of the ship's outside blazed with broiling heat.

A dancing luminosity shimmered in front of our eyes — and the rhythm of the hammer and scrape diminished like a weakened pulse. But at the very moment when the tediousness was at its most devastating point, I, as usual, ended up in the grip of absurd obsession. The rust spots had to be conquered, the surfaces ruled over, the sweat should flow.

That's how it is with work for me. It grows suddenly inside me like infatuation. Even the mindless pounding with a rust hammer against a ship's side awakens an excitement inside me. By forcing myself on the huge, dead, ugly iron, I change it. We grow together, the iron and I. We respect each other. There is enormous strength in a ship's surface. All that metal could defeat me. But I'm young and strong, and I happily let beads of perspiration run like chilly mops over stomach and back. It's a matter of finding the perfect balance, the ideal rhythm. Finally the iron and I become equals in strength. I solder my life into it and it returns hard energy.

And I admire myself. Yes, I love myself!

I am a crazy paid-by-the-hour laborer who merges with the monotonous work. Others hate such a conceited destroyer of the piecework idea. I could work myself to death just for the pleasure of the magnificent monotony. The first mate ought to be happy to encounter, finally, a lobotomized, seventeen-year-old, healthy, strong worker, since there are others who believe that work is a punishment to be done reluctantly. Guys like Svenson, for instance.

Amazed but pleased, he observed my violent hammering and came to the conclusion that as far as he was concerned he could relax, let his legs dangle over the edge of the raft, and smoke, while he criticized my work as being totally inefficient in order to maintain his superiority as seaman.

There wasn't a shark in sight. But by the time for the coffee break, I had devised a plan to scare the pants off Svenson. He would have to eat his own self-satisfied guffaws that had echoed in my ears when I plopped into the water earlier.

When we had climbed back up the rope ladder, I sneaked over to the kitchen's garbage cans and put cold cuts, old meat scraps, bones, and fish gut in a few rags, which I tied together into a small sack. Then quickly down to the raft, underneath which I tied my drippy parcel with a piece of wire. I counted on being able to push the tidbits into the water behind Svenson's back. Unseen by him. If the sharks were still in the harbor basin, my bait had to be irresistible.

I jumped into the water.

That's how I am. If you are going to do anything, you should do it well and quickly. I was back on the raft before anybody noticed, climbed up on deck, and walked dripping wet into the mess hall, where I looked at a row of dumbfounded faces.

Had I really swum across the harbor?

Oh yes, indeed. I bet the wages yet due to me that nobody would dare to repeat the feat.

An unnatural silence fell over the room. Soon after everybody began to cackle back and forth. Could there possibly be sharks in the harbor basin? And, depending on the answer to that question, what did that make me? Uniquely brave or an utter fool and madman?

The German declared that there were no sharks whatsoever in the basin, but that I was a fool and a madman anyway. Had I not come close to missing the boat in Cape Town?

Quick as a wink, Svenson decided to share that opinion. Just for the fun of it, he could swim clear across the harbor basin and back again. But why swim around in North Haven's sludge when one could walk over to Beach Taperoo? Where one may meet girls from good families and fuck for free if everything worked out.

Such a statement, inconceivable as it was, swept away all interest in sharks. Every man seemed to have his own story about meeting a girl from a good family in some corner of the world.

Admiration mixed with envy and disbelief greeted the tale of a Spanish family girl and her generously bestowed favors. The majority seemed dead sure of the impossibility of such an event. It fell on its own preposterousness.

I have read a few books during my life. Thanks to my beautiful and talented mother, I, at the age of seventeen, was rather well versed in what people call theological controversies. But all that hairsplitting amounts to zero compared to how sailors around a table in a mess hall are capable of turning and twisting the concept of girls from good families.

Throw a parched sailor in the middle of the Sahara and he will see a family girl flutter in a mirage rather than an oasis.

I felt entitled to claim that I was closest to girls of good families since I as the youngest had fresh memories of being considered a human being and not a fickle, faithless, seducing sailor in the perception of both girls and their families. But compared to the coarse descriptions flying in the air, my little accounts were weak numbers and nothing to write home about. So I listened and tried to learn something.

The problem seemed to be that every mate wanted to meet a girl from a good family who at the same time was something completely different. It made no sense.

I kept nodding and agreeing anyhow. Though mostly I was thinking of my sharks.

The terror and the commotion of the morning had acted as a centrifugal force that had vacuumed out my power of judgment. I thought of the sharks as belonging to me and hoped they were not busy chewing their way right through the raft. Sharks can smell blood miles away, and some blood could have trickled out of my parcel. The plan would fail totally if they were already circling the raft. Seaman Svenson had to be taken by surprise, exactly as a family girl — surprise combined with a large dose of imagination, all based upon meticulous planning.

He wasn't going to dare to put even his little toe into the water at Beach Taperoo.

Strangely enough, I did not think a lot about the German and his threats. Things were different between us. Perhaps he wanted to see me dead or perhaps he just wanted to give me a good scare. In spite of everything, I felt unwilling admiration for him. Almost in the same way as I did for the sharks.

The boatswain saw his responsibility as foreman slip through his fingers in the face of the colossal subject of family girls, and he interrupted the lustily panting mirages with a summed-up conclusion.

"In th'long wun ye pay 'nyhoo." Wise words, indeed, from a man with no teeth.

He spoke like that. Sometimes it was impossible to make any sense out of the sounds, which did not make me less of a fool in the others' eyes. The first time he allotted jobs, I didn't understand one syllable.

"Seep wi'ung" could only be translated as a command to us who were young to go and get some sleep.

Consequently I had turned back to my bunk. Finally I had met a truly sympathetic human being. He seemed good-natured even when he woke me up with a spluttered torrent of unintelligible words. It wasn't until he put his expensive false teeth in place that I understood his hatred for young punks who had their own teeth. That was the first and only time I saw him with his teeth in his mouth during work hours. The men whispered that he used them when he went ashore. Except that nobody had ever seen him go ashore.

Enough about the bosun. "Weiter!" as the German used to say.

I tried to hurry Svenson. We climbed down to the raft and continued our tedious work while he, in a splendid mood, related some of his ventures in the ports of the world. Girls from good families or not, one thing was sure: Port Adelaide was still the way the song described it. As long as you had money to spend, everything worked out just fine.

As soon as I could, I pushed the kitchen scraps into the water. The parcel dangled about a yard below the raft. Water saturated the torn cloth and soon frail veils of blood were visible on my side of the raft. A well-formulated invitation to my friends, I thought — as if they could tell the difference between a deck boy and a seaman.

To my utter disappointment, the surface of the water remained calm as a mirror. No triangular fins raced along, however many looks I threw all around the harbor basin. Instead Svenson began for the hundredth time to mock and ridicule my imaginary sharks. He threw his cigarette butt in the water and dove in after it, came up snorting, splashed wildly, and hollered kiddingly for help. An iron band closed around my chest. I urged him to climb back up quickly, my voice hoarse with tension. I fell to my knees and held out my hand, pleading with him.

It would be my fault if he were to be suddenly pulled under by man-eating monsters.

He must have detected something in my face. I was truly scared. He took my proffered hand and heaved himself up on the raft. He stared at me.

"Boy, you're shaking! Are you getting a sunstroke?"

"It's nothing," I said and returned gratefully to the dull removal of rust while he pulled off his shorts to let them dry in the sun.

His feet splashed in the water, and he rolled over on his back. To give his family jewels a bit of sun, was how he put it. Then he went into a long tirade about a birth-control method which, in short, meant that one overheated the balls and thereby killed all sperms.

"In case one runs into a girl from a good family," he said and pointed proudly downward.

He asked me to wake him up when "it" started to raise its head. That would mean it was Saturday night and time to go ashore.

I kept on knocking and banging.

And thought of women while the smacking sound vibrated in my ear. I imagined exactly how I would lose my virginity that clung like a leech to me. It was not right that I should be the one and only virgin, since all of me was actually drooling debauchery beneath the surface. Once a Spanish doctor in Las Palmas looked into my ear with a light. He emitted a whistling sound of surprise. I understood him perfectly: Lacking the real thing, my head had created its own pornographic movie theater. I was undernourished. It was time. High time. But I took the whole thing too seriously, as my brother used to point out. I had become stuck in the theology — the woman as a saint or not a saint — and would prob- ably have to sail the seven seas forever like a luckless monk. A part of me looked with horror and fright at everything people could and did do to each other, driven by carnal desires and raw lust. The other part of me romped around indecently with family girls and professional ladies of the night in one big voluptuous mess. To put it briefly, I wanted to be like Svenson. For him the whole thing was simply a matter of putting his trunk into the nearest available hole.

It wasn't fair that I should be the one with an overdeveloped sensitivity.

I cursed fate while the sun rose toward its zenith and threw bolts of fire at us. The work demon grabbed hold of me again, the rust spots shimmered in front of my eyes, sweat ran in torrential rivers, the blows resounded, and my head was boiling over. The monotony had put me into a hypnotic state. Forward. On and on. It would have been impossible to stop. I had to conquer the vast surface of boiling metal.

In this condition I got a sudden feeling that the sun had run off to hide inside a cloud. I was freezing. Chills traveled from the nape of my neck down toward the ice-cold hem of my sweat-soaked pants. I turned around to grab my shirt and tie it quickly around the waist in order to return without loss of time to my insane hammering. But the sun had not disappeared behind any cloud. And Svenson was sleeping peacefully. He was still lying on his back with his feet dangling in the water. No man of woman born would be able to have fun with what Svenson had between his legs now, courtesy the scorching sun.

I could easily imagine the sore seaman's new and cautious way of walking. My own heavily sunburned back was nothing in comparison with the look of his most dearly prized bodily parts. I exploded in irrepressible, roaring laughter.

Svenson woke up, confused and under the influence of the sun. He neither stirred nor tried to get up. He kept lying without moving while I tried to explain the reasons behind my attacks of mirth. The poor idiot didn't feel a thing yet, and I was unable to get comprehensible words out of my mouth.

Laughter folded me in two, and I took the opportunity to scrutinize the sun blisters on the severely burned skin and gristle scraps between his legs. What a wondrous sight!

In my head the laughter was hot bubbles appearing in boiling porridge. I fell to my knees, laughing. I could not stop, even when I saw my two sharks race toward the raft.

This time they attacked the way sharks are supposed to. With fins like superbly honed saws, they cut their way with terrible speed through the water. Laughing hysterically by Svenson's side, I managed somehow to get out a word or two about the sharks.

"Yeah, yeah," he said lethargically

He wasn't going to be fooled.

With no time to discuss the matter, I rolled him roughly onto his stomach and pulled at his arms to get his legs up on the raft. He roared in pain when his scorched sex organ chafed against the rough planks as both sharks hit the raft with a dull thump. Fighting for my balance, I was thrown down headlong and looked straight into Svenson's empty, staring eyes. He was gone. The pain had made him lose every concept of anything. Great confusion shone out of his eyes and cold sweat squirted out of his pores while he moaned that the sharks had bit him between the legs. Somehow, mysteriously, they had jumped up through the double planks and chewed the pride of his manhood to bits. I nodded in agreement. The two shark fins made a turn a few yards from the raft and plunged straight toward us again.

"It's the blood attracting them," I hissed and pointed.

He sobbed plaintively when the raft shuddered violently. I jumped up, pushed the shirt under him, bounced down on his bare buttocks, and yelled that if he did not want to bleed to death, he had to have a pressure bandage.

In any other condition, he would have seen things more clearly. But the heavy shock had an immense effect. It must have hurt terribly when I pulled him over the unplaned planks at the same time as the sharks thumped heavily into the raft. They kept whipping up the water around us and, in spite of my having reinforced the raft, it felt eerie.

Accompanied by Svenson's grunts and moans, I hollered for help.

Someone let down the hook, I fastened the raft to it, and we were lifted out of the water and away from the two beasts. My food parcel had long ago been torn away. In other words, no trace remained of my carefully planned revenge. With my foot on his ass, I stood on the raft and affirmed spiritedly Svenson's confused grunts. Yes, the sharks had bitten him in a very special place. And I had saved him without giving a thought to the danger to my own life.

The crew came running. The sharks were interesting, of course, but it was equally fascinating to see the mutilated seaman. The bosun tried to turn him over, but Svenson refused, remained on his stomach, and yelled bloody murder, while he pressed my shirt against his lower abdomen with all the strength he had left.

"D'n't b'a bib," said the bosun.

Which probably meant that Svenson should not carry on like a baby.

"He's had a nervous breakdown," I said, as humbly as I could. One should never exaggerate.

The second mate was pale under his tan but realized his duty as our ship's doctor. He ordered a couple of men to turn Svenson over on his back so he could assess the damage. Strong arms rolled over the recoiling and kicking seaman. After a tug-of-war using my shirt, he let go, totally exhausted. We formed a tight circle around him, put our heads together, and made the observation that the second mate was correct.

"Oh well. Nothing's bleeding."

On the whole, that was the only positive thing that could be said about Svenson's purply, swollen genitals. Some born-again wit insisted that he had seen similar damage on other sailors who had tried sexual intercourse with sharks.

Never in my wildest stretch of imagination had I dreamed of so much rehabilitating satisfaction all at once. The sharks were now a reality. And Svenson was shaking in every cell of his body. For the moment, his interest was concentrated on gingerly protecting what he thought he had lost forever.

One day he may begin to ponder what had actually occurred, but that day was as far away as the crew's interest in taking over his work duties. While I, naturally, jumped gallantly onto the raft the minute the first mate kicked up a row to indicate that the workday was not over, bravely offering to go on fighting rust spots. Whereupon he pointed at me and, to his own surprise, found himself holding me up as an example, worthy of imitating — an example of the old, responsible, honorable, self-sacrificing sailor corps.

As such a fine example, I was lowered down to the sharks.

The odds were not really against me. The raft was stable enough, as only I could know. Also, as one would expect, the first mate's pale visage was hanging over the rail most of the time. He was vain but not stupid. A lost and eaten deck boy would be a serious demerit.

When the sharks returned after a while and rubbed against the outside of the raft, as if expecting some special treat, he was the one who with his pipe tapped out the distress signal SOS.

I waved good-bye to my finned friends and climbed up the rope ladder. I left the raft where it was. The first mate patted my shoulder as he would a prodigal lost and found son. Beneath that loose skin palpitated a father's heart that, after a moment's hesitation, still refused to let me go ashore this Saturday night but was willing to make an exception so far as Sunday was concerned. I cheered up and tried to look as if I fully intended to go to church.

Saturday or Sunday, what does it matter? I thought. The main thing was that I, as the completion of my crucifixion of Svenson, was given a chance to put a crown of thorns upon his head by a matter-of-fact description of my pleasures ashore. Besides, it was high time for me to become a man. While I made a beeline for the nearest Eden to partake of tempting fruits, Svenson could always quote the Song of Solomon: "Look not upon me, because I am black, because the sun hath looked upon me."

I combined this pleasant state of affairs with the splendor of being a shark expert. As modestly as I was able, I reminded my shipmates of my earlier swim. That outdid even the captain's stentorian contribution to the conversation. With his twenty years in the trade, he had still not seen even the fin of a shark in any harbor basin.

He cursed the sons of Allah who heaved dead sheep overboard. He cursed strike leaders, agents, the sun, the heat, and the mess boy, who did not bring a fresh beer quickly enough after he had gulped down the first. A real captain, famous in every Australian harbor, ruled over us and our ship. He had even been given an Australian pet name: Woolakiiaan sagamaaroo. It means "the man who carries his table on the stomach." Beer belly is a milder version.

Our dear commander could be useful, said one mate. As a buoy if we were to go fishing for sharks. The crew continued tirelessly to discuss the immediate future of the sharks rather than take an interest in work. Some thought it would be impossible to fish for sharks from a given, permanent point. A shark would tear himself or the cordage apart when it was stretched. One sailor's suggestion sounded more feasible — to make a buoy with a hook and chain below, something similar to what was used in whale hunting.

Sunday.

"Sunday," everybody said in unison.

Because now we had managed to stretch out the Saturday afternoon to the finishing line and the fetters burst apart. To borrow the words of the first mate, a free weekend ashore was about as common as kangaroos turning into camels. Electric shocks of expectation went through the crew. The bosun even considered putting in his false teeth. An aroma of soap and shaving lotion fought in the insane heat against the musty stench of sheep from the Muslim ship.

I was sitting alone on the poop deck. Except for poor seaman Svenson, it looked as if there would be only myself and Woolakiiaan sagamaaroo left aboard.

That's exactly how it turned out.

Toward evening a cooling breeze fanned my face. The captain sat on the main deck with his beer mug on his stomach. I sat on the poop deck and kept an eye out for sharks. Everything in North Haven was peaceful and serene.

The same words can unfortunately not be used to describe my dreams that night. I have always had big ears for my age and thanks to my dear uncle's instructions, I learned to wiggle them. He ought to have taught me how to furl them inward instead so I could have turned off sailors' manifold tales of women and heights of ecstasy, burning disappointments and alluring promises, of farewells and tears, and, to top it off, mystical and indescribable venereal diseases.

Such was the stuff my dreams were made of while the rest of the crew, each according to ability, tried various kinds of amusements in Port Adelaide.

In the middle of one such dream, I was grateful to be awakened by a strange sound. I peered through the vent. Our ship's huge searchlights were turned on, the beams of light cutting wide rivers on the harbor basin's agitated water. The excited voices of the crew blended in with other sounds, like the screech of a gigantic washing machine whipping and reverberating in the water. I blinked hard several times. It took a few seconds before I realized what was happening. Protected by the dark, the crew on the Jidda ship had dumped a load of dead sheep into the basin. Every shark in Gulf St. Vincent had received a personal invitation to the bloody banquet. Hundreds of sheep corpses were torn to bits and ground down in the bloodred, spuming kettle.

The first wee hours of Sunday after a Saturday night ashore, you are used to hearing sounds of fun and merriment, bragging and crying, someone throwing up, someone laughing, someone fighting, and someone insisting on singing himself to sleep.

That is normal. And after such a remarkable shore leave as a Saturday night in Port Adelaide, the cabins sternward ought to rumble with liberated life. But after the first few excited voices, even the most arrogant and wisecracking mates fell silent. Perhaps the chilling spectacle lasted an hour, perhaps fifteen minutes. Or perhaps the loathsome feast went on until the first grayish streaks of dawn. I don't know. I remained right there on the bench, leaning against the bulkhead and looking out over the water as it slowly quieted down.

Nothing would ever make me dip even one toe in that harbor basin. I would prefer a bullet between the eyes.

But then, why would anybody want to, I thought, and began to scrub myself clean for my Sunday outing. I trimmed my toenails, shampooed my hair, and would have shaved my face, had I owned the right tools. The crew slept right through the sumptuous Sunday breakfast. The cook seemed to have counted on that. His bloodshot eyes expressed no surprise, only relief, when I asked for half a dozen raw eggs rather than fried ones.

Among the conditions for my Sunday adventure were my solemn promises to the first mate to be back aboard the ship before midnight. If I figured that the city's temples of pleasure would open around three o'clock in the afternoon and subtracted one hour for my return trip, I ought to be able to keep at it rabbit-style a little more than eight hours. Oh well, subtract another hour for changing partners now and then. I was determined to work through Port Adelaide's supply. Besides sufficient funds, raw eggs constituted a recommended preparation for such debauchery.

I was ready. Clean and innocent on the outside but filled to the bursting point with wild desire and hard lust within, I left the hung-over crew's speculations about catching sharks. From the telegraph operator I received cash and from the first mate a word of advice for the road. He stuck a piece of paper in my hand and mumbled something about a harmless place, but he seemed to have lost his fighting spirit.

I waved good-bye and walked toward Port Adelaide.

According to descriptions, this paradise was located beyond the harbor shacks and a stretch of wasteland. The heat shimmered over road and land. I moved cautiously so I wouldn't sweat. Like an aging crab, I worked my way along sun-drenched streets. It was so hot that the six raw eggs swilling around in my stomach turned into an omelet. Such things were mere trifles. Here I was, an unknown talent in this enormous country. Here existed gigantic opportunities to become, finally, the one I really was. Here the water swirled to the left in the toilet bowls and here I actually walked upside down. Why then should not my life take new and unexpected turns and trajectories, and why should not the bad luck ooze out of me and into space? My earlier fateful life may have been caused by magnetic disturbances from the North Pole, I reasoned optimistically while I shuffled along.

However hard I searched, I could not find one bar that was open, much less the kind of temples I had in mind. Everything was closed, the doors bolted. The Australian population had been blown off the face of the earth. No kangaroos. Not even an aborigine throwing a boomerang. Only weak tones from an asthmatic organ and human voices droning from something that had to be a church.

By and by, I began to understand the crew's interest in sharks as a Sunday amusement. They must be laughing in unison at the idiot who floundered about in the cinder-dry Sunday heat.

My worst misgivings turned into harsh reality when I saw the sign on the nearest bar door. In Australia, the church orders a day of rest, whether you want it or not. This very fact was cursed by a sleepy and angry drunk, whose foot had gotten stuck in the door after he unsuccessfully had tried to kick it open. I helped him get unstuck. He thanked me by using me for support, while we struggled toward what he called The Very Last Resort.

Even an inexperienced deck boy could see that this joint was the last outpost of humanity, but shame on the one who gives up easily.

I stepped into the hole in the wall along with the stinking drunk, mobilized all my courage, banged my fist on the rickety bar, and demanded a beer. In the semidarkness I could sense the others, my brothers in search of pleasure. Thoughtfully they swallowed thick saliva and stared at me.

Well-combed and clean, perhaps just a little sweaty and stinky after the contact with my new friend, I was still smelling like a rose in comparison with them. Consequently I was rather surprised when the man behind the bar amicably informed me that he did not serve minors, whereupon he listlessly threw me out.

As if he had touched something repugnant, he brushed off his hands and placed himself, broad-legged with authority, in front of the hole in the wall. Since the place was anything but attractive, I certainly had no intention of fighting to get back in. Besides, paradoxically enough, I was grateful. My playing macho and banging on the bar was only a decrepit defense action, not rooted in reality. The drunk and I had shared the path to the place, but his apparition had done its work. That was not the road for me, my mind told me shakily. What if I ended up like him?

Instead I would choose the first mate's harmless place. And make up a reasonably likely story about a girl from a good family. I fumbled for my crinkly piece of paper and asked the bar owner if he knew the address. His face lit up. He promised to call for a taxicab and stated that this would be the right place for me, if I turned to the left right after I had entered.

"Just like the water," I joked.

He did not seem to understand, or perhaps he was not interested in the enigmatic ways of water. Or else he failed to comprehend my dainty English. He himself sounded as if he had a mouth full of beer.

While the taxi went on its bumpy way with me inside, he was probably pouring more beer into himself.

Certainly no Swedish shipmate has ever been driven this far from Port Adelaide, I reflected, feeling a mixture of pride and worry, the latter having to do with the relentlessly ticking taximeter. The address was in the city of Adelaide itself. Now, there are cities and there are cities. If one blinked, one could easily miss the center of this one. Most of it consisted of huge suburban areas with parks and more parks in such numbers that I began looking seriously for kangaroos.

As I sat there staring out into the foliage surrounding us on all sides, a kangaroo jumped out. I yelled, "A kangaroo!"

The cabbie shook his head. What in the world had he picked up as a fare from the infamous hole in the wall? But I kept hollering and pointing. He shook his head more vigorously. I did the same, though for other reasons. The kangaroo had disappeared behind a clump of trees. In its stead a live camel strode across the lawn. I took hold of the cabbie's head to turn him forcibly toward this unbelievable magic trick. This made him really mad, and he threw me out of the cab, as soon as he had my money in his huge fist.

"Jesus Christ," he bellowed. "A shitty little zoo. That's nothing to make a federal case out of."

Shamefacedly, I realized that my Nordic foolishness continued to swirl to the right. I was the same as I had always been.

In a short while, however, I stood right in front of the first mate's harmless place. A hotel. Nothing but a hotel, though rather impressive with porches and slanted canopies and gleaming, etched panes in the revolving doors that slowly swung back and forth as if in training for some distant onslaught of human beings. I saw no sign, but that wasn't necessary since the whole front area was wrapped in an elegant aroma of tea and fruit cobbler.

I sighed and entered.

In order not to encounter any more kangaroos turning into camels, I acted according to the shady barman's friendly advice. I turned to the left right away and banged my nose on another couple of revolving doors. These were white with gilded mirrors. Graceful golden letters told me with flourish the message the doors intended to convey:

WOMEN'S LOUNGE.

That's what it said. The first mate gained several points in my estimation. He had loose skin, but obviously he had greater experience when it came to Australian niceties than anyone else aboard. Shiny door mirrors in golden frames, beautifully shaped letters . . . this was truly a place for connoisseurs, for people with class, who respected neither weekday nor holiday when the desire pulsated urgently. In short, in my simple soul I believed that this was a first-class bordello.

I had no idea that the Australians were closely related to the

Muslims. Exactly as the latter, the former separate women from men in public saloons. As it is said in the Koran, "Woman, your destiny proclaims that water slips through your hands while the man cups his hands and drinks from the holy well." One understands that men with such beliefs feel shame in front of their women. But that the men in Australia in the middle of the twentieth century behaved as Muslims was news to me. You can't know everything at the age of seventeen, after all. How that tallies with my knowledge of the Koran is easy to explain: Every sailor is filled with vague tales about that religion. That's how it is, pure and simple. You inhale it on the sea. Some is true, some is not.

Filled with desire, I took a deep breath in order to control my nerves and tiptoed through the doors.

The room was swimming in a green, dim light. To walk inside felt like diving into the Sargasso Sea. Just to be on the safe side, I continued holding my breath. The large shutters were pulled closed on the wall with windows, but a tiny amount of light trickled in. The opposite wall consisted of green latticework all the way to the ceiling. Voices and murmurs slipped in from the other side along with cigarette smoke and the clink of glasses.

On the wall across from the hinged entrance doors shimmered a painted fairy-tale landscape. A castle with pinnacles and turrets — and below it glens, ravines, and precipices beneath which flowed a river of silver. Over the wall painting drifted serpentines of smoke, as if an especially ordered effect. I let the doors swing shut behind me, fell down on the chair nearest them, and slowly let out my breath while attempting to assess the situation. Based on my scanty knowledge, this did not look at all like a bordello with style and class. Where were all the wanton women? I had imagined them lazily stretched out on red velvet lounges. In my fantasies they were dressed in light and transparent materials — a throng of skin and bodies multiplied by enormous, gold-framed mirrors. Over the splendor of it all, there would be wafts of mellow music. In other words, something quite like the illustrations to be found in *A Thousand and One Nights*.

Once again disappointment took root in me. As usual I was struck down by myself.

No matter. My boyish dreams contained realistic elements as well. Still, they were disturbing. I preferred to turn to other dreams, those tales woven of foreign, often Oriental, veils. Sometimes they were delicious and refreshing, sometimes heavy with musk and amber, intoxicating odors of myrrh, and smoke of incense.

Well, there was certainly enough smoke in this room. Quite enough. But that was the only thing that muffled the chipped elegance of the dreary place. Either Australian men were sired by tight-fisted Scots and reached satisfaction from the smoke of their own fires or else I was the victim of a massive misunderstanding. Meanwhile my carefully measured time for fun and games was wasting away, slipping between my desperate fingers as I continued my futile chase. Time kept ticking away wretchedly while I stared at the horrendous wall painting. It was just about as naive as I was.

"Garmisch-Partenkirchen. King Ludwig. Ludwig the Mad. He drowned himself in the lake you see down there to the left," said a soft, melodious voice near my ear.

The voice saved me from drowning right there on terra firma. Overwhelmed by disappointment, I had forgotten to breathe. Now I filled my lungs with air and turned toward the voice. And blushed beet red, since I had already indulged myself by sitting down at the woman's table. To her I must have looked like a puffed-up pig with big staring eyes. I stared because she was so beautiful. My eyes turned into eager cat tongues, lapping up her long, ash blond hair, deep gray eyes, straight nose, generous mouth, a simple linen dress, slender fingers that amused themselves by drumming against a tall glass. She sat in a high-backed rattan chair; a lace-trimmed pillow peeked out. She was a lonely mermaid on her throne in the Sargasso Sea.

She leaned forward and sipped something green and bubbly out of the glass through a straw and at the same time smiled toward me. It was a childish smile though it also betrayed an aura of no trespassing. In the sea green dusk, it was impossible to determine her age. Perhaps twenty, perhaps thirty. Absolutely no more. One thing was certain. She was a family girl of the highest order. I had gotten lost but had found what I was looking for.

Everything about her seemed white, as if she had been sitting forever in the shadows, the smoke, and the loneliness, at some distance from male murmur and clamor. I could not stop my staring, and she fell back into the shadows. My chances of introducing myself, as a normal human being would, were long since gone. I felt desperation and intense joy — and did not know if I'd dare to let out my breath in front of such a perfectly divine manifestation.

She held out her hand.

I took it, cleared my throat, and could no longer contain my breath. To my despair, I drooled saliva over her slim white wrist. "I beg your pardon." I hiccuped as best I could.

She laughed. And said she liked the fact that I had studied her with such profound interest.

"Others just sneak glances now and then. What are you drinking?"

She sounded like a genuine English lady. With cool perfection and without anxiety, she put forward such a tremendous question as to what I was drinking. Oh, good God, what was I really drinking? I suggested whatever she had in her glass. Obviously that was all right, since she knocked on the wall and shutters flew open.

Are all barmen in Australia ruddy, pale, and freckled? Do they all keep their mouths full of beer when they speak? Such questions occupied my feeble brain while I waited in terror for him to throw me out. But besides glaring suspiciously and asking if I was bothering the woman, he did nothing except hand me a glass of green stuff. "For the boy," as she put it. From their exchange I also learned her name. Else. It sounded as if she stemmed from the Bavaria of the wall painting. Else. A little vacuous for my taste. Else. No! The most beautiful name on earth!

Her laughter directed toward the ingratiating barman served to disappoint and infuriate me. It was the same smile and laughter she had bestowed on me, soft as a warm wind over peaking waves rolling in toward some exotic land. How could she? How was it possible for her to laugh exactly the same way toward this doughy, freckled relic from a penal colony?

Luckily, I managed to shove my disappointment down into my shoes before she turned back to me. With the same drink as hers in front of me, I was finally able to collect myself enough for a real introduction. I removed the straw and raised my glass.

"Ingemar Johansson," I said simply.

I held out my glass to toast her with suitable dignified elegance. But, horror of horrors, my hand began to tremble and to my own consternation it threw the drink into my face!

Total and utter fiasco. Nervous breakdown already in the first round. This business about not being able to hold on to a glass is an old affliction of which I had thought myself cured. It's the old shakes from my childhood, a kind of cramp that not even my beloved mother could prevent, in spite of her frequent and painful thrashings for the purpose of beating it out of me. Now the spasmic cramp had returned. It had sailed in my backwash from the other side of the globe while I meditated on water that swirls to the right or left. I could stop brooding. For me personally, all fluids jump straight into my face.

One might imagine Else laughing at me. She did not. Instead she began to cry. Quiet, dignified sobs. Oh well, I was used to all kinds of strange reactions since the real Ingemar Johansson lost the match against Floyd Patterson, and I was eternally grateful that she did not laugh at my sticky, green face. But for someone to take it so hard that our national hero lost match and title that she cried from the bottom of her heart was a new experience.

And a strange one to boot. If my mother's tears could be said to represent formidable reprimands so far as I was concerned, Else's seemed more like relieved exclamation marks. Hers were the kind of tears that greet the hero when he rushes down into a horrible prison hole and with one swift cut of the ax frees the prisoner from his shackles. It was the kind of crying you hear from somebody who suddenly sees the light.

"Excuse me," said Else in perfectly understandable Swedish.

In a certain kind of novel the people always jump or jerk or recoil when they are stung by astonishment, panic, or terror. I have always wondered what that looks like in real life, and I myself have tried many times to jerk or recoil in a believable way. It looks really weird, rather spastic and unreal. But at this very moment, I understood precisely how it works. You jerk or recoil on the inside. That's what it is. The soul reels around a couple of times and then stops in a totally new position, and you are no longer the same human being you were.

So I thought, while Else collected her tears in order to dress them in words. In our mother tongue's singsong tonalities, sometimes using peculiar sentence structures, she told her story.

She was as Swedish as I am. But, being married to Smith Allen, she had never been able to go home again, in spite of agonizing and recurring attacks of homesickness. Two hours and a few more glasses of green stuff later, Else had in turns painted this Smith Allen as a first-ranking wife beater and the world's unluckiest specimen.

She was a young au pair girl in London when they met. He was several years older but equipped with muscles and charm. He was also extremely successful in his profession as a stockbroker. An English aristocrat to the tip of his fingers; nobody could detect a trace of a proletarian background. Yet his father still slaved away in a coal mine in Wales. Eighteen years old and so much in love that it hurt, she became Mrs. Smith Allen and pranced about on the feathery clouds of high society. If her story has any moral, it must be that upstarts who create their own luck, destiny, and fortune find it more difficult to hold on to it all. Along with this goes an account of gradual transformation from human being to beast, if Else told the whole truth.

The fairy tale ended when Allen's father had an accident, deep down in the black hole of a mine. The company regretted the incident, but the corpse could never be brought up from the collapsed coal mine. Much too expensive. Mr. and Mrs. Smith Allen set out to bury the father symbolically in hallowed ground. Else had not met her in-laws before. Allen had prevented such an encounter.

Else remembered the funeral as a sad, sooty event. Immediately afterward, Allen had disappeared, leaving her alone with the widow. To speak with Allen's mother was like keeping up a conversation with a sackful of frostbitten potatoes. Outside rain poured down in buckets, the way it does only on poorly insulated English workers' dwellings. The gas stove emitted smoky fumes. Stubbornly, the widow kept the window open, just in case the company whistle would give the signal: "We have found him! We have found him!"

Else did not realize that. Shivering, she sat in the draft, one half of her body hot, the other half icy cold, while Allen's mother muttered spitefully about winds that blew whichever way they wanted in poor workmen's sheds. Allen did not return to his parental home until the wee hours of the night. For the first time Else saw him drunk. She described his eyes as dead and drowned in alcohol.

"Oh yes, the alcohol. That damned alcohol," I mumbled like some narrow-minded evangelist instead of thinking about the reasons for Allen's black sorrow.

They went to a luxurious hotel where they had reservations. The trip was as easy as snapping one's fingers, but it was then Else understood how far Allen had traveled from his origins. A will of steel, hardened by fuel his father had provided, had made Allen the career-obsessed man he was. The father's goal in life was, understandably enough, that his son would never set foot inside a coal mine. Such shreds of information were included in Allen's delirious ravings in bed, while she was soaking in a hot bath. He hollered, fell asleep, mumbled, ranted, and waved his arms while he uttered terrible threats, and then fell asleep again. As a married woman, Else was two years older now but hardly any wiser. She was lying in the sparklingly clean, warm, tiled bathroom, growing to catch up with herself.

"It was first then that I truly loved him. Isn't that terrible?" whispered Else in our green Sargasso Sea.

She was relieved to be able to speak to a fellow Swede after all these years.

From that day on, Allen began to slide downward as determinedly as he had climbed upward earlier. He went to expensive lawyers, threatened the mine company with futile lawsuits, gambled away other people's fortunes, and disappeared for weeks on end from the couple's expensive city home. She was the one to receive the eviction notice and the one who found a cheaper place to live. She was the one who exerted herself in the extreme, trying to bring a light back into Allen's extinguished eyes when he showed up occasionally, each time skinnier and more and more like the pictures of his father.

Their last resources melted away. Friends drifted off and disappeared. It took less than two years, and by then Else's love began to waver. Then one day, without forewarning, Allen came home with sparkling eyes and waved airline tickets in front of her face. It was the old Allen dancing around the bare room. It was a burning Allen, gushing sun and eternal warmth, speaking about a new and different life, a new continent. It was an Allen who, at a neighborhood pub, had bought a claim in a mine in Coober Pedy.

That was how Else came as a mine worker's wife to the promised land of Australia. The two of them would dig for opals. Allen must have realized that he continued the family tradition by digging deeper and deeper into the ground, but it was in order to preserve their happiness, he passionately pointed out. Down there in the sandy, cool chambers of the mine were immeasurable riches buried. After a few years, they would be able to settle down, have children, and live well.

Else told me how things worked out in reality. She told of Coober Pedy, where people went as far as building their homes underground, she told of opals that slipped through Allen's fingers as quickly as he dug them up, and she told about horses. Beautiful horses. Horses running like the wind. Untrustworthy racehorses with poetic names. All the reasons that they still lived in a hole in the ground. Allen gambled. Once a year they went to Adelaide and stayed at this hotel. Allen lost his opals, and they went back to their miserable life. This had gone on for more than ten years.

I added quickly in my head. She had to be a little over thirty — and had been unable to save herself during a span of ten horrid years.

Why?

As my father used to say, "If the shoes don't fit, buy a new pair." The world is full of shoes, but a human being is not a piece of leather with shoelaces. More like a hand grenade without a safety catch is a human being, tenderly, lovingly, and violently molded and forged by the parents. I understood that when Else spoke a few words about her own parents. She would not give them the satisfaction of saying, "Didn't we tell you? We told you, didn't we?"

One is most convincing when one lacks experience. Consequently, I lectured at length and quite eloquently about the lost but found child who returns home to old parents. They would slaughter the fattened calf in her honor, eat, and make themselves merry. I kept talking. And as usual, I had no idea what I was getting into.

I had also managed to get a word in edgewise here and there about myself. Else knew that I was a young man with presence of mind. She grasped my hand and said tearfully that fate had chosen me to save her. We ought to flee together. Or rather — I could help her to escape before Allen appeared and forced her to go back. In truth, they did not stay at the hotel. Allen could no longer stand being enclosed by four walls, so they were camping a few miles outside the city. Could I help her to get there and back? She had to pick up a few things. If I would only do that . . .

She did not exactly put her life in my hands. She jumped into them, as if from a tower in Ludwig's castle. I was benumbed and robbed of what little sense I normally possessed. To save her from a fanatic opal hunter seemed a lighthearted, easily snatched adventure. It goes without saying that any man with his self-respect intact would have had to say yes. The problem was that I did not have a driver's license. A rather disagreeable detail in a magnificent whole, I had to admit. She would have to drive. But she waved that away with a crushing argument: Allen's truck was not adapted to handicapped persons. She was in a wheelchair!

She laughed at my stupid pretense of being a law-abiding citizen. So typically Swedish!

"Go on. Push me so we can get on our way!"

I must have fallen asleep at some point in her story. My cheeks were burning. So that was why she had been sitting so still and why the chair looked different. And that was why she hadn't been able to get away. Allen really kept her prisoner. But why was she in a wheelchair?

In time I would find out, I supposed. I snuck up behind the wicker chair and grabbed hold of the varnished handles. With its small rubber wheels and stainless spokes, the chair felt ready to roll both of us to a gaping hole in quicksand. The barman was peering out through his aperture. He did not seem to react to any mentionable degree when Else chirped something to the effect that "the boy" was going to drive her around the park. Obviously Allen paid the bill. He would be amazed at the amount of green juice we had managed to imbibe.

The boy, meaning me, rolled Else out of the hotel without having any explanation as to why it happened to be open on a Sunday. What I mean is, had it been closed like other places, this remarkable story would never have happened. I decided to remember that as a good excuse when I met up with the first mate and his fury. It was already dark outside, the clocks would strike the midnight hour shortly, but even if I were to run so fast that I dropped my shoes on the road, I could not make it back to the ship in time.

I thought of that while I lifted Else into the small truck, well advanced in years, and put the wheelchair in back, lashing it securely in place with bits of rope left there for that purpose. Even her calling me a boy paled in comparison with the memory of her slight body in my arms. And even if Else's plan seemed far from thoroughly researched and I felt as if trying to escape with a pink elephant through the city, I would drive her wherever she wanted to go.

My head snapped around like an owl's. The car keys were in the ignition. The sinister Allen character could not be far away. And was he possibly her keeper from some mental institution in town? Well, OK, so be it. If that were so, he would have to take me, too, I thought, since Else leaned forward right then. It was sudden and spontaneous and not well planned, but it would all work out, she may have wanted to say when she planted a light kiss on my cheek. The small, dry kiss acted like a branding iron on a calf. Now I knew where I belonged and where I was going. It had nothing to do with bordellos and whores. An angel sat by my side. She may not be as young as I had thought, but an angel for sure. A girl from a good family and with purest Swedish blood in her veins. The memory of Allen vanished and all sense of time with him. My heart was pounding in my chest like a diesel engine, the pulse was a propeller-driven force, full speed forward without stopping, and her shy smile blinked like the lighthouse outside a friendly port, wide open, offering a safe haven for people with pure souls.

It was simple. I was a romantic idiot.

We sailed away from the cauldron of the city, up over the hills, and in among the trees. Here and there a kangaroo turned around to stare. They might have heard of Ingemar Johansson, avid boxers as they were.

Else touched my arm lightly when I should turn right or left. I have no idea how long we drove. Perhaps an hour. Meanwhile Else set forth her plan. In the darkness, it sounded perfectly reasonable.

She was going to pick up passport and money. I would drive her to the airport, and she would be on her way back home.

Finally we reached their camping place in a valley with a murmuring brook. With its patches and tears, the pale cotton tent did not look as if there would be money inside. I lifted Else down from the truck, carried her inside, and lighted a kerosene lamp. Allen had hammered down three stakes in a row along the middle to give Else support and guidance as she moved around. After a moment's hesitation, she asked me to wait outside. I could get some water from the stream, if I wanted to. She would wash up and change to more suitable clothing.

The stars of the Southern Hemisphere lighted my way, winking as amiably as the stars on the other side. The first mate did not spend all his energy teaching me the Morse code; he had also taught me something about those sparkling little pinpoints up there. Even at the tender age of seventeen, a poet lurks in the chest of every sailor. It is grand and agreeable to hurl one's questions, thoughts, and dreams into space. But never did I think that I would stand in the middle of the night in a valley among Adelaide's hills, dipping a pail into a stream to get water for my woman, while musing on the unexplainable mystery of love. In a strictly legal sense, she was of course not my woman, but it was dark enough outside that not a soul on earth could find his way here and demand his lawful wedded right.

I whistled in a typically male manner and trudged along with the water to the tent, considerately put the bucket through the tent flap's wavering opening, and walked a few yards away. I did not wait in vain. Even earlier I had seen Else's silhouette, as if in an old reliable shadow play, flutter against the tent cloth. I have to admit that I took my place in the first-row orchestra seat — partly curious as to how she would manage and, to a larger extent, because it was fun and felt good. I felt I had earned some reward for my efforts so far. Else had already pulled the dress over her head. She was leaning against one of the stakes. Sometimes her body became that of a gigantic goddess, sometimes a wavering stick figure. The arms came unstuck and played out their own enigmatic sign symbols — a temple dancer's slow gyrations, a giraffe with majestic movements, and there a snake wrapping itself around another snake.

My heart waltzed round and round during the performance, and I began to think of the next act with me as costar.

Then she fell.

There was a clatter of metal. She disappeared from the lighted circle created by the kerosene lamp. I waited. All was silent.

I stumbled into the tent. Else was lying on the floor with the dress covering most of her. She mumbled that I ought to let her try on her own. But then she pulled the dress from her face and said that actually the washing was Allen's chore. So would I be kind enough . . . ?

Save her? Yes, I wanted to do that. Love her? Oh yes. Even seduce her. I could imagine myself doing that. But to wash a thirty-year-old stranger's body? Wasn't that just a little too much? What if I discovered a lot of loose skin on her?

I stammered that of course I would, lifted her carefully so she could support herself against the stake, took hold of the sponge, and actually thought of my grandmother. Thousands of times she told of "The Large Washing of Refugees from the HORRIBLE WAR! They stand there as God created them. Nothing more to it. Easy as a butterfly's dance. And they are deeply grateful when THE LICE is washed off them."

"We have to start over again." I cleared my throat and began my new task with some trepidation.

It was not the same as scraping rust. And she did not look as if she needed red-leading or painting. She was smooth as marble, bone white in the light of the lamp, the shoulders thin, the breasts struggling upward, firm, with nipples like curious and fearless eyes staring into my own half-closed ones. Her backside was a song. The legs, too. Until dawn would break and the shadows flee, until the morning breeze would sneak through, I could have kept washing her body. I began to know a woman in a way I had not imagined. And then we would rest and take pleasure from each other, tightly embracing. And we would awaken and I would blow my breath on her and say, "Take your bed and walk."

I had hallucinations to such a degree that I mixed up the Song of Solomon with the miracles of Jesus and took it for granted that I would be able to repeat every trick and feat.

Why not?

All was possible. A kangaroo had obviously turned into a camel, right there in the city of Adelaide.

But a murderous opal hunter could be jolting along at this minute on the back of a kangaroo in order to shoot me like a mad dog and tie Else to the stake. It was time to leave. I kept washing, having almost turned into water myself, dissolved by nervousness as I was, when Else took my trembling hand and brought it to her breast. It was glossy and clean and burned heavily in my hand.

"Yes . . . yes," I said and cleared my throat. "Good as new. All we have to do now . . ."

I kept babbling. In vain, I tried to find something that would lighten up the massive solemnity in the deep shadows of her eyes. Help! Her eyes were flames that could melt me totally. And that was what she did. And I, as the imbecile I was, kept moving my mouth and making stupid noises until the eyes went out.

That is unforgivable stupidity, she let me understand, turning her back to me. I dried her, rubbing carefully and slowly, as if it were possible to caress the flames to life again. But no. The chance was lost. The moment was gone. In this other dress, she looked even more like a very young girl. She sat down on the cot and asked me to wait outside.

Perhaps she wanted to say good-bye. I went outside.

When Else let out a desperate cry, the Southern Cross gasped. Perhaps her exhausted pain could be heard even up there?

"He has taken my passport, my papers," she sobbed when I came rushing in.

She sat as if hit by lightning and rattled an old Ridgway's tea canister in her hand. In that small tin enclosure, she had hidden her life.

But why did the tin can rattle?

She smiled strangely at my question and I could see the hatred toward the man who had ruined her life.

"Because inside are the three opals I had in my hand when Allen was going to help me get out of the mine. I fell. Since then I've been unable to walk. He didn't dare to ask why I wanted to get back into the daylight so quickly. There are three of them, big as eggs. And they are mine!"

Else laughed and rocked the canister in her arms. Allen could gamble away his pebbles, but this fortune was hers to keep. Until one day . . .

That day seemed far away without a passport. Australia's passport police is harder than stone. We discussed the matter back and forth. She was inexorably stuck. What could we do? Go to the police? Find a lawyer? Sell the opals? If they were that large, rumors would start up and the truth would become known. A poor wheelchair-bound woman who becomes a millionairess is hard to hide. She would be a choice tidbit for all of Australia's tabloids. Allen would demand his share. A worthwhile trade in order to gain freedom. But no, Else did not want to let go of her stones.

"In Genoa, one can sell opals. And buy traveling papers really easily," I said without thinking.

The matter was settled anyhow.

It was so settled that nothing more needed to be said.

Else held the canister close to her breasts when I picked her up. A small distance from the camp, my own surprise went to sleep. I had not taken advantage of the poor woman's dilemma. And Else did not need to buy her freedom from me. But later . . . with her hidden in my cabin as a stowaway, we would have time to get to know each other. One day she would give me a sign. It could be the day we crossed the equator! What a wonderful christening, compared to mine the first time across. A mermaid, that's what she was. I promised myself not to hesitate another time.

It was past midnight. The first mate would be standing there, waiting. Wouldn't he be surprised when I returned, carrying a Swedish girl from a good family in my arms?

Meanwhile, I had not the faintest idea how I would get Else aboard the ship. If her plan was an old leaky barge, mine was ready for the ships' graveyard. But I could always trust luck. Within the last twenty-four hours, I had received my life back more than once. And I did not lack courage. Sharks and first mates, jealousy and madmen, what did all that mean compared to washing a woman such as Else?

I parked the truck a small distance from the port, pulled off the wheelchair, and lifted her down. By now we were like old partners in a routine criminal task. In silent collusion we moved forward, Else on whirring rubber wheels and I behind the chair. My head could as well have been a hollowed-out pumpkin. Fresh air blew right through it, and I did everything with good steering speed and precision.

The first mate stood stock-still by the gangway. That touched my heart. I parked Else behind some bales and hurried over to him. Boldly, I blew my breath toward his suspicious, sniffing nose. The smell of the green juice drink enveloped us like a cloud of sweet perfume. His surly grimace turned into a fatherly grin. I was stone sober. But what had transpired at the front?

I entertained him for a while, telling about my waiting at his recommended spot until late in the evening. Then an old cleaning woman came to do her thing. The beautiful and alluring females? On Sundays they go to church. Then it's time for Sunday roast. Grilled kangaroo tail. But on Mondays, they all return, as impious and round-heeled as always. Could it really be true? The thing about the kangaroo tail?

The first mate's eyes filled with tears. In other words, I was an innocent boy. For my own good, I ought never to go ashore but stay aboard ship and knock rust. I understood how to do that. That I understood nothing else should not give me any sleepless nights. There are few universally talented men. And every first mate has not as much consideration and care for an unimportant louse called a deck boy. But perhaps there weren't that many truly innocent boys left on the seas? Now he had seen such a one with his own eyes and could get his well-earned rest. We were touchingly in agreement and said good night as bosom buddies.

I looked after him. There my own truth went to bed, never to awaken again. He wasn't a bad sort, the first mate. It was uncomfortable to lie to him. I was a miserable, wretched human being. Inside me existed nothing but bottomless lies. I whispered my hope that the first mate might rest in peace for quite a while.

I, on the other hand, had a lot to do.

Quick as a river rat, I whipped back down to Else as soon as the coast was clear. I pulled my troubled friend out of the wheelchair and heaved her up on my back. Now or never. With legs moving faster than beating sticks on a drum, I ran up the gangway and further astern, while I silently chanted phony explanations for my burden in case somebody would ask any idiotic questions.

"Just a girl from a good family."

It was brave in all its simplicity. Of course, one may think that a girl from a really good family would not set foot on a ship's deck. A lot of loose rubbish, not to mention what was welded in place, seemed made to order for damage to family girls' tender extremities.

Outside the bosun's porthole, I shook with laughter. I practically went on all fours beneath it with Else on my back. The bosun was talking in his sleep.

"Catch that shark!" he hollered.

The clear pronunciation meant that he wore his false teeth when he slept. What good did they do? Perhaps his tongue would fall down his throat and suffocate him otherwise? That was a piece of information worth looking into.

I deposited Else on the only chair in my cabin.

We were bickering like an old married couple when I told her why I had laughed. She did not find it amusing. She was angry and embarrassed. Of course both of us were scared. She pulled herself up and hissed, the way people do in real marriages. I beamed. We were indeed growing closer. A few weeks aboard the ship, and we would be a true couple.

We argued about the wheelchair. I refused to carry it aboard. Better to roll it off the pier.

"It may float," I said. "Tired of your life, you have given yourself to the sharks. It lies there as a warning sign to Allen, something to think about alone in his hole."

"But you were the one who wheeled me out of the hotel," she pointed out.

She was right, of course. To rot in prison was not my goal in life. Or perhaps they went so far as to hang people in Australia?

So why argue?

I was catching my breath to deliver the next argument when the same thought hit her. She smiled and asked my forgiveness. The excitement, the heat, the feeling of safety — I don't know what, but suddenly we were like two empty sacks of flour, falling against each other. She was both heavy and light. Her chin rested against my collarbone. She raised and lowered her arms, and the dress draped itself around her feet. She kept her balance by leaning against me while I tore off my shirt. I felt her breasts, and her breath was warm and alive.

The next moment, there were loud bangings and reverberating knocks on the door.

Instead of putting her softly and carefully in the berth, I threw her in and pulled the curtain. The privacy of even a deck boy's cabin is supposed to be respected. I had to open the door, but to let anyone over the threshold was unthinkable. Not even the captain had any business in the cabin, other than to inspect after cleanup in the forecastle, and such inspections were not carried out in the middle of a night between Sunday and Monday.

I opened the door to utter a few well-chosen words but was instead blinded by a roaring pain in my head. Exactly in the spot where the corpulent cop hit me with his revolver. Red flames danced in front of my eyes. The Southern firmament could not compete with the stars I saw glowing in the orb of my head. But they paled at the sight of the crowd in the corridor. There stood the man who owned the hole in the wall, the cabdriver, the suspicious bartender from the hotel, looking like at least a cousin of the first; there stood the first mate and there stood a tall, brawny man who looked ferocious. For once, I am not exaggerating. It had to be Allen. All of them pointed at me and hollered in unison that I was the one!

"Who else would I be?" I asked, trying to sound sleepy.

But the game was lost. The cop drove the revolver up my nose in spite of the first mate's quiet remark that the ship was Swedish territory and that the crew was under Swedish jurisdiction. Even if it hurt to nod with a revolver up my nose, I agreed with him.

"Kidnapping topped off by murder knows no limits," hissed Allen. "You perverted turd! What did you do to her before you threw her off the pier?!"

There was only one thing to do. To deny everything.

"She jumped in by herself!" I cried out.

That was a rather stupid thing to say about a woman in a wheelchair. But with a revolver in the nostril, one thinks of the strangest things to say.

I was ready to swear that I was innocent, when a chilling female howl made everyone freeze. Nude and whiter than I remembered her, Else flew out of the berth. To everybody's amazement, she ran like a gazelle past the group of perplexed men.

The cop stared stupidly into the muzzle of the revolver. Either he was looking for what had been in my nose or else he was pleading with the bullet to choose its own direction. Allen's eyes were bursting out of their sockets.

"See for yourselves," I said. "She went on her own."

I made a mental note to remember that line. Evidently I would become famous all over the world, since I had performed a miracle. The closest my family had come to medical wonders was when my grandfather was operated on by the world-famous surgeon Professor Crawford. Grandpa let himself be known as the Crawford Aorta Constriction. Now I would be famous because my healing love for Else had actually made her stand up and walk.

Allen, however, wanted revenge. I should be shot on the spot, like a dog. He threw himself on the cop and wrested the revolver from him much too easily. To stay there and act the target would be not only stupid but dangerous to my life. I made a wild break, similar to Else's, and was out on deck almost faster than she.

What had happened to her?

How come she could run, fleet-footed as a hind?

To receive an answer to these questions this side of death seemed unlikely because right then the first bullet bounced off the sill of the fifth hatch. The midship aisle was straight and illuminated like a shooting gallery in an amusement park. Ten yards more and I would literally die in the middle of a leap, as my uncle did when he was goalie for the glass factory's soccer team. He was never really good at it. He always died in the middle of a leap, the old sports veterans said.

This was no time, however, to think of those near and dear.

I ran past the place where the painting raft ought to have been. It wasn't there. Otherwise I could have thrown myself behind it. And the rope ladders up to the boat deck were bathed in light. Allen's mad shrieks were closing in behind me, closely followed by yet another bullet that crackled into the midship structure. It was sufficient incentive to speed up my brain's decisive faculty.

I jumped overboard.

Even in such a robust construction as an oceangoing modern freighter, there is something called the exhaustion phenomenon. A gigantic ship can split along the welding seams, an enormous wave can rip the ship in two and sink it in ten seconds. Unfortunately, those who have experienced this phenomenon cannot tell us how it feels, since they are no longer among us. But I can imagine the experience vividly. It's exactly as if you for a moment are sure of having found the perfect hiding place from whizzing bullets — and in the next moment you reflect that nobody is stupid enough to jump into a harbor basin crawling with sharks. Only to discover yourself to be that stupid.

Among human traits there is a specific one: the attempt to do the impossible, such as to nullify the law of gravity or climb in the air. "Nothing is impossible. The impossible just takes a little longer," was my competent first mate's spirited motto. I would have liked to ask him what one does when there is no time to take a little longer. Does one tap the SOS against God's benevolent forehead? And what is the correct response if He taps "bon voyage" back? How many times have I not heard my grandmother talk about those who were not destined to live to a ripe old age. Perhaps I turned out to be one of those.

No! Not on your life!

I landed in the water with a splash, determined to keep on living, even if I had to bite off shark fins with my young, strong teeth.

An enormous splash too close to me interrupted such galloping plans. It was Allen. He had jumped in after me, determined to drown me. He was snorting and hitting wildly all around. I was nearly paralyzed but kept floating like a sour old piece of wood. I didn't dare move. With tiny, cautious hand movements, I kept my nose above the surface of the water and steered away from Else's murderous Allen, moving smoothly along the ship's hull. Its surface felt like rough, slimy skin to the touch. Allen had the same idea, of course. He treaded water a few yards away and listened. I moved along, my nails digging into the ship's metal, pulled at some sea-weed, and got scratched by tiny shells, while the crew kept shout-ing up on deck. Everybody was awake by now. Presently they rearranged the floodlights. Thanks a whole heap! To be drowned fully illuminated in front of a fascinated viewing audience — what more could I want? Why not a couple of sharks to complete nature's inevitable food chain? To be reborn as a molecule in a shark, was that my future?

Oh well. Things could be worse. Buried in the ground like ordinary people, I would in time be nothing but manure.

The raft? Where was it? Somebody must have moved it. Sternward or toward the bowsprit?

A meaningless question under the circumstances since Allen was in my way if I wanted to go sternward. I scraped on, with each inch bidding my young life farewell. The closer I got to the raft, the greater the risk of a date with sharks.

Not that I have any notion of the conscience of sharks, but somehow I felt it would be fairer if they only chewed up me. Sure, Allen had pulled his wife into a hole in the ground. But what did that have to do with me? In order to play hero, I had pulled an innocent human being into my magnetic field of foolishness.

Suddenly I hit my head against the raft. Simultaneously the people on deck had become organized. A light swung out over the side of the ship. Anxious voices screamed for us to get up. A shot rang out. First I thought it was Allen shooting at me, then I understood that the corpulent policeman was aiming at approaching sharks. Allen was swimming in a furious crawl toward me and the raft. I did not dare pull myself up. We had no intentions of exchanging friendly hugs, nor of pounding each other's backs and spitting in unison on stupid, elongated shark snouts. No, Allen would be the first one to throw me right back into the water. I might as well stay where I was.

I took advantage of the darkness to wriggle in between the raft and the ship's side. My toes felt the reinforcements I had made for the raft with my own hands. I had used rough-hewn planks, and the space between the four oil kegs was more than half a yard, so there was at least half an inch of airspace for breathing. I had no time to think. I squeezed myself in beneath the raft. A few nails tore my back and splinters from the planks embedded themselves in my skin. Was I safe between the deck of the raft and the planks beneath it?

The floodlight's intense glare threw a gruesome trelliswork of light through the fissures between the planks, and I imagined the sharks studying a well-illuminated morsel ready to be served, whenever they decided to take a flying leap. Pure and tender meat of lamb instead of tough sheep, dead from more or less natural causes. . . .

Allen's hand hit against the raft. His heavy breathing wheezed a few inches from my face. Could he see me? No, he was letting himself down a little in order to gather himself for the jump up on the raft.

That's when the shark hit the raft. There was a dull thud and it felt like a pressure wave in the water against my whole body. The raft lurched. I swallowed a lot of seawater. At first, I thought I was the one screaming bloody murder, but it was Allen, hollering in pure panic.

The first mate came swinging down on the hooked chain cable. A brave man was he. Nobody else did have the courage to try to get down to us. I heard the clatter when he hooked up the raft. Once more the violent shark thudded against the woodwork right in front of me. Allen was shrieking, as if possessed by demons. The raft danced around, smacked against the surface of the water as if unwilling to leave the games instigated by the sharks, but then it took off along the ship's side. Something warm and sticky ran over my face. The sweetish, mawkish stuff must be Allen's blood.

When the raft flopped down on deck, I realized that nobody had discovered me in my hiding place between the planks. Allen's mutilated legs attracted all eyes. There was less than half an inch aperture between the raft planks, but I could see enough to follow what was taking place. I was probably not the only one who was shocked when the first mate hollered to our potbellied captain to remove his pajama pants. The bosun however understood the need for such an action. Awakened from deep sleep, he still wore his false teeth.

"Yes! Do that!" he said, his words clear as crystal.

Except for the captain, the first mate was the only one with pants on, though he had already pulled them off. The man with his pot in front of him took off his silky pajama pants, slowly and hesitatingly. He threw them from the boat deck. They fluttered down. The first mate, himself nude, wrapped his pants around what remained of one of Allen's legs. Quickly the bosun did the same with the other leg, using the captain's silk pants. Somebody held out a knife for the first mate to lash the bandage in place. The bosun grabbed hold of an iron bar that happened to be lying around. That way they got leverage to tie the cloth tightly against the leg stumps.

Allen was quiet. He had fainted long ago. Soon he was carried across the deck to the ship's other side. The cop ran ahead. I wanted to call out and recommend that they use the truck but was struck silent by the sight of bloody bone pipes beneath Allen's thighs. I closed my eyes. It's possible that I fainted.

When I came to, my old enemy Svenson was sitting on the raft, sobbing loudly. The bosun bawled him out, but the German defended him, saying that unreliable scum like me would probably just poison the sharks and reappear as pestiferous seaweed during the trip home.

No, better to be dead than having to clear up the mess I had managed to make of everything. I was beginning to feel that it wasn't so bad to be dead since I was still alive. To get involved in their discussion from the other side of life seemed not only stupid but meaningless. The German's earlier threats rose in my ears like rancid old seawater. Let bygones be bygones, I thought — and by that I was referring to myself.

But why was seaman Svenson so unhappy?

I peered through the fissures when the bosun and the German left.

What I saw made the blood freeze in my veins. For a few seconds I'm sure that I was really dead, had anyone bothered to check the matter. Svenson was sitting with an enormous shark head over his shoulders, trying the jaws against his throat. Inside it, he mumbled thickly how intensely painful it must be when it happened for real. Now I understood the bosun's excited speech. Clearly, the crew had managed to catch a shark. That was why the raft had been left outside the ship. Svenson had put the head of the shark at the foot of my berth to get back at me. And Else must have put her feet into the jaws and been so frightened that she had run away in spite of not being able to walk.

Just like me, Svenson had quite a bit on his conscience.

Obviously my power to heal was nothing compared to a couple of slimy shark jaws. As my grandmother used to say, "To do magic is all right, but to be proud of it is destructive."

My spirits were low. But that was nothing compared to Svenson's genuine sorrow. He sat there for so long, snuffling and clicking the shark's jaws, that I was almost ready to tell him that things could be worse. For instance, he could have been me.

Finally he left me alone to ponder my fate.

Even dead, I had to depend on the laws ruling life on earth. The first thing was to get away from the raft and hide in a safer place until I could be resurrected. Once we were far away from the dangerous land of Australia, I could jump out. Who knows? The first mate may even be glad to see me.

A piece of advice to anyone who plans to hide in a lifeboat: Bring along a flashlight. I tried to open a tin of canned goods and broke my nails in the process. When I finally put its whole contents into my mouth, it turned out to be a fishing line with quadruple hook and float. I spent many a sweaty hour trying to ease the hook out of my gap. It wasn't fun at all.

The days passed. And the nights arrived with regular intervals. It was the worst strike in the history of Australian dockworkers, which is saying a lot. I had no concept of time, but I believe that we remained anchored four weeks more. Little by little, I was able to plan and execute small thieving expeditions during nightly hours and managed rather well in the lifeboat. After a while I became brave enough to use the commander's toilet. It was quite luxurious. In the afternoons, he sat under the lifeboat and conversed with the beer mug on his stomach. One thing he could not understand: Why did he seem to keep forgetting to flush the toilet nowadays? I could have called out to him that flushing would have awakened him.

I spent most of the time thinking about Else. I came to no conclusion. That is a recurrent problem in my life.

After a considerable number of days, the loading began. It went fast. One morning I awoke, feeling vibrations in the lifeboat. The main engine was alive and running. We were finally leaving Port Adelaide. We were going home. I rejoiced and peered out under the cover of the lifeboat. Exactly as I thought. The hatches were all closed. Ready to sail. I felt almost like waving farewell from the lifeboat but quickly pulled back my hand. Right in front of my nose was Allen, moving past in Else's old wheelchair. As soft and neatly as if on clouds with springs, the German with the help of winches lifted him up through the air and aboard, in spite of Allen's rantings and ravings while he waved the small leg stumps.

Else's voice reached my ears from the gangway. It sounded sure and happy.

What was this? What were they doing aboard the ship?

The captain's stentorian voice explained the whole thing.

"It's the least we can do!"

Aaaah! My sins paid for their tickets. All guilt and blame had conveniently been placed on the dead one. I felt like resurrecting myself on the spot in order to speak a few words of truth regarding Else's part in our disastrous plan. She was the one, wasn't she, who had seduced a poor innocent boy? No, I had to be careful with Allen aboard the ship. Who knew what he kept beneath the wheelchair plaid? Perhaps a sawed-off shotgun, perhaps a knife meant to nail and carve ghosts out of deck boys. I argued back and forth with myself a few rocky days while our ship set off at full speed for the Red Sea.

One afternoon the ship stopped.

Help! Lifeboat drill, I thought, and cursed the zealous first mate. From my hideout, I had heard him trying to teach Svenson the Morse code. He even used my quick ability to grasp things as a worthy example. I nodded in agreement. Svenson couldn't even tell the difference between a dot and a dash most of the time. The first mate could have tired of those lessons by now and turned his attention to the crew, wanting to get the men involved in new activities.

I shut my eyes and waited for the lifeboat cover to be ripped off. Then my skinny-but-still-not-eaten body would be revealed before the congregation's astonished eyes among the remains of my thievery.

But nothing happened and nobody appeared.

The ship seemed deserted. I peered out. A ship moving forward in open sea is familiar and secure. But stop the engines and let the ship roll in whatever swells the sea offers, and the ship turns pitiful. Worse than I felt when I saw my shipmates in their finest ashore clothing, standing at attention on the astern deck, waiting for the captain. I understood that I was going to witness my own funeral.

Naturally, there was no body to wrap chains around. The bosun had no nose to put the last stitch through after sewing the sailcloth shroud. But the steward had thoughtfully contributed a Christmas tree from cold storage, and the kitchen staff had artfully arranged the branches into a wreath with silk ribbons and written messages that waved farewell. A short piece of chain was fastened underneath the wreath so that it would sink in place of my already presumedly consumed body.

The captain's words were brief and vigorous. The desolate wind carried them to my ear. He described me as a curious and gutsy young man. When the flag was lowered and the wreath slipped into the water, at least my eyes were not dry. So much bother on my behalf.

Below the lifeboat, on the lifeboat deck, stood Else behind Allen in the wheelchair. She sobbed beautifully while he irritatedly asked her to stop. Else found it absolutely terrible. I had been "just a little boy."

Not so little, I thought. Disappointment, jealousy, and a perfectly normal question pained my chest, as I was lying low in the lifeboat.

What would have happened, had we not been interrupted? Would Else have been able to call me a little boy afterward?

Questions flitted about as uneasily as lost souls. But ghosts did not exist in my head only. Many aboard the ship felt there were unearthly visits. I roamed around just about everywhere, thinking that perhaps it would be good to be discovered. One evening I went astern, to my own cabin. It was empty. I wasn't there. On the bunk was my worn cardboard suitcase with the lid open. Inside the lid the first mate had glued a list of my belongings, witnessed by the bosun. I recognized that trick. A good system. Then one can be absolutely certain.

Furthest down on the list the first mate had noted one Ridgway's tea container with three stones, rather large. Worthless, he had added in parentheses. A gutsy little man he was, and very neat, too. But obviously he had never seen opals in the rough. I took the container and sneaked back up again. My thought was to put it on the boat deck so Else would see and recover it. After all, she was the legal owner. But things did not happen that way.

Later that evening I was awakened from my dreams in the lifeboat by agitated voices. Else and Allen were having a heated argument. The stiff breeze tore their sentences into small pieces so I never heard any distinct words. Suddenly the chain running along the deck underneath the lifeboat clattered. I managed to stick my head out on the same side. There was a free fall to the water under the lifeboat. I could do nothing. With full speed Else pushed the wheelchair with Allen in it over the edge.

Since he was turned toward the ship, I could see his face. He looked perfectly content.

Else wavered close to the perilous edge like someone intoxicated. Desperately I pulled at the lashing that held down the lifeboat cover. Sometimes it took me endless minutes to open and close it so well that no observant eyes could detect any loose pieces of rope. I bent and twisted trying to get out quickly. I even called out. Too late. Else was already suspended in air and soon disappeared.

I will never understand why both of them longed for the bottom of the sea.

So this is the story of how things turned out when I tried to visit a bordello in the fair city of Port Adelaide.

The opals in the tea canister?

I snuck ashore in Genoa and sold them for three hundred and fifty billion lire. I got a false passport as a bonus. That was OK. But the money did not even cover a train ticket home. It was counterfeit and of no value whatsoever.

ALGERIA
1976

Louise was magnificent. Toward sunset she drove up in a four-wheel-drive Landrover. To the best of my knowledge, she had no driver's license. I rushed out to shop, picking the ultimate luxury-food items the place had to offer: lamb cutlets, wine, salad, a can of condensed milk, and "la vache qui rit" cheese cubes.

My hospitable Frenchman was away. We had the house to ourselves, but still we ate among the spiny bushes next to the cracked pond. Some children were drumming stubbornly on tin cans, and the hard contrasts between light and dark melted and merged in a warm blush before everything was shrouded in the blackness of night. I wanted to paint her face, without shadows and with that precise softness, as if rosy childhood skin had been magically restored. Louise had gained a few pounds. She looked healthy and strong. She was also calm and collected in a way I did not recognize.

I introduced my friends and patients, the turtle and the schizophrenic dog. The dog presented the greatest problem. Running around in the neighborhood, he had received so many beatings that friendly words and fingers scratching his fur actually seemed to intensify the attacks of violence. He crawled on the ground, wagged his tail, snapped at the air with drooling jaws, and tried to keep his eyes closed at all times. I took his unwillingness to look me in the eye as indicating feelings of shame. It would be possible to get a wedge into the mind of the big male beast, if only I could isolate him from his surroundings. The other day I drove off a small boy gleefully throwing rocks at the dog. The boy's mother appeared and misunderstood the situation totally. She removed one shoe and began to bang it on the boy's head. His head started to bleed. The boy screamed. The mother's frenzied, shrill voice scared off the dog. I tried to stop her, but by then we were surrounded by other women and children. In a matter of seconds, I would have been the main course for the incensed females.

Luckily Omar appeared, and even he had difficulties in toning down the rage. He voiced the informed opinion that the women were upset because I could be seen among children and dogs in the middle of the day. I ought to hang around a café like other men.

"Omar," I asked. "Why do you beat your dogs? And why do you hit your children, as if they too were dogs?"

"It's simple," answered Omar. "Children and dogs — it's the same thing. We hit them to teach them obedience. The day we are old and have no strength to hit them, the memories of the beatings are so strong that they obey anyhow."

Omar smiled. He was proud. In his universe everything had its preordained place.

*   *   *

The evening progressed with both Louise and me, in spite of every-thing, succeeding in avoiding the shadows that existed behind us. I was careful to discuss neither the present nor our future. Instead I proudly related my latest method for repairing turtles and showed the old shapeless creature with new plastic padding stripes in the cracks made by the dog's teeth. Louise wondered what would hap-pen if the turtle grew. I had not thought of that. I had always seen the turtle as ancient. I promised to chisel out my mending fillings.

Then I asked the turtle to tell a tale from Adelaide. It just stared stupidly with watery eyes, pulled in its head, and could not be bribed even with fresh pieces of lettuce. The effect was the desired one, though. I managed to awaken Louise's curiosity.

I told her the truth. With nothing else to do, I was attempting to find myself. It was slow going. I had never formulated one single opinion about my own person. I was unused to doing so and expe-rienced feelings of embarrassment. But since I was far from my former place of work and consequently had all the time in the world, I might as well do what she had urged me to do. In other words, I had tried to speak to the turtle about my life. Unfortunately I got stuck in Adelaide.

"What happened in Adelaide?" asked Louise.

I told her.

We drank wine while the North African night enveloped us and a glowing moon rested on the rooftops. I laughed a little at myself as a comical figure while sorrow and a feeling of loss groped around inside me, trying to get into the light, as if other memories were pulling me down into a well of pain. My desperate tries to sneak the distorted mirror image of our relationship into the story did not ring true. But behind all the garbage, we both existed, I and Louise, if only she would listen. If only she would smile and think of the two of us and when we really met.

HOW IT ALL STARTED
or
First Encounter with Louise

Up to the time I met Louise, my life was a torrential rapid of events and happenings. This is how the last bit went.

I do everything too late. It was the same with the military service. I was forgotten and never put on the rolls, but I managed to muddle into the military life anyhow. To my consternation, I was placed in a secret elite unit of the navy. The first few months were rather fun. We shot holes in cardboard figures, cut straw dolls into pieces, dynamited tree stumps, broke into indicated places, and learned to do a multitude of things blindfolded.

One day we were to learn dog defense, meaning the art of neutralizing a rigidly trained beast who attacks in order to kill. It's rather simple: The dog leaps toward your throat, you drive your left hand with full force between the dog's jaws and press downward, turn counterclockwise against the animal's body while you place your right arm around its neck, grab hold of the lower jaw, and jerk it as hard as you can. Dogs have no strength in their lower jaws. They can easily be dislocated. After this, you grab hold across the nose and break the neck in the same hold by hitting the dog's back against your right leg.

For weeks we practiced on a stuffed German shepherd who flew at us from a catapulting mechanism. The elite specialist was mighty proud of it. The sides of the poor stuffed dog were totally worn out, the lower jaw was disjointed, and the neck wobbled. The elite group stood in a line and, one by one, we stepped forward and killed the stuffed animal while the instructor howled and growled as realistically as he was able. Every time he threatened that the next one might be a real dog.

After a few weeks of practice, the instructor's face acquired a

---

suspicious expression and his sharp eyes began to follow me with extreme caution. He was absolutely correct. I always stepped out of the line and went behind the next man in order to avoid the brutal handiwork. The instructor shouted the way military men do, while I stressed the meaninglessness of killing a dead dog. Not even if it were alive would I want to kill it.

The instructor was foaming at the mouth. Without hesitation I had cut holes in hundreds of straw men, throttled dolls of cloth with a piece of wire in the darkness, gone swimming across straits, exploded marked tree stumps, and blared blank machine-gun shots against cardboard enemies — why then would I not break the neck of a dead dog?

"Because I feel sorry for it," I answered.

"But you don't feel sorry for the straw figures?" he asked shrewdly.

"No."

That's as far as we got.

He failed to understand how I could feel sorry for a dead dog, and I could not explain why. For my refusal to kill the stuffed dog, I was transported to the military prison in Stockholm, where I was placed in a cell for a few months. The only time I was let out was when the crown prince reached the age of majority. We military criminals were commanded to fire a salute. It remains one of my most solemn memories. On a glorious day of spring, the bunch of us pale, drawn, and inferior creatures met. One had taken one pat of butter too many, one had been intoxicated wearing a uniform while he raked leaves, and so it went. In spite of these heinous crimes, on this day we were allowed to melt into the nation's harmonious unity.

Shortly afterward, I was cross-examined by an admiral. I explained how distasteful I found it to kill a dead dog, and he tried to convince me that military training is just a kind of preparation for a reality that nobody wishes to experience. The exercises were like games and not to be taken seriously. So I asked if it would be possible to practice on a stuffed teddy bear instead. Such a one can be bought in any large toy store. A teddy bear is less real than a stuffed dead dog, falling more into the category of the straw figures, which I willingly, even cheerfully, had cut into small pieces. I offered to return to the training camp and do that particular part of the course over again, using teddy bears.

The admiral had slithered into a discussion he could not handle. He capitulated and sent me back to camp with a box full of teddy bears.

I was given free hand when it came both to color and to size.

Our secret patrol was lined up in front of the catapult machine. To be on the safe side, I had not mentioned the teddy bears to our instructor, only that I wanted to repeat that special phase of our training. The rest of our group was forewarned. I waited, murderous and broad-legged. Out of the catapult and toward my throat flew a pink, cuddly teddy bear. I wrestled it as realistically as possible and even hit it against the ground a few extra times for good measure. Everybody except the instructor cheered the bear killer.

My happiness was not to last though.

I was discharged from the navy about the same time as the admiral asked for early retirement. There are limits to the amount of derision and ridicule an admiral can take.

Such is chance — or indescribable fate.

Because had I, like everybody else in our small attack group, chosen to dislocate the jaw violently and break the dead dog's neck, I would probably not have ended up aboard a banana boat. An inner yellow thread runs through my life, I'm sure of it. Why else would I find myself on a banana boat?

When I was little, I always fantasized that my father worked on a banana boat. He carried out a heroic deed; he was an unsung hero. While my mother was dying and we children were scattered by the winds of ill fortune, he was bringing bananas to the Swedish people. Every time I saw someone eating a banana, I felt of noble and elevated mind. In a way I felt as if I participated in this necessary bringing home of bananas, since I had relinquished my father to the duty. I felt included in his heroic fight on behalf of the Swedish people.

There ought to have been some kind of gun salute, as I set foot aboard my first banana boat.

Instead I found myself face to face with a dear old friend, the first mate from my eventful journey in the Australian waters. That in itself is not remarkable, since the cold storage ship sailed under the same shipping firm's flag. More remarkable was the fact that he had not yet become a captain.

Quite a few years had piled on top of one another and somewhere, in some roundabout way, he may have heard about my wondrous resurrection, but he did not seem to recognize me. The formerly so energetic little man was now gray and passive, looking ready to lose himself.

We were leaving Göteborg to get a full load of oranges in Cape Town, unload these in Europe, and then continue our roving ventures in the Pacific's cold storage market.

A small group with placards and banners had gathered on the pier in Göteborg. They had misunderstood something and were demonstrating against importing oranges from South Africa, in spite of the fact that we had not yet picked up any. Aboard the ship the opinions about the morality of loading South African fruits were as varied as the opinions regarding the human qualities of the demonstrators. Personally I had seen more than enough of ugly racism and abominable separatism. But, being an employee aboard the ship, it would have been difficult to join the demonstration.

Standing there watching it all, the first mate suddenly reverted to his old self. His anger rose to a boil, he roared abusive invectives against the demonstrators, and cast off the moorings at the same time as the tugboat on the other side received the signal to pull outward. Big forces are set in motion when six thousand tons take off. We had not had time to bring home the cable spring. It slid along the pier and got stuck. A few coils were lying loosely in big rings around the bollard. The first mate was leaning against the sloping edge of the bulwark, waving provokingly, before he jumped straight down to the bollard and the cable coils. These were pulled to one side with a smacking sound and went right into the first mate's right leg, cutting it clean off immediately below the knee joint. He fell down on the deck with a thud. Surprise and pain flashed in his eyes, and his blood pulsated forward in a hard rhythm. The steel wire creaked, snapped off with a loud noise, and flew at a rattling pace up through the air.

Everybody except me rushed over to the first mate. I tore off my pants before elbowing my way over to him. I wrapped the pant legs around the lower thigh of the bloody stump to stop the bleeding.

For an instant something glimmered in the first mate's dull glance.

"You?" he moaned.

"Yes," I said.

Nothing more was said between us. He was brought ashore along with the sheared-off piece of leg. Past the lighthouse of Vinga, I was still pantless. At Skagen, a new first mate was lowered aboard from a helicopter, and three weeks later we were loading oranges in Cape Town just as planned.

It is a rather common occurrence that one or another aboard a ship breaks down and goes crazy, shows pictures of his children, drops soiled love letters like leaves in the wind on deck, drinks, cries, fights, or suddenly disappears overboard one night. All that is part of the everyday life at sea. But during this trip down, the whole crew, from deck boy to commander, drank like demons in desperate fits of shivering chills. Never before have I encountered a whole crew swilling alcohol and getting sentimental shakes. To my own surprise, I began to drink as well. I played cards, cried, and got into a couple of fights, while life ahead of me seemed like an eternal, rocking and bouncing, gray-as-lead ocean.

However good care I took of my legs, I'd never be able to walk on dry land and lead a normal landlubber kind of life. Home, wife and children, a cottage porch to sit on, a hedge of lilacs to piss on, and a Swedish flag to raise every time it was the king's birthday — all that was lost forever. I was not built for the seagoing life of escalated stress. I had run out of juice as a human being. At the age of twenty-three, I was trying to forget everything, to drown my past in alcohol — and by age twenty-four I'd be a babbling wreck, boring everybody with broken promises to stay sober. It was time for a lengthy sick leave. Or at least time to sign off this ship.

At Cape Town, I never even went ashore. I gave notice. Three weeks later I left Bordeaux for Sweden.

Where would I go when I arrived in Sweden? My home was my suitcase. I debated this question with a Swedish girl who happened to share my train compartment. She was irritatingly worldly and sophisticated as she conveyed to me that she had grown weary of living with an artist. He had forced her to crawl around on a painter's drop cloth drenched in oil paints. Like drunken eels, their naked bodies had wriggled and entwined, after which they were supposed to press their paint-saturated selves against huge pieces of canvas hanging around the walls of the atelier. Now she wanted to do something with her life, go back to school, and work with the unfortunate in society. She guzzled wine unceasingly, ate the provisions she had brought, all wrapped in a red-checkered scarf, cut pieces of chicken with a large pocket knife, smoked Gauloises, and dribbled chewed-off chicken bones all over my suit while she confided the facts about real life in France.

"The French are so existential," she explained. "Life and death go hand in hand. Always."

As a child of the working class, I had been taught that one does not take a train journey dressed in work overalls. Consequently I was dressed in a three-piece suit. But I had not been taught how to use five- or six-syllable words without embarrassment. One was not supposed to flaunt a wide variety of complex words. Language should be like a finely honed ax that you use to fell dreams. Nothing else.

"There's a lot to it," I said, smoking Marlboros, drinking whiskey, feeling nauseated and sweaty in the late August heat while my thoughts kept returning to her slipping around in oil paints with that artist.

In Hamburg, I went to buy more wine for us. In the space of a few hours I had turned into a full-fledged existentialist. I floated through the door, slipped on the step down to the platform, and dropped my sunglasses. Of course, I got it into my head to pick them up between the platform and the train car, and fell down. Louise screamed, thinking that the train would run me over. A couple of cars had to be derailed before I could climb up. That adventure left my suit black and sooty, and it slowly stiffened over my nauseated, sweaty being. Louise said that I reminded her of someone. A little boy she had been unable to forget. His mother was dead, his dog was dead, and his daddy loaded bananas on ships on the other side of the globe. A rather droll uncle of his took care of him.

"For that little guy life and death really joined hands!" Louise said, laughing.

Because the girl was Louise. I had not recognized her but fell in love at first sight. She sketched out her life story. As the daughter of the Bible-spouting grocer at the glassworks, she was compelled to run away from home. Naturally. At the age of seventeen, she cajoled her way to Uppsala with an artist twice her age. The memories of her father's stinging belt and the religious restrictions in the home combined to keep her going like a thunderbolt. School did not fall within her sphere of interest.

We fell into each other's arms as soon as we rediscovered the childhood years we had spent together. And there we remained. Louise had enormous steering speed. I went into her backwash and trotted along to the institution of adult education while questions banged together in my head. For instance, what was an institution of adult education? And what would I do there? I was the only one arriving in a vested suit and consequently was considered somewhat underdeveloped. It didn't matter. Louise was equally confused. Her red-checkered scarf, her Gauloises, and her existentialism were totally condemned. Karl Marx was the only one who counted. We clung to each other while we went into intensive training and soon were a formidable elitist couple on the political left edge. Louise played left quarterback, I played left defense. I wanted her to play toward the center of the field, but it would soon be evident that she always wanted to dribble on the outer chalk line.

And that is, in short, also the reason why we find ourselves trying to talk to each other in such a remote and strange place as Bordj El Kiffan, Algeria.

ALGERIA
1976

With the exception of the dogs who barked their eternal replays from block to block, everything was quiet in Bordj El Kiffan. Even Louise was silent as a clam, after hearing my Adelaide story. The candle had burned down. Darkness had draped itself like black velvet over us. Something rustled in the grass. The turtle floundered about and made the dog tremble with contained excitement. I nearly stopped breathing when I became aware that Louise was crying, silently and absentmindedly. Her voice reached me, as if from another world.

"How can you sit there and tell me such an idiotic mess of fantasies? Why do you try to hide? This isn't you at all! Why do you turn your life into a series of anecdotes? How can you do that to yourself? You're not a dinner guest, there's no yawning company to entertain with jokes and funny stories. There's only me, right in front of you. And I know this isn't you. You know who you are? You're like my dad. My daddy washed dishes one single time when I was little. I may have been ten years old and came home from school too early. He got flaming mad and threw me out of the kitchen. But I had time to see that he hardly knew how to do it. I snuck up to his office and sat down by his desk and went through every drawer. In one he had a lot of change. In another one he had condoms. I opened each and every condom wrapper and put the coins inside the condoms. Afterward he gave me a thrashing with his belt. That's how my dad was. A strong individual who was involved with his money or sat behind locked doors in his office and counted love according to the number of fucking rubbers. You're just the same! Punishment, work, and responsibility . . . with love measured in how many times we hop into bed together. There's no difference. Other than the fact that you've a freedom that my daddy never had. I've prioritized you too damn much. And been left alone at home with all the work."

So it went. As usual it grew from quiet crying into violent rage.

Remarkable. Louise always plunges straight into the dishpan the minute we talk to each other. She forgets that she herself has never given many minutes to housework. She has no time. She has taken too many courses. With her level of ambition she ought to have her own half-hour television program to explain to us ordinary mortals why the world looks the way it does. Instead I am her test audience, forced to admire her capacity. After half an hour's introduction in a new course subject, she has absorbed all the latest findings and integrated them into her personality. She rearranges her whole intellectual world in the time span of a coffee break. Even when she whizzes around in a Landrover, spending my hard-earned money thousands of miles from our home, she lands back in the dishpan again, sloshing around and crying her wretched heart out because I have not behaved like a totally domesticated man. Where the hell has she read how I should behave?

Probably in some sociological study of women in low-income positions. Isn't there one single report about privileged women who never have had to take responsibility for themselves? I have worked my tail off so she could keep on studying to become the world's foremost expert on questions of relationships, and the only thing she has discovered is that her husband works too damn much!

I have awakened by the side of a woman who during the day had no idea where Jerusalem is located but who overnight became an expert on the problems of the Middle East.

And I have made love to that same woman the preceding night, in spite of her supplying information in the middle of the act from the most recent and incredibly wordy report on human sexual behavior. Doubtlessly such a report makes it clear that I am a sexual tyrant, an egotistical, ejaculation-fixated spray painter of her shimmering cervix. In passing, she jabbers something about it being a fact that our whole earthly existence is linked to this very same cervix, and that I, generally speaking, do not reach her G-spot. It takes me three weeks of diligent work to find the G-spot theory among the yards of books dealing with the latest news on the female front. I find that the theory is not as yet scientifically tested and proven.

With my eyes smarting from reading all the small print, I let out a breath of relief, only to awaken the following morning to the information that our marriage has stagnated. I remain calm. What man would make a move voluntarily with a tornado in the house?

Louise is like her mother. My mother-in-law is a cleaning tornado. A white, whirling entity. She rips everything out of drawers and cupboards every day. By midnight everything sparkles and is put back in place. I understand fully why my father-in-law has a small room set aside as a home office. Where else could he escape during her violent cleaning attacks?

Once we lent them our apartment in Stockholm. Never again! We couldn't even find our quilts under the taut, wrinkle-free bed covers. The stench of cleaning fluids hit us with a vengeance wherever we looked. Finally we gave up and called them. Our quilts were put under the mattresses to keep the covers perfectly smooth. Of course!

Louise is the same kind of tornado. The only difference is that her scouring powder is every new theory she comes across, and the object to be sanitized and spot-free is me. I am the one to be spring-cleaned and to have my furniture rearranged. Like I said, she insists on playing at the very edge of the football field.

"I feel as if I'm the only one who keeps developing," Louise says.

"How the hell do you want me to develop when I don't have time?!" I scream savagely and observe that I have extreme difficulty containing my incandescent rage.

Where did our camaraderie of so long disappear to? What happened to all of our practical agreements? Why do I feel like choking her?

My favorite daydream is an absolutely magnificent blueprint for murder. I would dig a hole in the sand and put her there. Everybody on the beach would see it as fun and games. Louise, too. Once I had her imprisoned by the sand, I'd keep shoveling more and more of it over her. And when everybody else had left, I'd fetch ocean water and pour it into her. Then I'd dig her up and throw the body into the sea. Drowned. Not a trace. Ingenious.

Such are my dreams behind the locked door of my workroom, in actuality a closet and much worse than my father-in-law's office. He has hunting rifles, moose heads and medals for marksmanship, comfortable armchairs worn to amiable perfection by a multitude of behinds, and probably more fuck-rubbers and more coins to count.

I, on the other hand, sit in a closet and fantasize about cutting up his daughter, placing the pieces in the freezer, and later boiling her, piece by piece. The problem is, who would eat Louise? Not even a dog could be tricked into gulping down such feed, which would probably make any sane animal raving mad.

Nothing of this happens. Silent and industrious, I return to my intellectual treadmill. Steel doors slam shut; a chill lowers itself over my diligent and dutiful self. Why don't I offer any resistance? Why do I slave over meaningless papers, lectures, and meetings while she flops around like an exotic parrot and imitates everybody and everything? Why must she always shit on my head?

But in Bordj El Kiffan, there was no work hole to which I could retire. Since I couldn't turn myself into a turtle, I expressed my thanks and went to bed. She was welcome to fill the old dried-up pond with tears all by herself.

Something pulsated in my body, as if reverberations from a distant pain. It happens when Louise fails to understand that I must search for and find my way in my own strange manner. I need masks and disguises. And I do need laughter — otherwise I will disappear in an ocean of tears. Did she not grasp that what I told her about my zany life was a gift? Did she not understand that beneath all that garbage existed a portrait of me? Is it my fault that one single day in my life sounds like a cock-and-bull story? Why don't my experiences fit in anywhere? And why can't I simply tell the truth? I am afraid to lose her. I am so closely intertwined with her that I will die if she goes away.

She is as crazy as my mother.

I crawled into bed, exhausted, and fell asleep just like that.

What was Louise doing? Washing the dishes, probably.

Drenched in sweat, I awakened to Wagnerian notes. A row of crystal-clear pictures were still doing somersaults on my retina. Cape Town. A dream. I tried to organize the bad dream into some logic, having to do with the reason why the German wanted to kill me in Adelaide a long time ago.

SOUTH AFRICA
1962

I am sitting crouched down by a tiled wall, holding my head in my hands, my eyes tightly shut. Inside, a day and a night rattle. I ought to hurry up. I am late. There will be one hell of a row aboard the ship. But I am unable to move a muscle. Outside the toilet there is a sign stating that only whites may enter. It seems somewhat exaggerated since an identical sign was posted at the entrance to the bar itself.

Here I sit. I am two people: myself and also another — we are separating. It is weird. I stand over by the wall and look critically at the poor devil, hunched down with his head in his hands.

I try to console him. "It wasn't that bad, after all. You're only seventeen and there's plenty of time to forget it." But he keeps sitting there, and I keep standing here.

Somebody has rent asunder his inner balance wheel.

He can't go on sitting like that. The mirror image greets him with an ugly grimace when he gets up. A steamy spot spreads on the mirror. The face is ashen. Clear pearls of sweat appear at the hairline. The gums are pink and there are small white spots on the tongue. Everything becomes enlarged by the sun, catching fire in the mirror, having entered through a window placed high up.

Slowly I melt together with the other one, who is now grimacing apologetically toward himself.

I remember the walk.

The German and I have gone ashore. He is off to rent a car. I stand on the path along the shore at Sea Point. The wind howls through a crystalline, refreshing day. We headed into Cape Town through turbulent breakers after the worst storm in history. We have heard that a South African ship has hit a reef out there. I am stubborn and get our taxicab to drive past it. The German continues on his way. He has promised to pick me up later.

DANGER — EXPLOSIVE GOODS is proclaimed on the kegs the sea carries toward the coast.

Police are guarding the beach and keep us curious onlookers at a distance. I melt into the large, inquisitive mass of people. Above us a helicopter is buzzing with its human cargo from the wrecked ship. She is a small, neglected ship in the coastal trade. She seems to be whimpering in the enormous breakers. We are a human mass, groaning every time the ship heaves and pitifully reveals its lacerated metal. Every breaker throws the ship against the sharp reef. We follow her movements with our mouths wide open and let out, as one body, an "ooooh" when the ship splits open against the black cliffs and keeps opening up, more and more.

Down on the beach stands the rescued captain. He is throwing out his arms in a regretful gesture as he explains to the reporters. His mouth is a gaping black hole. An echo from a gigantic breaker rises out of our bodies and the captain turns around. Together we watch the ship topple over slowly — she curtsies gently and slides down into a depression between two huge waves, turning the gashed metal bottom up.

The captain forgets to lower his hands. It looks as if he is blessing his black crew, who were to be saved last.

The German picks me up in a car, calls me chicken-hearted and overly sentimental. Here it doesn't follow that women and children are to be saved first. Here it goes: first the whites, then the blacks.

He grins and drives on, says that he has planned our day. What am I doing here with him, really? He drives like a madman.

Table Mountain — the intense heat and light hit against the side of the mountain. The road is a black ribbon, sometimes draped on precipices, blasted into the rock, crooked and shimmering in the heat as if it wanted to lure us out over the edges, straight into the mighty sunlight — a bluish white field of light with the sun suddenly jumping out from behind the next promontory or the next piece of cliff jutting out.

Between us stands a case of beer. My job is to open a new bottle as soon as the German has emptied one. I am scared. He is of the opinion that the beer balances the driving and that the winding mountain road craves a great amount of beer. He blows his beery breath toward me and holds the wheel with one hand, snorting laughter, then turns back in the last moment and grabs hold of the wheel. The car lurches, we skid through the curve.

Above us hang the cliffs, profound and silent. Beneath us are jagged declivities.

This is Victoria Road, a glistening black tendril along the sea. Red, weathered, crumbling mountains, yellow mud that is cracked and reekingly dry. The narrow strip of sand far down there, the dizzying steeps. Every once in a while one can spot a human being by the sea. The sea is icily blue. The white breakers are like frozen lines against the yellow-brown sand. The distance is confusing. The quivering air distorts the vision. The ocean has congealed into a stiff surface with hissing, white lines that threaten to blast loose and break away.

Banty Bay, Camp's Bay, Bakoven, Llandudno, Mount Bay. The road goes on and on. Always a new promontory. The point is hiding. The moment hesitates while I wonder if we will reach the Cape of Good Hope alive.

I let out my breath when we arrive at the wildlife park. Now the road is straight as an arrow. Everything seems deserted; falcons are floating above us except when they sit down for a rest on the only telephone wire that goes out toward the cape.

The wildlife sanctuary is divided into two parts, one for blacks and one for whites.

Black, uniformed guards stand gawking at the gate to the point. They carry long, thick, knobbed sticks to fight off the mountain monkeys. Even at this woebegone end of the continent, the country remains divided into two worlds. Only the monkeys leap freely and without mixed emotions between the signs. As a mat of fur and chatter, they suddenly cover our car completely. A guard saunters leisurely over and hits indiscriminately with his knobby stick, roars a few unintelligible words, and drives the monkeys from the car. The German grins.

"Probably speak the same language," he says and swings out of the car, several bottles of beer in his hands.

I don't know what to say.

We are almost the only ones there. A few other cars. A path juts out toward the precipice, a white dress glimmers between the dry bushes, the monkeys scratch themselves and skip and bound around. Alone or with one companion, they are shy and hop away. As soon as there are more of them, they sit bravely and gawk at us while we walk to the end of the path and look at the lighthouse far down there.

The ocean itself is separated. The Atlantic and the Indian oceans are on either side of the Cape of Good Hope, which is a boring cape, a monkey cape. The ocean is blue as ice. It looks as it always does, without boundaries or names.

I turn around to go back and discover that the German has disappeared. Perhaps I stayed too long. The woman in the white dress is gone, too. In the dwarfed trees, the monkeys swing on the branches. Something disturbs them. It's the German. He is throwing rocks at them. The monkeys jump down and come at me at full speed. I stand rooted to the spot, frozen. Below the precipice, the ocean remains coldly blue and my retreat is cut off. Then the guards appear. They wave their knobby sticks at the monkeys.

"It was just a joke," says the German.

But it wasn't funny.

We drive back at twilight. I am quiet and still wonder what it is he wants.

Cape Town glimmers in the night when we return. The German invites me to a restaurant. The best in the city. The exchange rate of our money and the cheap labor force in the country make us as rich as all other whites. We move straight up, floor after floor of the hotel, and are presented with all the lights in the bay as a spectacle when we look out through the rows of windows in the restaurant.

Turtle soup. An Indian stands alertly behind the chair all the time, ready to be of service. The soft wall-to-wall carpet muffles all sounds. The German explains to me that anything can be bought, provided you have money. He demonstrates that one may even eat the flowers on the table if one wants and dares to do so. He laughs and urges me to drink more wine. Drunkenness is a membrane all around me. I sink into the chair, eat steak, and point to the tables that seem to be constantly moving. Finally I float out on the wall-to-wall carpet with the German's brotherly supporting arm around my shoulder. He supports me all the way down and pours me into the car. Absentmindedly I note the lights playing hide-and-seek on his face as he drives through the city. I am not afraid any longer but wonder how he is able to drive with all that alcohol in his body.

When we stop outside a house, I finally find out what I am good for.

"Whatever you see and whoever approaches, just honk twice. Understand?"

I nod. The German did invite me for dinner and paid for the meal. What he is going to do has nothing to do with me. Besides, it sounds thrilling, like a spy movie. And I am included in it, just a little.

The few streetlights reveal a rather seedy area. A dog barks in the distance. The German leaves. I keep looking eagerly for the slightest shadow on the deserted narrow street, but nothing happens. A herd of elephants decide to sit down on my eyelids. I hadn't dared refuse when the German kept offering me more wine. For a seventeen-year-old who doesn't drink alcohol, I have imbibed abnormally much. Both the car and the street start swirling around and around. I tip over backwards and fall asleep.

I awaken when an old woman knocks at the car window with a beer bottle. She is heavily made-up, smiles, and wants me to open the car door. Should I honk now?

No. She has come to get me.

The night has gray edges. Through a creaking door we enter a backyard. Clotheslines with waving washing are above our heads. In the kitchen, the faucet has a chronic drip. The woman opens a beer and nods for me to sit down. The walls are impregnated with yellow dirt. Giggles and mumbled voices reach us through an open window. I walk over to it. A black woman walks into the backyard. She is nude but quickly wraps a piece of cloth around herself.

At first, I believe it's the place where we entered but then realize that I'm looking down into the backyard on the other side of the building. The woman disappears, swallowed by the gray darkness. The German comes out. He is also stark naked. He throws away an empty beer bottle and pisses on the cracked concrete while he looks up in my direction.

I understand why he wanted me along.

But by then it's too late. Hard boots clamp up the staircase. A cone of light hits the German, somebody whacks him from behind. He falls. It looks strangely unreal when he does. His legs jerk spastically when a bluish black figure aims a kick toward his midriff. I see a stripe glimmer in the light, but that's all I have time to see. A weird sound buzzes in my head. Amazingly enough, I have time to feel surprise that it doesn't hurt any more than it does before I drop into merciful blackness.

Not until I come to is the hurt there, a harsh pain radiating from a spot in the back of my head. The stone floor is filthy and feels rough against my cheek. An intense light blinds me when I try to look around. Laughter and bloodcurdling screams echo in the big, bare room. Within a fraction of a second, I manage to see everything that is happening and wish I could force myself back into the black oblivion. The screams won't stop. The toe of a boot prods me and I turn over. The German is tied down, lying on his stomach, on a narrow, rough-hewn table. He is nude. Legs and arms are stretched out, spread-eagle fashion. Behind him stands one policeman in shirt and pulled-down pants. He moves back and forth absentmindedly while picking his nose. Another is holding up the German's face with a leather whip, while a third one spits, barks, and threatens the German with his penis, which he has brought out and holds in his hand. The German screams again. The cop in front of him turns away, suddenly. We look straight into each other's eyes, the German and I. We fall into each other, and I understand that he will kill me if we survive this. I know already how the humiliation will work inside him, like a revving engine.

By this time the barking cop has already turned his attention to me. His pink face and downy upper lip partake in an expression of sinister delight. His penis is a white monster against the dark blue uniform pants. In the large, bare room, sounds echo and multiply, and they keep hitting my thudding head. The man standing behind the German is through. He spits on him. I don't understand what they are saying, but it seems obvious that I'm their next plaything. They come to stand in front of me, elbowing and pushing each other. A giggle bursts from me, I jump up and try to bite a police leg, right through the rough uniform cloth. I hang on and get a hard kick in the stomach. Everything turns black again. Perhaps it only lasts a brief moment. Because I see the legs move apart when the door is thrown open. A slightly built man with his hair combed straight back bends over me. He is a bit of a dandy and seems concerned as he licks his thin lips.

"My boys do the strangest things. Do you understand what I'm saying?"

I nod.

"Do you understand what you have done?"

"No," I answer and hot shame burns my innards as I try to put intensity in my look toward the German.

The man in front of me glances toward the German.

"What are we going to do with him?"

My stomach quivers on the edge of nausea. To amuse them I suggest that they let us go. The cops grin superior, self-confident grins. They wait. So long as the slightly built man is there, they are powerless. He seems to consider my suggestion, nods, and gives a few brief commands in Afrikaans to the men.

"That's exactly what we're going to do. As soon as you've learned that nobody laughs at us. Do you understand?"

Understood. There wasn't that much to understand. One of the cops was already soaking the leather whip in a pail of water. He brought it up and held it out toward me.

I understood that I was chosen to flog the German.

The cops threw me out first, and I floundered about in Cape Town, ended up in a men's room, and finally found myself on a bench outside the Botanical Garden on Queen Street, my body stiff and trembling but law-abiding since it was proclaimed that the bench was only to be sat upon by whites. The German appeared in a taxi. He had been driving all over town because of me. He yanked me into the car and took my hand. At first I thought he meant to console me, beg my forgiveness for having lured me into the strange affair with the black prostitutes. But instead he took a good hold of the thumb on my right hand, stared into my eyes, and swore that he would kill me if I uttered one syllable. Then he pulled. A violent jerk. The pain was excruciating.

I did not utter a word when he explained to the hopping-mad first mate that he had run around like a crazed rat trying to find me, all night and all morning. Our departure had been both delayed and prevented. The captain had planned to leave Cape Town without us. In South Africa, however, everybody plays the same note. Even if the harbor authorities could not tell that, for the moment, we were being tortured by policemen, they knew very well that they were not allowed to let the ship take off without us aboard. Time is money. Those hours were costly. I had to pay them back with interest.

ALGERIA
1976

That was not how my dream went. It was disconnected, got caught in retakes, disappeared, and froze into one single picture that stayed stubbornly right there until I, still deep into my dream, managed to force myself awake. In the dream, my main feeling was curiosity. I don't know how I could know that, since it was a dream. But in all my dreams there exists an interested and involved second person. Like an avid movie fan he sits there, unable to close his eyes.

I reorganized my dream. It was easy. The ending was a simple case of double exposure — two events melted together into one. The event with the German who is flogged stems from Cape Town. In the dream, I'm the one forced to carry out the task. As if there were some guilt, in spite of everything. But the humiliating rape is a totally different story from the time I was in Algiers, at the age of sixteen. Perhaps it has worked its way up to the surface since I am back in Algiers? In either case, I just want to forget what really happened.

I keep thinking about the German. That asshole. I nearly missed a whole continent because of him.

But why keep delving into such things? My future life may be healthier if the past stays buried.

Louise was still playing Wagner. The music boomed through the house, and I ambled into the weird living room. The stone floor and the bare walls surrounding the enormous model train setup emitted desolation and coldness, as if Monsieur Verdurin had grown up by mistake and had no idea what to do to create a home.

Louise was not alone. She was lecturing poor Omar. Her way of throwing back her hair, her lively gestures, and the fiery concentration she evidenced had totally hypnotized him. He might be illiterate, but he knew how to dream of European women. Monsieur Verdurin had probably shown off his bedroom walls to him. But watch out, Omar! All the Playboy bunnies with their bare asses and silicone tits may do for one-man orgies, but in reality those taped-up angels of Monsieur Verdurin's are just a fabricated product by men and for men. That kind of woman does not exist. They are only dreams that make it possible for us to get through the everyday humdrum. Perhaps we will talk about this one day, when my poor Volvo is repaired.

I nodded sadly toward Omar. He looked perfectly at home, kept twirling his wineglass, and listened attentively to Louise's renditions, like a true gentleman. I felt sorry for him. Soon she would get to the graphic description of how she and the artist squirmed and wriggled around in oil paints. That story lived its own life nowadays. It developed in step with new friends, new conversations, and new expectations. Not even Louise knew anymore what was true and what was not. It belonged among her myths, her youth, lost but constantly recaptured in her Paris memories.

Actually, I didn't lag far behind her. When I told of my years at sea, I didn't know what was true. Everything gets worn down, sandpapered by time, so that one can catch the essential feeling of inner turmoil. The events become a representation of reality, in which the inflexibility of my youth is the heart and core. I search for the original truth. Every reality is therefore deadly serious but, unfortunately, not always scrupulously truthful. Like Louise, I have a tendency to lie a little about myself whenever necessary. Perhaps there weren't quite that many sharks in Adelaide. But it sure felt like it.

She if anyone ought to understand a slight exaggeration. All of us have the need to spin a few myths around our lost origins. We look for truth in our wounds, put spider webs and healing balsam around them.

I sat down, muttered something unintelligible, and tried to look as if I understood French well enough to follow the conversation — or lecture, rather — since Louise remained on her soapbox the whole time. She was not at all in Paris playing snake with an artist. She was in the middle of her favorite subject: The Male.

Perhaps I failed to understand the finer points, but she had obviously found a metaphor for what she wanted to express about the one-dimensional creation that is man. She called him The Concrete Man and thought of the male psyche as an enormous armor of concrete that contained an inner, stormy ocean of pain and confusion, especially when confronted with female attacks on the patriarchal society. The question at hand was how the two sexes would go about disassembling these mighty male armors in such a way that the potential strengths and powers did not seep out and disappear. Because the dangerous, insensitive man enclosed in the concrete armor owned also potentially positive power and strength.

Total and utter nonsense, in other words.

Whose armor is she out to get if not mine? She wants to dismember me into small parts from which she can rebuild her own wishful dream of a man with total control over diaper changes, thought-provoking essays, and rich emotions. But how on earth would we have been able to survive and get the necessities of life had I been running around like a portable reservoir of pain and confusion, trying to find myself?

The confused one is Louise. She has almost three degrees in every subject that cannot be combined into a sensible profession. If anyone is leaking, she is the one. She could use a few armor plates for her existence, even though right now she, in contrast to me, may look utterly stable and professional. I have to confess that it was my armor that had cracked back home in Sweden.

Wisely I kept my mouth shut while Louise delivered her long-winded theory of The Concrete Man. I did not want to spoil a possible conciliatory celebration in bed. Whatever opinions I harbor regarding Louise, our reconciliations have been festive gala numbers. I also kept quiet because Louise only fucks men who share her opinions. A change in that area was not to be hoped for. The one who is not on her side is excluded from the sanctuary. She began with the existentialist artist and continued with me as a genuine worker and socialist. If she only dared, she would by now fuck only her sisters at the university. It is from that direction that I, these last few years, have been given a distinct feeling that it's no longer quite all right to be a man. Perhaps that's the reason I have not been feeling well and have grown rather quiet. Only a tiny part of my earlier life would probably suffice to put me on the rack.

Such concepts would not be understood by Omar.

Blinking his eyes, he nodded silently, like a real natural man.

I think he said something about women being the power — as long as one kept them at home. With several wives in the house, the man was stronger than ever. Omar could well imagine himself buying several, if only he could get together enough camels.

I nearly choked on my newborn joy.

Finally a fundamentalist of the purest order!

Louise would of course force Omar to admit that he was a true Concrete Man. She would attack Omar as a simple oppressor of the female sex and refuse to see his reality.

Silently I wished her good luck, fell off the chair, and crawled on all fours out of the room, laughing uproariously. My God! She probably still believed that it was a question of hours before Omar would be a convert, change his sex, or buy a couple of how-to books on the art of finding oneself as a house husband — and at the same time become immersed in the struggle to liberate the Western woman. There are times when I believe that Louise is a cartoon figure. If she doesn't already exist as such, she ought to be one.

"Go ahead and laugh," Louise sneered after me. "But walk on two legs like a normal human being. Otherwise Omar may put you back in prison again. He knows what you tried to do in Sweden. Erik told me how you went about it."

Louise has this remarkable ability to transmit several surprising pieces of information simultaneously. In other words, Omar was a regular secret policeman. And who was Erik? A man with so much power that he could get people thrown in jail in other countries?

I kept on crawling.

In the hall I met the regular dog of the house. He licked my face affectionately while I bared my throat to him. Perhaps it was a secret-police dog I had in front of me. I offered my throat to the dog and asked him to take a substantial bite. He would probably have enjoyed planting his teeth in my throat but did not dare to reveal his true identity. He growled and crawled backwards, the yellow eye-teeth foaming in saliva. As if he knew he wouldn't have a chance against a teddy bear killer.

The nausea overwhelmed me and I lay down on the worn linoleum floor.

I who used to brag about being cross-examined by the FBI couldn't even recognize a secret policeman when I saw one! And who was that Monsieur Verdurin who so easily opened up his villa to a total stranger? Why did Omar constantly carry off parts from my dear old Volvo to have them repaired? Was it a clever form of house arrest? I felt dumber than a Swede and wanted very much to know what it was all about.

Why did I, who generally speaking was without guilt, lie on the linoleum like a stupid dog?

Looking back, I would want to see this exact moment of my life as a shining high point, my last big and hysterical laughter. There I was, and I really admired myself for being able to block all truths about my own person so totally! I was still capable of seeing myself as nearly perfect. I mean, it takes quite a bit of courage and a lot of energy to maintain such a viewpoint long after the moment of truth with all its force has crushed your day-to-day existence.

And yet . . .

Gleefully, on all fours on the floor, I could suddenly see another microscopic truth. A truth that was amazingly simple. It traveled toward my heart like a small silver bullet and hit me with this:

Imagine if I were wrong??

That would make Louise and all the others on her side right!

Yes. Right.

Nobody but myself kills myself. I am both the hunter and the wolf.

After this knockout blow I had to lie in the hallway awhile longer. Again I thought of the day that was the beginning of the end for our family.

SWEDEN
1975

My father-in-law looks pleased when I come rushing out into the yard with the double-barreled shotgun under my arm. For a moment I believe that Louise has told of the despicable rape in Stockholm.

"Good," he says. "Finally."

"Now, goddamn it," I say.

"Want me to help you?" he asks.

"No. You don't have to get involved in this," I say.

"Are you going after them one by one or will you take all of them at once?"

"There's only one," I say, a bit confused.

"On the ground? Yes. Of course," my father-in-law answers and walks toward the warehouse while he shakes his head at my agitated state.

He has reasons to do so. My father-in-law is rather hard-of-hearing after all the shooting contests. Of course he was speaking of this summer's big bone of contention — the five kittens.

I am trapped.

I see Jonas in the kitchen window. His face quivers with disappointment. I am the one who is betraying him. We have spoken of it for months. My father-in-law has refused to dash the kittens against a wall. Now it is too late. Louise has, as she puts it, studied the subject. Very loudly and at great length, she has complained that we men cannot even get rid of a few kittens. My mother-in-law refuses categorically all responsibility. Meanwhile, both the kittens and Jonas's love for them have been growing. There has been an eternal tittle and tattle type of thing going on about who is going to kill them.

My father-in-law reappears with a can of liver pâté. He opens the can and serves the last supper on the pebbly ground. Then he fetches the kittens, who start gulping it down. Five of them, almost four months old. Can I do it with one shot? It depends on the distance. I measure it out. Four yards means good diffusion and enough power to get through two, should one stand behind another.

I take aim. My father-in-law has gone inside. Only the kittens and I remain. I shut my eyes and press the trigger. It's not especially dramatic. I go to get shovel and broom, a garbage bag, sweep a little gravel and sand over the pieces, and rake it all up, leaving no trace. A few minutes later I have deposited the small, broken corpses in a hole behind the warehouse, covered them with dirt, and put the tools back.

All the time I keep telling myself that I am like my own grandfather, large and secure in a matter-of-fact attitude when it comes to killing a hen. We grandchildren stand in front of Grandma, who tries to remain steadfast against our fascinated attempts to look through the large and light kitchen window.

Grandpa's heavy steps outside. The chickens clucking around in panic. Our shrewd tiny steps in order to witness the Sunday death of a hen. Grandpa, large and heavy, who lets the ax fall, and the hen who shudders and jerks, almost leading a headless life for a moment.

That memory is not at all dangerous. This one is. Jonas can't understand how I could kill the kittens so easily. A few minutes of precision work and rational thinking. Small and burdensome lives versus large and comfort-demanding lives. The neighborhood cannot be overrun by cats just because we do not take care of our own.

Silence and gloom reign in the house. I see Jonas scurry through the hall. He disappears into thin air when I walk into the house. My father-in-law is gone too. Probably standing in the cellar, pouring alcohol into himself. Louise sits at the kitchen table. She stares at me with loathing and amazement.

"I can't believe what I've just seen," she says.

"But you wanted me to get rid of them. Didn't you?"

"That you could do it just like that, cold as ice. Just murder them. Get things out of your system by murdering a few innocent kittens."

"I've only done what you've asked me to do for weeks on end."

"That's what everybody who puts the blame on somebody else says. Why can't you ever stand up for what you do?"

I have only one shot left in the gun. It swings up against her breasts, carelessly oscillating back and forth. From this distance of about one yard, there would be a considerable hole in her splendidness. Of course, it's just a game. But I am furious. Always the same illogical demands. Her mixed and contradictory signals crush me. Enclosed in my own eye of the storm's calm center, I see her go pale and at the same time there is a new glitter in her eyes. It's irresolution mixed with contentment. Finally she has me at a point where I am visible and unyielding. I calculate my violent swings with the gun in front of her and press the trigger. The shot buzzes out through the open window beside her. The detonation feels as if a couple of wet woolen mittens were pressed hard against my ears.

The first sound that reaches me is a strange gushing one. Louise sits straight as a pin on the chair and looks totally blank while the gushing continues. Suddenly she smiles, then begins to laugh. She stands up and walks stiff-legged out of the kitchen, holding the wet dress against her legs.

"You wipe it up!"

My mother-in-law materializes in the dusky hall. Her eyebrows are black and reproachful dashes drawn in coal. I crawl on the floor under the table and wipe up after Louise with my mother-in-law's kitchen towel. One accident is no worse than another. Besides she must be rather inured by now. Also, she has her God to pray to. We don't have that.

When I get upstairs to Louise, she stands there, washing herself. I sit down on the bed and watch. It never fails to give me pleasure. Louise treats herself with practical and loving care.

She seems to like having somebody watch her. Without knowing why — perhaps it was her story about Axel — I ask her what she thought of when we were making love.

"Of someone else," she answers.

"And when you make love to someone else?" I wonder.

"Then I think of someone else."

Although she drives me crazy, I have to admire her logic. It slips through like an irresponsible, whirling ball that without even a moment's hesitation breaks an expensive Ming vase.

I laugh. She walks over to me and softly presses her hand against my face, forcing me down on the bed. She purrs and whispers that she is strangely excited. I can understand why, can't I? There are tempests raging around us. Her breasts are smooth and slippery, still damp and a little cold. She adheres to me with suction, as if she finally found something to hold on to.

Much later, when we lie completely still, she says softly, almost inaudibly, that I ought to understand. She has wanted to leave me for quite a while.

"Axel?" I ask.

"He's enough for now," she says.

"He's still going to get a hail of bullets between his legs."

I say it almost gaily, looking forward to that chore.

"Don't be stupid," says Louise.

Am I the stupid one? I don't know. A pulsating pain is associated with the act of getting dressed. How many hours have passed since Jonas and I went down to the millpond to fish? Four. Perhaps five. It is a remarkable day that has not even happened yet. And now Louise plans to take Jonas from me. I am sure of it. But she is not going to succeed.

Mechanically I pick up the receiver, having rushed downstairs to stop the insistent ringing. Of all people, it's Axel. It gives me certain pleasure to describe in minute detail what I'm going to do to him. My mother-in-law comes into the hall. She has no more facial expressions left. I'm babbling on. Axel takes it calmly and reasonably as always.

"OK. But before you perforate my tender and highly valued body parts, I want to speak to you about your speech at the conference in Harpsund. 'The Third Man' . . . ? Even the title of the talk is questionable. Wasn't that an old movie?"

"Oh yes," I say and think so hard that my brain squeaks.

"Just a piece of advice, if you don't mind. I don't believe it would be very wise —"

"Not very wise!" I scream. "It happens to be the truth. Which I believe our dear prime minister should hear."

There is some static on the line. Axel keeps sounding as if we were having a regular telephone conference. I cannot understand how Louise can let herself be raped by such an insensitive oaf.

"OK," Axel says. "It's your funeral."

There is nothing strange about that line. He always says that. That's why he is a professor. But then he says something strange.

"I think you should have a long talk with Louise. We've spoken about you. You ought to grow up one of these days. And I have to stop being your father."

He hangs up.

Who does he think he is, really? He has not done anything except saw me into small pieces. What kind of fatherly care have I received from him? Raping my wife — is that what fathers do for their sons?

I feel sudden disgust faced with the approaching conspiracy. Axel's mild warning regarding the conference with the prime minister ought to be taken seriously. I should be careful not to play the seer.

As a representative of the labor party, our prime minister has been listening unusually keenly these last few years, meaning that he and the inner government circle have met frequently with so-called select groups. People from commerce and industry participate as do a few prominent professors with the right party colors, such as Axel, an occasional sociologist such as me, and finally some authors and assorted screwballs thrown in for good measure. One talks endlessly, puts forward hypothetical theories, drinks heavily into the small hours of the night, and generally behaves like a swine, becoming bosom buddy with people one otherwise wouldn't want to spit on. That's the whole idea. Because next time you debate with someone in front of the whole Swedish population, you'll remember how the guy on the other side, the poor devil, dissolved in alcohol fumes, revealed intimate and sentimental details about his life. Who can crush a man who once told you, tears brimming his eyes, that as a child he never could learn to swim?

I came along as a kind of Jiminy Cricket when I wrote about farmers' organizations centralizing the collectively owned refinement units. That's been one of the forerunners in depopulating the same rural areas that their party in such eloquent sentences keeps declaring that they want to guard and protect. My criticism was appreciated by the Social Democrats, who thought I had forgotten their own idolization of large-scale production. I had not. However, a little screeching is good for them. The upcoming election results were of personal interest to the prime minister: Should he stay on as the leader of his party or put his energy into an international career?

I must humbly report that I enter this picture somewhat. The politicians know that I have kept a sharp eye on the devastating destruction of the old glassworks. They would like me to become a spokesman for the opinions of ordinary citizens. Naturally, I don't know a thing that the government doesn't already know — or ought to know. The glass workers have done everything to call attention to the problem. They have demonstrated outside the minister's office doors. An inane theatrical drama was performed in Stockholm in front of jaded city folks and with compulsory attendance by the minister of culture.

Everyone knows or ought to know. But the knowledge is too simple; it has to be ritualized and rewritten in acceptable sociological language. That's what Axel and I do. Unfortunately, personal or political motives always exist behind the supposedly objective opinions given. Axel has his motives as I have mine, and he does not like my proposed contribution to the next conference. I don't know why the prime minister shouldn't hear what I have to say. I am going to find out why. And confront Axel at the same time.

But that has to wait. He will be allowed to live this weekend.

I watch my father-in-law working in the yard. He has dug a large hole in front of the rowan tree and keeps digging deeper, tenaciously and rhythmically. I walk over to the hole. He doesn't say a word about the shot from the kitchen window. When I ask if he wants me to relieve him, he nods and climbs out of the hole. I try to sniff discreetly when he sweeps past but can't tell if he has been drinking.

He goes off and I dig.

After ten scoops of dirt, I am aware of how tiring the work is. I have lost the ability to do monotonous muscular work, as well as the pleasure of simple tasks and pure physical effort. My head is spinning. My body has grown used to sitting down in one place.

Damn it all.

I increase the tempo and let the sweat pour. Then my father-in-law stands there, the toes of his boots by the edge, and scratches the back of his head. I take a break, panting. He looks at me with his brown, hard, small eyes and asks me where Jonas is.

"How would I know? I'm standing in this hole, digging."

I suggest that Jonas may have gone over to visit my uncle. The latter is still a warm, joyous, and irresponsible sort. Children are fascinated by him. He wiggles his ears, shows his tattoos, tells hilarious stories from his years at sea, and is generally childish. I love him — and it irritates me that I'm ashamed of him. He never wants to grow up and he can't drink. It gets awkward when he insists on dancing with Louise, making my aunt run upstairs and slam doors. Things are exactly like they used to be. The only difference is that my uncle keeps his bottles in the cellar nowadays.

I smile a little to myself. It seems there are plenty of folks in Småland who have problems with alcohol in combination with supervising wives. My father-in-law looks questioningly at me, but I can't tell him what makes me smile. He is still thinking about Jonas's whereabouts and doesn't see that as something to laugh about.

"The fishing rod is gone," he says.

An indefinite chill deep down in the hole grows up along my legs and freezes them to ice. The handle of the spade is smooth from frequent use. No, it's impossible that Jonas has taken off for the millpond by himself. I stand still and note my own slowness, my unwillingness to realize the truth: Jonas has gone down to the pond all alone.

Suddenly, the paralysis wears off. I leap out of the hole and start running, hollering to my father-in-law:

"Follow me with the car!"

I trust that he understands what I mean. My lungs are on fire while I run. I recall what Jonas and I said about the stream that goes to the millpond. I explained where the free-fishing boundary went, and how irritating it was, since the large beasts were probably lurking right in the pond. Now, if one were to walk out carefully, a balancing act on the rotten, unsteady wooden bridge below the pond, one could reach them. Couldn't one? We had been nodding like two cunning, wily fish poachers. I see the scene in front of me while I run along the slope, throwing myself through brushes and vegetation. The forest swallows my frenetic calls. His name disappears between the tree trunks. Finally I reach the stream.

Everything is quiet and serene.

The water pushes its way over the rim of my boots when I wade along the edge of the treacherous stream, deep with cloudy cavities in places. The reeds have elbowed their way in from the sea. They cover and hide the old, muddy, steep edges. Fifteen years ago, one could stamp one's feet on the tottering grassy mounds and scare out herds of crayfish. Now the water is dead.

When I was thirteen, we went swimming in the pond. I can still see the rays of sun streaming through the brown water when I swam upward, having dived in from the sluice gates. I see my skinny and sinewy body — white at first and then slowly browner — as it falls slowly into the dark, frightening pond. Beside me Jonas is falling. He is fully dressed. His boots are too large, he has a stunned expression on his face and asks with wide-open eyes why he was not allowed to live.

"Jonas!!!"

I bellow his name out over the pond. The bridge is empty. The wet, half-rotten planks are loose. And at the furthest point lies our fishing rod.

I fly toward it, slip, and fall against one of Jonas's boots, which has gotten stuck at the very end, between two rotted planks. It takes a few seconds before I realize that Jonas is actually hanging there, his foot still in the boot. I slither to the edge and see his body, the head under the water. How long has he been struggling? An hour? Two minutes?

After a moment's frantic effort I yank him up. He is lifeless. I have no idea what I am saying or doing. I hit his chest with my fist and plead with him to wake up, to speak to me, say something, tell me if he caught anything. He is blue and white, frighteningly white. Then I become calm and work methodically. I blow my breath into his nose and mouth. I hit the spot over his heart with hard, calculated blows.

Nothing happens.

I sling him over my shoulder, his head hanging down, and run toward the road. Perhaps the shaking will make the heart start working again. My father-in-law has not yet arrived with the car. I swear and I cry, running along the pebble-strewn road, past people who stop and look questioningly. My voice sounds like a saw working against marble, a thin and cutting sound, as I keep hollering.

"He's not dead! He's not dead!"

The car has been brought out of the garage and is parked in front of the house.

My mother-in-law and Louise stand outside it, pulling at the door handles. My father-in-law sits in the front seat. He has locked himself inside the car. I understand. He probably jumped into the car, drove out of the garage, and all of a sudden realized that he was not sober. Now he thinks he can hide that fact by refusing to open the doors.

I throw Jonas down on the ground and yell to Louise to keep giving him artificial respiration. I grab the spade and break the side window. It takes me one second to pull my father-in-law out of the car. Sobbing loudly, he crawls on the ground, while Louise jumps into the backseat and I place Jonas in her lap.

We drive.

Glancing at the back mirror, I notice that she wants to stop giving Jonas artificial respiration and indulge in her own sobbing instead. My voice is a roar.

"Don't give up!!"

ALGERIA
1976

The one thing I have wished hard for in this life is to be a father who is there for my son. I cannot understand how Louise could even think of divorce and of taking Jonas away from me. We ought to talk intensely about such things, Louise and I. But instead I am sitting in the hallway, staring into Monsieur Verdurin's kerosene heater. The flame is waving on half-mast inside the soiled glass. The North African night is devilishly cold in the beginning of the year. I ought to put more kerosene into the heater, but first I must ask Louise who the hell Erik is. If she doesn't answer, I'll go and hide in the Landrover and then appear suddenly. Unexpected meetings and quick farewells are my specialty. I got that from my father.

NIGERIA
1963

The chain cable thundered out of the capstan. Its roaring noise was quickly absorbed by the stifling, threatening jungle foliage on both sides along the river. The anchor hung suspended in the sluggish water of the yellow, muddy Niger and then swung up in the direction of the current when the plows began catching on to the sludge. The din and the smoke from the capstan burned like a stinging iron ring in the nose. I tightened the brake lever. We were there. All the chain cable that ought to be out was out. Through the loudspeaker, our captain tried to cut holes in the quiet morning, but nothing could tear apart the deep silence. The third mate answered, while I jumped up on the heel of one of the bollards and gazed out over the river.

At some distance, perhaps not more than a hundred yards away, there rested our sister ship, sprung from the same shipping firm as ours.

My father stood in the midship aisle.

The anchor was still sinking slowly through the black mire. The chain cable bent and straightened. Slowly, we were moving closer.

I was a little over eighteen years old and had sailed on West Africa for the last six months. This was my third trip. I had not seen my father since I was fourteen. We were always sailing past each other. When he was at home, I was away. And vice versa. In time I had fostered a feeling that he no longer existed. I knew that he sailed as engine operator on the sister ship, but we were always weeks apart in our minutely planned trading routes along the West African coast and the ports in Europe, including Scandinavia. Something must have happened; otherwise we wouldn't be riding anchor side by side in Nigeria's humid, stinking jungle.

My father lifted his arm in greeting.

The anchor was getting a more tenacious hold. The thick cable creaked. Its thickness matched my father's lower arm.

The distance between us shrank to a little over fifty yards. He didn't look as large as I remembered him. The air was absolutely still. The temperature had already risen to above thirty degrees centigrade and total silence reigned. If you believe that West Africa's jungles and marshes are filled with shrieking life, think again. It is silent and hot. Everything rots and gets moldy, grows and dies in a violent cycle.

I looked at the figure who was my father and thought of the last four years. He had grown smaller but was dressed, as always, in one of his pale blue and well-worn overalls. A faint smell of oil and gasoline assaulted my nostrils. But that was pure imagination. That acrid, slightly raw, and pungent odor mingled with that of detergent and perhaps sun and wind was nothing but a memory. When I was little, I sometimes clung to that smell. It came from another world, a world into which both my father and my maternal grandfather disappeared. Mostly it was my father's world since Grandpa's overalls smelled more of oil and dirt. It was a thicker, heavier smell that he arrived and left with in an unbroken rhythm: morning, breakfast, dinner, and night. My father's overalls, on the other hand, were always clean and packed in a suitcase. If I secretly brought out one of these overalls and pulled it over me, it wasn't just the size that swallowed me. Those odors of sun and wind, perhaps of foreign detergents, came from Africa, from America, or perhaps from the Pacific Ocean. That hole in the pant leg was mended in Conakry, that white spot from corroding droppings stemmed from an albatross who sailed across the ship on his way to Australia.

The suitcase was unpacked and packed. He came and he disappeared.

Now he stood there, short and thickset with his sturdy rib cage bursting out of the overalls. He looked like his own father. But my paternal grandpa was not an overalls type of person. That grandpa smelled of elegant importance. For a long time I believed that he was better than the rest of us. Coffee, spices, and cigars from foreign countries combined into an excellent odor for a short, broad man with graying hair and a well-groomed mustache. He was a driver at an import firm. First horse and cart, then truck, and finally the executive car — he drove it all faultlessly. That was his contribution, along with the fact that he supported eight children and took care of a home with a constantly complaining, sickly wife. He did everything with a sort of sullen kindliness. The few times he opened his mouth to speak, he was surprisingly funny.

Was Grandpa's fate the reason for my father's unwillingness to stay at home with us kids when Mom took ill?

The ship shuddered. It felt like a sudden push beneath the soles of one's feet. The main engine was turned off. We had come to a stop and rode with a slight roll at anchor. Actually we were too close to the other ship, but everything was immobile in the suffocating heat. What could happen? We waited. And I observed my father disappearing into the midship aisle's black hole. I suppose he had things to do.

I could have called out to him, could have asked him across the river Niger's yellow, slow-moving water, "Why didn't you stay home with us?"

Instead I turned to the third mate, who had come to stand beside me.

"That was my father."

I pointed toward the black hole. He was gone.

"Is that so?" said the third mate.

To him there was nothing strange about my experience. To a sailor, nothing is strange. In fact, everything is so peculiar that the one who takes every event to heart will soon go crazy. Those who survive have become hardened and keep forging layer after layer of indifference around themselves.

The third mate was pale under his tan, red-eyed and shaky. I probably looked even worse. We had a few days and nights in hell behind us. Only Eight-Finger Karlsson — for the sake of simplicity simply called Eight — the river pilot, the third mate, and I were awake. The rest of the crew slept or had perhaps just opened aching eyes after forty-eight hours of search and lookout, all in vain, ever since Stockholm, so-called because he was from that city, had disappeared.

Our captain, who was well aware that we called him Eight, rasped in the loudspeaker again. I was given the command to show up on the bridge. That was expected since I was the only one who had been present when Stockholm jumped.

Eight sat on the bridge in the high, bolted-down wooden chair meant only for captains and pilots. As I understood it, he had only moved from it once in the last forty-eight hours, which in itself was a feat. He rubbed his eyes with the paddle-like hands where all the fingers had been cut off in line with the thumbs and consequently were only about three quarters of an inch long. Usually jovial and happy, reminding me of the stereotyped Mexican movie bandito just before he puts the knife into the back of an unsuspecting victim, Eight did not have much grin left now in his fatherly face.

He had sailed on West Africa for more than twenty years. Disregarding the fact that he was mad as a coot and had stumps for fingers, he had done rather well for himself. He was of athletic build, and there were rumors that he could move an eight-thousand-ton ship with his bare hands. I know that trick, too. The key is to be sober when you do it. But that's another story.

In spite of his age, Eight's inky black hair curled without any gray wisps. The nose was a big, meaty bulb that arose between sea green eyes. Those always twinkled merrily when he asked if one had "throttled any black ones" during the course of the day. Everybody knows that sailors have their own poetic expressions for bodily functions. He became exorbitantly happy if one's answer was affirmative, clucking and asking, "Is that a fact?" After several months aboard, I finally realized that Eight had knocked up against and entered a world where real black beings were actually strangled.

Having an insane skipper aboard is not an immense problem. It's worse to have a mad first mate, a screwy bosun, or — banish the thought! — a demented cook. As long as Eight received his daily reports as to how many black ones the crew had strangled during the last twenty-four hours, he remained relatively calm. And the sailors' descriptions of a visit to the toilet became loaded down with more jokes. Common euphemisms were "bend a cable" or "write a poem." Especially the latter had a mirthful meaning within our ship's bulwarks.

Long ago a motorman aboard this ship was constantly complaining about his troublesome stomach and consequently he spent hours of his workday in the john. Purple-faced from anger and high blood pressure, the head engineer timed the motorman and came to the conclusion that he was actually worth only a third of his wages. But, since things are not handled that way, the motorman got his full pay. Of course, he signed off before too long.

About a year later, the motorman published a collection of poems, *Black Drums*, and told in an interview how he had written the poems in the engine room's toilet. The article reached the ship, forwarded by someone, perhaps the motorman himself. The head engineer was still there. But only so long as it took to read the word portrait of "the poet with engine songs in his blood." Then the head engineer had a heart attack and died on his feet. I have to believe this to be a true story, since I have used the toilet in the engine room and read a poem scratched into the bulkhead. But that, too, is another story.

Eight was sitting on the bridge, and he wanted something from me. Here in Sapele, the nerves to the absent fingers were bothering him and his luxuriant heartiness was replaced by inward brooding. I stood there, my eyes glued to his face, waiting a few eternities. Perhaps I slept standing up since I was rather drained after the two heartrending days. Perhaps I was even dreaming.

Anyhow, eternities kept flowing right through me and I felt as if I truly understood him. Tricky nerves is something that happens to everyone. I myself never slept anymore except when I was awake. Soon enough I will explain why, since Eight plays a definite part in such a preposterous statement. But first I have to tell how his fingers were sheared off.

As a relatively young second mate, Eight took the ongoing thievery in the cargo hold to heart. In every port the world over, part of the cargo disappears in strange ways. In Palermo, New York, Tangier . . . a long list of black holes where just about anything can go up in smoke in spite of watchmen and heavy locks. And every single port along the Gold Coast qualifies for a top place on that list.

Eight realized that locks and guards were rather unsophisticated thief-catching methods. The thing to do was to break tradition and resort to methods employed by those governing Africa's corrupt political meshwork. Tools such as the Leopard Men in Sierra Leone use. Sudden and unexplainable diseases or death. A leopard's paw scratched as an ominous sign on the ground outside the afflicted one's house. Scratch marks appearing on the chest of a corpse. That's how the Leopard Men govern. That's how they have ruled for a long time. So perhaps it wasn't overly remarkable that Eight figured out his own leopard pattern. Simple, yes, but so shrewd and so violent that the word spread like wildfire from port to port.

Eight let one of the heavy iron lids of the cargo hold stay wide open during the night. A hasp on its back prevented the lid from accidentally closing. From that hasp he stretched a thin fishing line of nylon up to the bridge wing, and from the edge of the lid he stretched yet another nylon line. It was a stretch of a little more than fifty yards, but, with two sturdy rods used for deep-sea fishing, he had the strength and flexibility to jerk it taut. The lid became a highly perilous variation of a simple bird trap.

Eight sat on the bridge wing with his night field glass — and waited. He did not have to wait long before he saw his first victim sneak across the deck and crawl down. At the exact moment that the thief lowered his head, Eight yanked on the nylon line. The hasp flew up and the lid flew down and cut off the thief's fingers.

Afterward everything was quiet as the grave since the victim had also been hit in the head by the heavy lid, knocking him headlong four, five yards down to the ladder pit. All Eight had to do was to climb down and remove the nylon lines. The cutoff fingers and the victim were left until the next morning when the stevedores came aboard and discovered the poor devil. The message spread rapidly.

After a number of similar accidents, the ship acquired a reputation of fighting back by its own magical power. With the exception of the mutilated and sometimes seriously injured small-time thieves, everything was fine. The one who advanced in his career faster than anybody was Eight. Both bolted down and loose property aboard his ship remained untouched.

Once he was made captain, Eight was no longer content to savor his secret in silence. At one time he had picked up a ring finger and dried it in the sun. The turner was ordered to make an artfully ornate brass ring at the finger's cutoff surface and drill a hole through it. Eight put the resulting ornament on a leather string. Right outside the deck office was a cupboard with a glass window for the key to the fire equipment, in case of a fire aboard. Eight substituted the finger for the key and changed the written message to read: "In case of thievery."

He overdid it.

He took away the unexplainable, the eerie magic that everybody along the coast had swallowed tooth and nail. His joke was too gross. The men feared that revenge would hit blindly. It did in Sapele, and it hit with grim exactness.

Nobody knows precisely how Eight lost his own fingers. He awoke one morning as usual, seemingly healthy and whole. Then he felt something sticky on his hands and lifted one hand to pull off the sheet. First he saw all the blood. When he saw his hands, the story goes that his screams were so loud that the whole crew could hear them. A long line formed all the way to his cabin. A screaming captain with eight cutoff fingers was something everyone wanted to see. Some claimed, of course, that they just wanted to see what a captain's cabin looked like. That may be an equally likely story. Many of them would never have a chance for an exclusive viewing again. A little blood and some injuries are things most sailors get to see too often, but a glimpse of a captain's cabin would be almost like getting an idea of how Our Lord lives.

There were some strange things about Eight's cutoff fingers. The turner complained later that he had lost a bolt cutter, so the tool was obvious. But how had the revenger been able to cut off Eight's fingers without Eight feeling it? And why did Eight keep screaming that he had heard a clicking sound?

Explanations and interpretations of this event have outstripped the wind across the seas as they have raced from ship to ship. Some were of the opinion that Eight in his sleep had *heard* when the bolt cutter snapped off the fingers. Others thought that Eight had been anesthetized quickly and effectively. What spoke against that version was that it was not pain that had made Eight scream like that. Others said that the clicking sounds were some kind of hypnotic signals.

Whatever the case, Eight became a legend.

Much earlier, a November night in Cartagena, Spain, I had heard of the thief catcher's fate but had dismissed the story as drunken ravings. I had forgotten it by the time I signed on for the West Africa trade route. It wasn't until three weeks later, right outside of Monrovia, that I laid eyes on our captain. There was nothing unusual about that. Like all other gods, captains rule most efficiently by remaining invisible. I was standing at the helm and had almost written the figure eight in the backwash when he put himself right in front of me, scratched his eyes with a crippled hand, and asked if I had ever throttled a black one. Since he was grinning, I took it as some kind of a joke and answered affirmatively. He liked that but expressed the opinion that I steered like a garden rake. Then he stared at me with his jovial and dangerous smile and admonished me to lie absolutely still if I heard clicking sounds.

I nodded and agreed with everything.

So we had a mad skipper aboard. Best to treat him normally — with respect and keeping as much distance as possible.

Before long I owed this deranged man a considerable debt of gratitude. If Eight had not made that strange remark about lying still when there were clicking sounds, I would not have been able to sleep even when awake. Then I would have been as dead and as meaningless as a Swedish telephone pole in Monrovia. The simile may seem strange, but the fact is that we really did unload Swedish telephone poles in Monrovia's port while it rained cats and dogs. The telephone poles were deck cargo and stank of tar and some oily impregnation matter. Many four-letter words were pronounced applying to the idiot who had ordered wooden telephone poles to a continent that has more wood than anyone can imagine.

Somebody pointed out the ingenious part of the undertaking. It must be as difficult to sell wooden poles to West Africa as to sell snowplows in the Sahara. We shrugged it off, happy to know that they would finally disappear from deck. They were long and slippery, which made them a nuisance, dangerous to unload with our own booms. But the stevedores in Monrovia were far from stupid. They rigged holds in pulleys and drove like mad with five, six poles in every sling.

The rain was of the heavy, steady kind. We kept slipping as we crawled around on the greasy poles. It was a tiring undertaking.

At the end of the day, I tore off my clothes, threw myself down on my berth, and fell asleep immediately. A few ports in West Africa had already taught me that it's hardly worth the trouble to go ashore. Getting whacked on the head and robbed gives you headaches. Safer to go to sleep and save the money for healthier amusements in other ports.

Sometime during the night I was awakened by a clicking sound. It clicked clearly and distinctly. I was wide awake but tried to imagine myself still dreaming since I was scared. What was that sound in the darkness? A black hypnotist who would snip off my fingers in a moment? Perhaps I was already hypnotized to feel nothing, to be unable to move, only to lie there as a tranquilized but fully awake piece of luggage?

I had been at sea almost three years. Bit by bit, that time had filed off some of my uncontrolled curiosity. Being now a little over eighteen years old, I did not take everything indiscriminately to heart anymore. But since I had just heard about the mysterious clicking, I couldn't help it if my imagination ran wild.

I lay there for a long, long time, quite paralyzed. Possibly I trembled the way mice do when they sit, stiff and frightened, in front of a snake's hissing gap. With my nose toward the bulkhead, I ordered my unencumbered left ear to sail off on a scouting trip in the dark. Nobody there. Nobody there. And nobody there . . .

And yet, perhaps somebody was right there in my cabin?

His breathing sounded exactly like mine, and he was stinking as much from the slippery telephone poles as I was. He was so close that I got a whiff of dried cod. We had tons of fish aboard, having loaded them in Bergen, Norway. It rained there, too.

I shut my eyes tightly and tried to think back to Bergen. I had good memories of Bergen. She also smelled of cod. But perhaps that was only because we had been smooching under a tarpaulin that covered tons of it. Just like me, that load was waiting to get aboard and out of the rain. But this girl did not want to be counted among those who accept invitations to go aboard ships. We had to stand under the tarp and kiss as well as we were able while the stench of cod brought waves of nausea into my throat.

Perhaps it was just the memory of that situation that had awakened in my nostrils?

I turned over on my other side, facing the darkness of the cabin, and laughed softly, a small neighing laughter, at my own wild fantasies. Naturally I would be the one to imagine that I had a bunch of clicking blacks in my cabin. The neigh froze against my lips when I opened my eyes to affirm that I was alone. The whites of two enormous eyes gleamed just inches from my face. The owner of the eyes was squatting next to the berth, waiting for me to sit up and look around the cabin.

It was a rather shrewd thing to do. But my staying immobile for so long had made him curious to find out if I was asleep or not. He had just snuck his head close to mine when I turned over and opened my eyes. Being that close, it would be easy for him to stab me with his knife, should I happen to discover him. The blade of the knife glinted in the dark. What could I say? Excuse me, sir, but you must have taken the wrong turn!

There was no time for me to figure out a suitable polite phrase. I felt the air movement caused by his arm when the knife came at me.

Quickly I rolled off the berth, right on top of the man. The many breathless seconds I had spent waiting and listening in the dark had pumped me brimful of adrenaline. The strange clicking sound had prepared me.

He was wearing only a pair of shorts and a hard hat. Perhaps he had heard about Eight's iron lids that fell on people? We rolled around, fighting, for a while. Having crawled across the sticky telephone poles he was greasy and slippery as an eel. Slithering around with him in the cabin made the fight seem like a bad joke. It was like both trying to protect myself and hanging on to an enormously strong and alive gigantic soap. Plop! He slipped away. The knife clattered on the cabin floor. I understood that he was groping around for it, so I scrambled to my feet and jumped as high as I could in order to land on his back.

It worked! The air went out of him. He stayed inert a few seconds. Strangely enough, the hard hat was still on his head. Its sharp edge had torn the skin on my forehead. Blood pumped out over my eyes. I had trouble seeing, as I tumbled down on his slippery back and took a steady hold of the helmet with both hands. Then I pulled it back with all my might. As I had figured, the leather strap cut in under the chin and toward the throat. He let out a death rattle. I pulled and yanked. The seconds ticked away like hard New Year's counts against my heart. I aged and was born a hundred times before the body grew limp and collapsed underneath me.

Had I strangled the nightly intruder?

There was no time to make sure. I slammed the door hard behind me and locked it, turning the key twice. There! Now I had imprisoned my burglar. Perhaps even killed him, I thought the next moment. What should I do? It did not feel like a barrel of fun to go to Eight, shake him awake, and tell him that I had just throttled a black one. We would probably get stuck in a complicated debate as to whether or not I had really done it.

The problem was shoved aside, at least temporarily, when I happened to glance down at the floor under my feet. Either my lone scoundrel had danced a preparatory hypnotic dance on his bare, oily feet in the aisle or else there were more of his kind aboard.

The cabin beside mine was occupied by a man from the island of Gotland; he was called the Islander. An old but hardy fellow who seemed to have sailed the seas since the days of the Flying Dutchman. I yanked the Islander's door open and caught sight of yet another hopeful lad crawling on the cabin floor. Quick as a wink, I pulled out the key, slammed the door, and turned the key twice from the outside.

Now I had two thieves and one Islander locked in. All hell broke loose in there. It sounded as if the Islander were practicing discus throwing with the thief.

Then my eyes discovered more footprints. They led all the way to Stockholm's cabin. Stockholm's real name was Karlsson, but since we only had one man from the fair city of Stockholm aboard, he was the target for everybody's distrust and envy of the Swedish capital and its inhabitants. I repeated the locking maneuver with his cabin door.

The place teemed with black, oil-impregnated, and stinking robbers and burglars. All of a sudden I had caught three!

Stockholm let out loud cries and protests. He wanted me to remove the thief from his cabin.

"Why should I?" I yelled back. "He'd just run away!"

"I've got no clothes on!" Stockholm roared in answer.

I had trouble understanding what that had to do with anything. Especially since I myself was completely nude. I looked as if somebody had rolled me in tar and clotted blood. I could barely see, due to all the blood flowing from the wound in my forehead, but in spite of this I ran around locking in thieves as if my life depended on it. We argued back and forth about who should fight Stockholm's thief while the rest of the crew came running.

Most of those further aft were from Göteborg, historically a rival of Stockholm, and those witty lads demanded immediately that the poor thief should be let out of Stockholm's cabin for purely humanitarian reasons. As a punishment, it was too tough, just one step from being sent to the gas chamber, to be forced to spend time in the same cabin as a nude and hysterical man from Stockholm. After some palavers and considerable gaiety, all serving to put me as the hero in the center, the watchman, the first mate, and even Eight himself came down.

Eight was holding the watchman by the ear, saying that this was the same old conspiracy. He promised to hang the whole bunch of us from the yardarm. That was funny since we did not have any yardarm.

I thanked him sincerely for the warnings to remain still whenever there was a clicking sound. He looked somewhat wonderingly at me, as if I rather than he were the crazy one.

"I was talking about the compass! You should keep still and not weave back and forth so much!" he hollered and snapped his fingers in front of my face. It looked rather amusing since he had no fingers to snap with. Still I swear that I did see him snap his fingers.

The explanation may be that I thought it was painful for him not being able to snap his fingers. At times I wonder where my soul has its center and habitat. Mostly it seems to fly around like an agitated and compassionate ghost inside other people's troubles. It was the same thing when my mother coughed so horribly that she died. I could actually see my own small lungs constrict in cramp and sympathy. And now it happened with Eight. I giggled a little nervously and wanted so very much for him to be able to snap his fingers. When he kept scowling, I consoled him with the fact that, be that as it may, he had still saved my life.

He proceeded to become the jolly Green Giant. In order to avoid having to embrace me like a long-lost son, he pulled my ear. It hurt like hell. Horrendous strength lived in the remaining small stump of the index finger. He lifted me several inches off the cabin floor and urged three cheers for a real live throttler of blacks.

Then the Islander came out. That is to say, he yanked the door open with such force that splinters flew. He had finished the battle with his thief but was still belligerent and confused. He growled and fumbled for new human beings to use and throw as a discus. Unfortunately he chose me. I guess he didn't understand why the men were cheering someone whose ear was being pulled. Besides, I was nearly black from all the tar. He took hold of me and threw me into the bulkhead. Lucky for me Eight let go of my ear, otherwise I would have had to live out my life with one ear dragging on the ground. I was made of elastic material and it would probably have stretched like chewing gum rather than broken off. But my elasticity only went so far. I had had it. I stayed right there on the floor and fainted.

When I came to, the bulky Islander sat like a worried and tall monolith beside my berth. Bloody and torn, he still managed a small, almost joyous smile when he noticed that I was awake. On my stomach was placed the thief's hard hat, standing upside down like a chamber pot. The Islander winked with a bluish, swollen eye and fished around in the hat. As I was wondering what I might look like, he hissed with his cracked voice, "You don't drink strong stuff. But Eight sent down some goodies anyhow."

He unwrapped the shimmering green tinfoil on the first miniature liquor-filled chocolate bottle.

"Brandy. After that we'll try a little Swedish punch. And then a small cordial. Which we rinse down with another cognac."

After thirty-eight bottles, I felt both intoxicated and hyperactive. So I fell asleep. And that was the first time I fell asleep while awake. An extremely cold and alert person existed inside the seemingly sound-asleep one. Like a coiled steel spring, I reacted to the tiniest sound. I tried to strangle the Islander twice that night, the minute he made the slightest movement. He fed me several more chocolate bottles and sang a lullaby about big mountains and little trolls who couldn't find their way home. Very beautiful. I think I cried a little against his broad shoulder. He was better than my father had ever been.

When I awoke in the morning, he grinned broadly.

"Morning, Strangler."

An unpleasant truth to wake up to, but I took comfort in the fact that things could have been worse. Imagine waking up in Monrovia being both dead and robbed!

With nearly forty centiliters — or thirteen and a half fluid ounces — of sweetly sticky hangover in my body after the Islander's insistent and considerate refills, I crawled with painful difficulty up on deck for breakfast and saw the world anew, having throttled my first black one. I noted exactly how it looked.

Suddenly I remembered a boatswain, Bengtsson by name, who for a long time had been like a father to me. He was far from religious but almost sounded as if he were when he summed up his life-acquired wisdom. "If a human being is truly good, he will be crucified." It was eloquently expressed. I thought of Bengtsson and wanted to cry. But I braced myself and did not let one single tear through. I managed rather well, according to the Islander. A few more years and I'd have the makings of a real sailor, able to drink through the night and still work a full day. As I said, he was rather old-fashioned. God knows what he poured inside himself, but he always smelled of old, sour jungle juice.

It took me a full week to figure out if I had killed a human being or not. The crew stubbornly insisted on calling me the Strangler. It did not help that I finally was told that the thief had recovered and been put ashore. It remained eerie.

I have had reasons to consider these kinds of dilemmas before. Since the day I was old enough to understand spoken language, my mother kept telling me that we children would be the death of her. It wasn't much fun when we finally succeeded.

Generally speaking, it isn't much fun to keep brooding over the question of whether one has brought death to someone or not. Equally terrible is to plan another's demise. And even worse when people die right in front of you with no one caring.

When I was little, I didn't think that growing up would be like this. I believed that my soul would open up like a flower since I would be strong enough to defend it. Of course it was childish arrogance to see one's soul as some kind of white lily that would burst into bloom later.

I had probably acquired my arrogance from Grandma's outhouse. Since she knew that I used to sit there and read, she prepared the outhouse with religious parables in cheap editions. At least half of them told of small children who on the very last page were transformed into saintlike creatures. It was very beautiful and convincing, and I simply awaited my turn.

Unfortunate circumstances made me instead snuff out my mother's life.

At the age of eighteen, I had long ago forgotten my childhood and all silly notions of my lily white soul ready to burst into bloom. It's rather amusing. During the teens, you need to remember your childhood's holy oaths to rehabilitate and reconstitute the natural and healthy parts of childhood, but then the hormones take over and produce a thick mess of sperms as an efficient cover, placed right over the possibly innocent images you have of yourself. You simply don't want to remember yourself as a child. As a teenager, you betray your childhood without thinking, and even if it burns in urgent flames, you don't see it. I believe this story may be about how I as a teenager managed never to betray my past, even if the rocky, often violent drive of destiny did its utmost to mold me into an image as like my father as possible.

My perception of him when I was a child was that of a metal bullet. My own hardening process was not far behind his. So what would it sound like when we met? Clank! Clank!

The fact that I as a memorial to my fierce struggle and honorable victory in Monrovia had been tabbed the Strangler and then been able to associate on friendly terms with the strong-as-an-ox Islander without toppling over backwards when he engulfed me in his fetid breath were parts of my final exams before the inevitable encounter with my father. The only missing piece would have been my own imbibing the Islander's jungle juice.

*   *   *

That is how far back my thoughts transported me while I stood on the bridge, waiting for an all-clear signal from Eight, when his face suddenly split in a broad grin and he said, "Jungle juice."

"Oh yeah," I answered as flatly as I could.

That was a lesson I had learned: Conversations with madmen should be conducted with inflections and voice totally devoid of passion. Eight may have loved jungle juice or perhaps he hated the home-brewed concoction or he might want me to reveal my own relationship to the cheap brew.

"Stockholm. Of course he has been drinking that goddamned half-fermented mash. Was it the Islander who served it?"

I remained silent, thereby taking the risk that Eight would twist my ear. But who can betray someone who has sung lullabies about mountains and trolls by one's berth?

"Were it up to me, I'd rather portion out bottles of honest-to-goodness Swedish schnapps," Eight said with a sigh. "But then the folks back at the shipping line would think I had gone crazy. And we don't want them to know about that, do we?"

On that point I could only nod reassuringly. I had no reason to write home to the shipping company about it.

We stood there for a while and talked back and forth in that uncertain way you do with madmen. All the time, I nourished an eerie feeling that our conversation was about something totally different than the missing Stockholm.

Finally Eight let out a deep sigh and said that there wasn't a thing one could do about it.

"You ought to go to sleep. Or why not go over and see your father? A good man. He has decided to be especially kind toward all children since he can't be sure which ones are his own. We've sailed together. Do that. Go and see him. I'm sure he'd be happy. Here are some cigarettes — to pay for the round-trip. But don't give them the pack before you're there. People have died for less here on the river. A few years ago an Englishmen lost three men on his crew. They were going to follow in separate canoes to go swimming."

Eight laughed uproariously.

"The devil made sure they got to swim!"

It was weird to hear one of my father's standing jokes from the

lips of Eight. The one about the children. Eight had no way of knowing that I used to have a totally different understanding of that joke.
The punch line was that my father in actuality was kind to all children always, except his own. With growing amazement we had
observed his predilection for giving presents to other children.
A flashlight, a pocketknife, or a considerable money gift for some
cousin's child's birthday seemed to appear frequently in front of our
stupefied eyes. He wanted to stay more popular with the children of
our relatives than with his own. Why that was so, we never managed
to comprehend.

"What about Stockholm?" I asked.

Eight didn't answer. He slept, his head rolled down toward his
shoulder. I stood there awhile and studied him. Even when he slept,
there was a cunning expression on his face. Or perhaps the whole
affair with Stockholm had warped my judgment.

We were on our way into the mouth of the Niger. The river opens up
in an enormous delta toward the sea. An endless lowland with
marshes and swampy ground, dead and yet alive: During unfathomable stretches of time something totally worthless has kept producing
a rich secret — oil. High fire flames from the new drill towers licked
the sky. That made Eight swear as he walked back and forth on the
bridge in the darkness. The drill towers made navigation a shaky
business. It was hard to make out the faintly blinking fairway buoy
that is the meeting spot for ships and pilots.

The first time I saw the pilots, I had trouble masking my laughter.
They came in four, five open outrigger dories with outboard engines,
and each one contained a raggedy, colorful bunch, costumed in a
multitude of stolen shipping flags.

The steersmen hollered and tried to ram each other while the
pilots themselves authoritatively waved soiled letters of recommen-
dation and loudly began to negotiate their price with Eight. To no
one's surprise, he chose the cheapest one, a small, crooked man a bit
over sixty with running, purulent eyes and lacking a right leg. The
explanation voiced aboard ship was that Eight and the pilot were
brothers in their respective handicaps. We couldn't care less.

The pilot brought his own steersmen along, two strong young

men, who effortlessly climbed up a thick piece of manila rope like monkeys, one of them carrying the pilot on his back.

"Look carefully, Strangler," said the Islander. He happened to stand beside me on deck when the steersmen with the pilot scrambled aboard.

The Islander emitted his usual stench of jungle juice. He panted loudly over my hair, and I wondered if he could function as flamethrower if ignited. I felt my hair go limp from the noxious breath and moved a few feet away while I asked what exactly he meant.

"That's how they do it. Ten men with big hooks fastened to ropes. In an outrigger like that. They catch up with us during the night, climb aboard, cut the crew into dead pieces, and load all the stolen stuff aboard their dory. They're gone before anyone notices a thing. Besides, how can we notice if we're dead as doornails?"

He laughed out loud and met one of the steersmen's outstretched hands with his enormous clenched fists. Instead of taking the proffered hand, the Islander continued the movement and took a good hold of the man's throat. He yanked him up the last foot over the railing, clucked noisily, and let the young man's robust body fall like an empty overcoat on the deck.

"But then we'll strangle them, won't we?"

I nodded, agreed, and laughed as raw and heartily as I could at the Islander's joke while the young steersman crawled up to the bridge quicker than a whip's lash. What else could I do but laugh? Ever since the night in Monrovia, I was considered the specialist when it came to strangling natives.

That was the first and only time I laughed at these masterful professionals. The one-legged pilot and his two steersmen handled our big freighter as if she were a canoe racing forward through the river's sharp bends. In places the Niger was hardly wider than our ship — we would almost have needed hinges on her to manage the narrowest parts.

The worst was to stand anchor watch, prepared to let both anchors go simultaneously should the pilot or his steersman miscalculate the river's capricious new furrows and sandbanks.

Standing at the tip of the bow was like being placed one yard from a movie screen with a mad projectionist in the back rolling a Tarzan film at abnormally high speed. I never saw Tarzan, just a lot of green stuff flimmering past the tip of my nose, and I was hanging on to the capstan's two braking cranks as if it were a question of life and death every second. Bit by bit I got used to it and relaxed a little. I discovered that it was better to look astern. That way I received a reverse picture, an impression of standing on the only nonmoving spot. The poop deck looked as if it were wrapped in tenacious lianas and suspended branch work. Miraculously enough, only now and then did a branch get stuck. I was standing there, imagining the crew awakened by a terrifying thunder, rushing up, and staring, only to say hello to their brothers, a mass of paralyzed and frightened monkeys.

As usual, I found myself in a precarious position whenever I started to laugh at others. Through the loudspeaker Eight hollered his command to let down both anchors. I whirled around and stared in panic at the bow, already ploughing the dense greenery.

"Behind which tree should I drop anchor?" I called out to Eight.

"Select one you'd like to hang from," he yelled back.

He could only appreciate his own jokes.

I dropped both anchors, jumping around in a hell of smoke and sparks while I turned the brake cranks and attempted to stop the thundering anchor cables without yanking the capstan apart.

The sun hurried to hide behind a drenching shower of leaves and branches. The pregnant silence that followed seemed almost like a rumbling hell. When I disentangled myself from the slippery, sticky greenery, it sounded as if a large animal had tumbled down from a branch. I stood stock-still. A more desolate sound I have never heard. As if thousands of crocodiles were burping all at the same time. We were stuck in the sludge. The jungle had already begun to swallow us. We were being screwed down in the swampy sand, inch by inch. The burning deck under the soles of my feet was sinking downward.

The ship did not have enough buoyancy to withstand what we had brought about. We were stuck in a gigantic wedge of suctorial ooze. The smacking sound returned, the ship was pulled down, down, down . . .

I began to contemplate from which tree I would be hanged. The whole thing was my fault. Everything. I had gotten involved in thinking of a stupid joke for exactly the number of seconds needed to stop the ship in time.

Eight's voice on the loudspeaker calmed me. The only thing he demanded was for me to find the capstan underneath the rubbish of branches and lianas.

"Remember to look out for snakes. Those little black devils kill you in ten seconds," his clucking voice rang out over the quiet jungle.

He found that funny.

My eyes searched feverishly for the little black killers. Any branch could be a camouflaged snake. When I started to clear out the stuff, the Islander arrived, large and sure, with a fire hose on his shoulder. He waved me away, connected the hose, and put the mouthpiece on high pressure. Sure enough, here and there a small black snake wiggled down into the anchor hold while leaves, twigs, and branches flew in every direction.

I shivered in the damp heat, as if the snakes had wormed their way under my shirt. The Islander then drove the capstan while I leaned out over the railing and rinsed off snakes, leaves, and branches. Half inch by half inch, we made our way out. It took hours before we were liberated from the jungle's deadly embrace. Slowly, the black, stinking mud came up along the cable and, as slowly, we glided out into the river.

Once back in our right element, we could see how the bow had made a cut, sharp as the edge of an ax, into the jungle's black sludge. Trees and bushes had been mowed down. Anyone passing would have found the enormous slash into the jungle's green hide totally mysterious and without rhyme or reason. But I knew that by the next journey, three months later, the wound would be healed.

Perhaps life did the same with me. Most days and nights disappeared in endless monotony, but then there happened one second of crucial importance; it expanded and developed into minutes, hours, and days, which put a gigantic wedge into me. But the events came and went and along with them disappeared all visible traces. I would never be able to point to these deep, huge dents in my life and make them understandable.

One West African port after the other went past, in flickering speed. Every port, every day, and every night had, of course, its special quality.

We glide through a bluish white and incandescent flowery meadow under the Southern Cross. I cling to the rope ladder on my way up to the bridge wing. Once up there, I am in another time and upon another ocean — I sing a mad and loud song over Biscaya's wheezy wave tops. A flash of summer lightning strikes the foremast. A pale, surprised face is visible during a tenth of a second, then everything drowns in blackness again. It's warm. Europe disappears out of memory as a piece of melting ice under the sun's welding flames. Offshore the air is almost dry. I lean forward, toward the surface of the bridge that is exposed to the wind, stand still, and feel the hairs on my arms rise to greet the cool wind that floats past.

The views change, coasts sink into the ocean, mountains break up the eternal horizon, every day is different.

But one thing remains eternally the same. I have no choice. The ship is both my home and my prison. For a few short hours I may be allowed some carousing ashore. But my time is carefully premeasured.

One night, as we pass an illuminated city, I want to step off, simply walk straight overboard. Perhaps that is the night when I think of my father, the years he has traveled, and the time both of us now sail through in the same manner. I begin to understand him more and more. The inconceivable indifference he has always displayed toward those closest to him is at least partly shaped by his years as a sailor. He is a surface that has been hardened by thousands and again thousands of days of disappointment.

I understand that I am learning to relate to reality as the jungle relates to us when we injure it. It heals its own wounds. Nothing is visible. My compassion for myself and others turns inward. I can't do anything about it. It lies deep inside and pants, like a beaten puppy, while we pass continents, ports, illuminated cities in an eternal continuity. Everything is the same thing. There is nothing out there to long for or to awaken emotions. I break the habit of thinking of home since I am my own isolated home. A shell grows all around me with frightening speed, and I understand that my desire to go to sea may have to do with crawling beneath my father's hard surface. The price I have paid is that his reality also shapes me. And yet, I have sworn never to become like him. By following in his professional footsteps, I am indeed making things hard for me.

Such thoughts ran on like a screechy record in my head one night. Or perhaps many nights. I don't believe that I thought a lot of them at one and the same time. Perhaps I wondered what my father was doing at that moment, that night. Perhaps I stood at the helm, aware of Eight wandering about, muttering, and perhaps we were on our way to connect with the Sapele pilots while West Africa's new flame-throwing oil drill towers make life harder for all shipmates and captains.

I don't know if my real story begins here in the inky West African night. Perhaps it doesn't really begin until two days later when I meet my father in Sapele. But since our encounter turned out the way it did, I also want to relate the suppositions and premises. That means that my story must also reach backwards at times.

When I was standing at the helm outside the river Niger's delta, I had no inkling that I would see my father again so soon.

Neither did I know that my indifference had grown to the extent that in just a little while I would let Stockholm jump overboard with my blessing.

Less than an hour was left until midnight. I was relieved at the helm and swore softly to myself while I danced down the rope ladder to the galley to put on some coffee. I cheered up when I remembered that I did not need to throw out that heavy monster of a pilot ladder. The Sapele pilot and his steersmen climbed aboard using a rope. Why couldn't all the pilots in the world's ports learn such a simple trick?

While the water for the coffee was boiling, I went back out on the deck and stood for a while by the railing. We were almost at the panting light of the buoy. On both sides of us glimmered faint lights from the shore, tiny glowworms in an endless sack of blackness.

I went back to the galley and poured the coffee, took off the kettle, and ran out to lower a rope to the pilot. That was not necessary. The one-legged pilot stood already on the deck. One of the steersmen was leisurely rolling up the rope with its big hook, and the other had his head over the edge of the deck. He swung himself over the rail without effort. I nodded and they smiled amiably back. Although in the back of my head lived the Islander's warning about treacherous pirates. Look how simply, quickly, and soundlessly they had reached us with the help of the dory's large outboard engine. It took them seconds to come aboard.

Their little demonstration, coupled with the night in Monrovia, reaffirmed my wise decision never again to sleep except when fully awake.

It was time for the next watch. They would have a few easy hours ahead. No turn at the helm and no lookout. Well inside the river's wide mouth, we would probably weigh the anchor and wait for the dawn's early light.

I went sternward to wake up Stockholm and Vappu, the Finn. The two together were called Light and Dark. Vappu was Light and Stockholm was Dark. Other than the difference in coloring, they were confusingly similar in looks, as if forged in the same mold. Both were broad and large guys with so many muscles that you wondered how they could keep track of them and worried that they would lose any of their playful equipment. Their greatest pleasures were to pump iron and to drink large amounts of jungle juice.

Stockholm used not to drink more than a glass now and then on special occasions, and since there weren't many of those aboard, he was almost totally dry. When Vappu came aboard, the picture changed. In contrast to Stockholm, he soaked up jungle juice like a merry sponge. But nothing showed. At most, he would sing some melancholy tune and lift a few hundred extra kilograms of weighty scrap iron. He could drink all night long and yet work his full twelve hours during the day in the suffocating heat, so long as he got something to drink now and then. Since it was not enough for Stockholm to emulate Vappu in their shared athletic interests, he drank, too — and became darker and darker in his moods.

I had occasion to reflect over their mental states when it became clear that the crew had gathered in Vappu's cabin. It must have been a special occasion since everybody was yelling, roaring with laughter, and filling glasses to the brim with a rather unctuous vintage smelling of fusel oil.

It turned out to be Vappu's birthday. His twenty-second.

Didn't that mean that he was two months younger than Stockholm? somebody asked. And couldn't one see how deterioration had begun in the older one? That was the right of creeping age, certainly, but it wasn't a pleasant sight to observe a triceps fall down over a biceps.

In that vein the talk went with veiled puns coined by those from the rival city of Göteborg, while the man from Stockholm, called by the city's name, slowly developed a face to match his raven black hair. When I entered the cabin, he had taken on an almost deep purple color of resentment and nausea. The latter was because he couldn't stomach the Islander's jungle juice very well. Suddenly something boiled over inside his thick head. Brutally, he grabbed Vappu's friendly waving hand and demanded the Islander as judge supreme, outside of all contests as he was.

Here would occur a trial of strength. Arm wrestling.

I have noticed the same tiresome phenomenon thousands of times. I don't know what secret ingredient there is in alcohol, but it seems always to be bringing out two extremely boring kinds of behavior in the entire male species.

One is an irresistible desire to shake hands with anyone who is to be convinced of something that cannot be explained verbally. As words and whole sentence structures are flushed away by that mysterious substance in alcohol, the shaking of hands increases. It's as if the intoxicated one, with the help of the ongoing handshakes, wants to pump forward whole oceans of agreeable understanding. If both the handshakers are equally drunk, this looks possible. Never have I seen women shake hands in that way. This is why I have come to the conclusion that there must be some special element in alcohol that only affects men.

The other behavior is a strong hunger for arm wrestling. It breaks out as some kind of rapidly spreading epidemic in the members of the male sex as soon as they drink alcohol. On the surface, it's an innocent, harmless contest. But even the most pure-hearted athletes can become entangled in each other pretty much the same way as reindeer bulls do when they measure their strengths head-to-head.

Light and Dark had long ago become enmeshed in one another. It was high time for arm wrestling. Room was made, in spite of Vappu's friendly disinterest.

"No. Shouldn't start wrestling. It'll take all night," he said and smiled.

But the cabin was filled with human beings who had all the time in the world to watch the duel till the break of dawn if necessary. Vappu sighed and moved forward the bulging tree trunk he called his right arm. Stockholm's arm already stood there, rooted to the table like an iron bollard, the red and blue tattoos waving threateningly. The Islander counted, and the wrestling began.

I fell right into a hairy dilemma. Like everybody else, I did want to see this match. But I suspected that this contest of brute strength would take time, probably until far beyond midnight. I ran back to the galley and the coffee, got a cup for the third mate, and hurried up on the bridge with it. The third mate was already there and asked why I and not Stockholm or Vappu came with the coffee. My explanation sounded farfetched since it was true, but he accepted it with the added condition that the two contestants break for a strict sobriety control on the bridge.

"I'll see what to believe when I get to see them," was how the third mate expressed his opinion.

A rather reasonable request, considering the reputation of the two.

I slid happily and eagerly down the ladder to convey the message. First when my feet touched the deck did it occur to me that the third mate would probably tumble backwards if both Vappu and Stockholm were to let their breath escape in the direction of his face. I have an absolutely extraordinary ability to do everything wrong by eagerly trying to please everyone.

Well, I didn't have to worry about it. Stockholm was already standing on the deck in the dark night, staring out over the river toward the faintly glimmering lights ashore. He was shivering, as if from a chill, when I dared to touch him. I could have sworn that I heard someone sobbing in the noise of the wind.

Then he became unmanageable all of a sudden and yelled that he could walk on his hands along the railing around the whole damned ship, if he so desired. He jumped up on the railing and rocked back and forth.

I have experienced that kind of thing innumerable times. Without asking for it, you are handed a bunch of cards that you can't read. It's a poker game with a deck of cards invented for the moment. The one invited to play inevitably does it wrong. But to save the life of someone who wants to jump overboard can never be wrong, a beginner in the game will say. Ha! He doesn't know the first thing about the rules. I must discuss that another time. Now I had to deal with the grave matter of Stockholm. The problem was that he was unbelievably big and strong. I didn't dare to get too close in case he'd get the brilliant idea to pull me along. I took a few steps away from the railing and suggested that he climb down. It was his watch; he should take his turn; I had neither the time nor the inclination to accompany him all around the ship while he walked on his hands.

"Which I'm sure you'd be able to do," I said.

A glint of surprise forced itself to the surface.

"You believe that?"

"Oh yeah."

"But not that I'd be able to swim ashore?"

We were hanging from a cliff above a gaping abyss with our fingertips touching lightly — just half an inch more and I would have saved him. That's how it was, in spite of me standing two yards away from him. A few words more and his madness would have lifted its wings and flown away. I drew a blind card in the mystifying game and thought I was on the right track when I appealed to his common sense.

"You wouldn't get very far away from the starboard side. I mean, however far out you'd jump, you'd end up in the propeller suction. There'd be nothing but gristle left of you."

"So that's what you think!"

It was over. I had only one card left. I turned away and took another step away from him.

"Jump then. If you're so goddamned stupid."

Such total lack of interest combined with cool disdain ought to erase his need of revenge. There was nobody looking now. Further astern, Vappu's party was in full swing. Who cared about the disappearance of a guy from Stockholm, I thought, but wished he would quit the grim game.

I pulled out my trump card, took a few more steps in the direction away from where he stood, icily determined not to turn back but to show that he had to play on his own, without an audience.

As I reached the rope ladder leading up to the boat deck, I whirled around anyhow. Stockholm had jumped. Perhaps I had heard a faint scream and a splash through the roaring of the wind. Perhaps I only imagined it.

With a few leaps, I was on the boat deck, yanked loose a life buoy, and threw it into the rushing water. Then all strength leaked out of me. It was not even twenty yards to the bridge. In a few seconds I would hear my own voice holler, "Man overboard!"

But my legs turned to lead. I had to drag myself up the next rope ladder. The scene with Stockholm kept running over and over in my head, at the same time as large parts of my brain tried to erase and obliterate the whole event. It had not happened. He had not jumped. Why didn't I do anything? Why didn't I rush over and pull him down?

The twenty steps seemed like a mile-long walk to a court of judgment where the verdict had already been handed out. I saw Eight in front of me, his finger pointing, even though he didn't have any. To what punishment are people who don't care condemned?

Or had I done the best I could?

Could I have done it differently? Could I have used other words?

In actuality, the twenty steps took just a few seconds. And my voice sounded exactly as I had imagined it. It broke as if I were still in my early teens, though I was all of eighteen. And Eight swore exactly as much as I had expected. As a real captain, he made decisions before anybody else had time even to think about it. He threw himself on the engine telegraph and stopped the engines as he ordered me to drop the anchor quickly. There was no time to lose. We could not be adrift in the middle of the river's current flow many minutes before we made contact with some sandbank.

Gratefully I worked off some of the heavy questions. The steel cable clanged harshly in the black night at the same time as the tocsin resounded its signal over my head. "Every man on deck! Hurry! Hurry!"

Everybody seemed to be shouting.

But really, what was there to do? If Stockholm had not been sliced to bits by the propeller, he must certainly be moving outward with the tide and the current, somebody reasoned, and made a gesture over the dirt yellow river water, which by now was bathing in light from every available light source.

I was quite a distance ahead of the others in the development of events since I had more or less recommended Stockholm to jump. Irritated by their sluggishness, I yelped between clenched teeth that we must get a boat in the water. Crew hands wavered uncertainly over the lifeboat apron.

Was it really any use? Especially since none of the men were sober.

Of course I had forgotten that. What I took for slowness and general paralysis was the result of that damned jungle juice.

A weak wind huffed a few warm breezes over us. From the skylight down to the engine room, the large main engine growled in a subdued voice. As many as possible of the earlier so boisterous party participants clung to the headlights, letting them sweep over the water. The rest did their best to avoid having to bring the lifeboat down into the dark and ominous water. I wanted to fall to my knees and plead for some action to be carried out in order to erase my guilt. But since I was the only one who knew of it, that seemed exaggerated. Why throw such burdens on others?

Along with other seamen by the railing, I ultimately got used to the thought that everything was already too late.

"When it comes to folks from Stockholm, one more or one less makes little difference," someone muttered and spat into the water.

I was inclined to agree when I happened to glance sternward. Vappu was working feverishly with the jolly boat that was hanging on the upper poop deck. Vappu! Yes! With him I could share my guilt. If Vappu had not forced his melancholy buddy's arm, they might have continued to pump iron and slurp jungle juice for the rest of their days.

I flew sternward toward Vappu. Several of the men followed me.

The jolly boat was of course much more suitable for putting into the river than the ungainly lifeboats, which needed ten men with a sober sense of rhythm at the oars. The difference from the lifeboats was also that the smaller workboat had an inboard motor.

Soon enough we were lowered. I threw off the mooring line and we drifted out with the current into the darkness while Vappu tried to get the motor going. He swore long tirades in Finnish, the water clucked against the sides of the boat, and our strongly illuminated ship seemed soon much too far away.

"He couldn't stand that you won the arm wrestling," I said in order to transfer my burden onto Vappu.

He looked up over the motor.

"No, no. I didn't break down his arm. I let him win. But maybe he noticed."

"Guess he had too much to drink. He may have tried to keep up with you, Vappu. You pour a lot of that stuff inside you."

I kept jabbering. I couldn't stop.

Vappu straightened up from the stone dead motor. He looked out over the water and gestured for me to be quiet.

"I don't drink a lot. In Finland, we drink a lot."

Vappu stood there like a concrete block in the boat, immobile and yet as if ready to jump in after Stockholm. His weight slowly seemed to press the boat down, toward the bottom. Slowly, slowly it sank through the river's indifferent surface. Suddenly I felt water far above the ankles.

"Vappu! We're sinking."

"Damnation! The stopcock!"

We threw ourselves down and fumbled around in the dark. Somebody had probably unscrewed the stopcock so that the boat would not fill up with rainwater. Vappu grunted, fell to his knees and tore off his shirt, ripped off a few strips, and groped around until he managed to press the rags down into the hole. He stood up. For the moment we were safe, but we drifted with rather alarming speed away from the ship. The tide played with us as if we were a piece of cork. Again Vappu stood there, silent and inert. Shouldn't we try to do something?

"Shouldn't we try to call him?" I asked.

"What's his name?" Vappu asked in turn.

"I don't know. I don't remember."

Vappu was right. It felt wrong to call out "Stockholm" and let it reverberate in the darkness. Out of a little more than thirty crew members, I didn't know the name of more than possibly five. We knocked against each other like old beer cans with long-since-rubbed-off labels. We lived and worked together in the ship's microcosm, making dents and scratches in one another, and these served as name tags rather than the old association with regular names bestowed in a christening or similar rite. Had I jumped overboard, the rest of the crew would be faced with an identical problem. Who would stand there and holler "Strangler!" into the West African night?

Sternward only Vappu kept his name. I don't know why. Perhaps because he so determinedly pressed it into each hand when he introduced himself. Also, to our Swedish ears, Vappu sounded pretty much like a brand of beer.

We kept drifting. We heard or saw no sign of Stockholm. Finally Vappu sat down. He let out a long sigh.

"You Swedes are fucking funny. Never happy when you drink. Why not?"

"Vappu," I said. "We Swedes want to be very happy; we're always happy. A normal Swede radiates joy, health, and prosperity. There's no place for sorrow in our country, no room for tears. We cry too little and laugh too much. Our jaw muscles are worn stiff from all our smiles. That's why we drink and get melancholy and gloomy. We need help to handle our sorrow. Look at me. I'm happy and jolly all the time. I've such an enormous and unrestrained sorrow inside me that I simply don't dare to drink. Imagine if I drowned in all the tears that have never been let out."

In the dark I glimpsed Vappu's thoughtful face.

"No. Yeah. But couldn't they listen to beautiful music instead? Sibelius. You know him? I listen to him every night. Then I cry. Cry big rivers. Just like the music. Try it."

"But Vappu," I protested. "You don't have a record player."

Vappu hit his bare chest with the enormous club that was his fist. "Oh yeah? Inside here."

He motioned for me to come over. I did. I bent over him and put my ear to his hairy chest, exactly above the heart. A whole symphony orchestra played inside the muscle-armored ribs. The sound was exquisite. Soft and expansive with a sadness strong as cold-rolled iron. Vappu ruffled my hair a little.

"Well, can you hear it?"

"Vappu," I said. "You're overworked. You've a whole symphony orchestra in your chest. You hear hallucinations."

I was still lying with my ear glued to his chest. Sibelius must have been a big man with large, masculine tears. Rapids must have spurted from his eyes. The musicians in the symphony orchestra played as if enchanted in there; fir trees whispered, silvery lakes glittered, ripe wheat fields waved. It was a solemn, noble sorrow. In spite of the obvious danger of the boat overflowing, I had to press out some tears.

While I lay against Vappu's broad chest, sense memories of my father emerged. My own father was equally big and wide as a church door. He was a Swedish version of Vappu but with no symphony orchestra in his chest. I thought of the Islander who had fed me miniature chocolate bottles; I thought of an electrician who had saved me from a knife fight with a Spaniard. And I thought of Bengtsson, my very first bosun. He was like a father to me. Everybody had been like a father to me, but now I was eighteen years old and ought to become an adult and forget my father. What I had not received, I would never get.

On the other hand, if I ever met my own father, I could kill him.

Or at least punch him out, so long as he in reality was not quite as big as Vappu.

Yes, indeed. Sibelius must have been a dangerous man, I concluded against Vappu's chest as the symphony orchestra kept playing Sibelius's mighty music. And the sorrow transformed itself into the West African night.

All fell silent and there were movements against my ear as if the musicians put away their instruments and went home. But it was Vappu who had started rowing. I must have fallen asleep. He kept on rowing with long, rhythmic movements. The boat croaked and clucked along, and I realized that Vappu had given up. Searching for Stockholm in the dark was a futile undertaking. After a while I felt guilty and offered to take the other oar. We tried to match each other's strength or lack of it but just kept rotating. When Vappu tried to put as little force behind the oar as I did, we got nowhere. So he took over the oars alone again. To make up for it, I bailed water as we approached the radiant ship, illuminated as if for a celebration.

I wondered what to say about the stopcock. And about the motor. We could have gotten lost and been killed, too. It ought to be put in the log. Negligence. Goddamned sloppiness. The first mate did not keep things shipshape.

"Now you're fucking Swedish again," Vappu commented. "Stockholm won't come back, we're afloat, and in just a little while we'll get breakfast. What more do you want?"

I wish that Vappu had been right about all of that. Oh yes, the gray dawn arrived and the darkness scurried off across the longitudes. Before we set foot on deck, the sun glittered forward its first welding-ray tongues. And from the cook's domain, a rich odor of eggs and bacon floated toward us. Sunday breakfast was served as a small compensation for the night's hell. One said thanks and lapped it up.

Everything Vappu had said before we boarded the ship was correct except one thing. When he promised that Stockholm wouldn't come back, he was wrong.

On the bridge Eight paced back and forth when I was sent up to inform him of the nightly events. He was profoundly irritated. That we would have had to drop anchor anyway, he had forgotten. Stockholm would have to pay — three months off his salary. It was expensive as hell to have a full crew work overtime all night long. And a crew to boot that had the stomach to insist that it was the men's right to be drunk during their time off.

Eight would be holding forth about our worthlessness to this day, had not the second mate slipped in that the crew under no circumstances could count on overtime. The safety of the ship had been endangered. Through his negligence in not taking his watch at the correct time, Stockholm had put the whole ship in distress and peril since it was indeed highly dangerous to navigate in narrow waters with one crew member missing. According to the letter of the law. Period.

The second mate was an extremely ambitious man, a reserve officer, and an incurable romantic. Two things made the world understandable and worthy of living in so far as he was concerned: maritime law and immaculate white detachable collars. In order for his collars to stay clean longer, he used to put them on the bridge in the dark of the night. The first chance we would get, we would rub our fingers, having made them sooty first, against the snow white collars. We had nearly managed to drive him to a nervous breakdown. Now, having a chance to show off his knowledge of maritime law, he radiated tightly packed self-esteem.

Eight developed an aura of joy and relief as well. Those words about "the letter of the law" and "period" put him into a state of elation. He couldn't have said it better himself. At that very moment, the mess waiter arrived with the breakfast tray — eggs and bacon. A lot of coarse salt on it. And a misty glass of milk. And juice. The real kind, chock-full of vitamins. And black coffee. I could only congratulate Eight for what a sailor considers a reasonable breakfast. In comparison with that hearty repast, I became uninteresting. Perhaps his cross-examination of me would be a small dessert to stimulate his jovial goody-goody mood.

Consequently I waited and stole glances at Eight when he grunted orders between chewing mouthfuls.

No time to waste. Weigh anchor and full speed toward Sapele.

The pilot and his steersmen were ready. Had it been up to them, we would have left at the crack of dawn. The lost hours meant, in fact, another night of waiting on the river. Sapele was far away and there was a chance that we would not make it there before dark.

While the capstan grated away, two men in a small canoe were paddling in front of us across the wide river. Suddenly they stopped, swung around with splashing speed, and paddled frantically back in the direction from which they had come. It looked so weird that Eight brought up his binoculars to see what had frightened them. After an incredibly long while, he lowered the binoculars, put them down, took a piece of bacon, and chewed it thoroughly, not saying a word about what he had seen. To presume using Eight's personal binoculars would be as blasphemous as spitting on his sunny-side-up eggs. But I reached over and grabbed the binoculars. I don't know why. Perhaps what was coming closer, being carried toward us by the current, was so strong that it could reach us all the way up on the bridge. Oddly enough, Eight let me take the binoculars, merely throwing me a quick glance and smiling slightly as he kept on chewing.

It was Stockholm. There he was, lying on his back with his arms stretched out in the water, floating comfortably back and forth with the tide. That meant he had not drowned and still had air in his lungs. But he was dead. As stone dead as you would expect to be if you made contact with a propeller blade right through your skull. The face had been split in one clean cut all the way to the neck. One could see the water slosh right through him. Eight did indeed have an excellent pair of binoculars.

Far away, as if from another world, the anchor cable was still clattering. I wondered why Eight did not order the capstan stopped. It would be easy to fish Stockholm out of the river and put him in cold storage. The binoculars were bringing him so close that I could read his tattoos. They looked as amateurishly done as always. Sailor's grave. I'm sure he would rather have invested his money in a hard hat, had he known how things would end. For once I had to admit that my father had been right. It's not worth spending one cent on tattoos.

Eight pinched my ear amiably with his hard finger stumps. I handed back the binoculars. He had a fried egg in his mouth as he followed the body's movement through the binoculars and let his words splutter out. The thin egg white moved about like an extra tongue when he commented that the blacks ought to be able to afford to bury their dead.

"Instead of just throwing them in the river. Where will it end?"

Eight sighed and put down the binoculars. He swallowed the egg and nodded to the second mate.

"It's hardly civilized."

Our second mate did not look well at all. His detachable collar seemed to have shrunk quite a few sizes. His face was white with bright red spots when with a trembling hand he put down his binoculars.

I ran out on the bridge wing and took several gulps of fresh air on his behalf. From there I had a clear view of the decks both fore and aft. As if transmitted by an invisible herald, the message had gone from man to man, and now the whole crew stood along the railing while Stockholm's body drifted by, floating as if on a cross beneath the surface. More than one stole a glance toward the bridge, listening to the clanking anchor cable and waiting for the command to retrieve the corpse.

When it had already floated quite a bit toward the stern, everybody understood that Eight had no intention of losing any more time. What they did not know was that Eight had already declared that Stockholm, through a propeller slash to the skull, had been magically transformed into a black native of Nigeria's sump mark.

All of us were paralyzed. Nobody protested.

We let it happen.

No, Vappu ran toward the stern and lowered the flag to half-mast. At the same time I heard through the loudspeaker that the anchor was weighed. I climbed up above the bridge to the flagstaff mast and waved to Vappu. He understood immediately. Following his example, I lowered the Swedish flag to half-mast. The flag on the flagstaff mast is smaller than the one sternward. When I had climbed down to the bridge wing again, it looked terribly small, like a soiled handkerchief.

I did not sleep the next twenty-four hours.

I did not dare go to sleep. As soon as I closed my eyes, Stockholm's body turned up on the retina behind my eyelids. In the split face, small shoals of fish peeked out triumphantly while they busily cleaned out the contents of the head. A bird pecked its way through an eye, not at all frightened by the many and threatening tattoos on Stockholm's arms. Arms that never again would lift weights or have its muscles bunch into hard knots during a contest with Vappu.

In my dream, Stockholm kept twirling in the mouth of the Niger, moving back and forth with the tide, as if neither sea nor river wanted him. He drifted out there while we worked our way further and further into the humid and suffocating jungle on our way by the same river to Sapele.

*   *   *

As I have previously mentioned, we cast anchor in Sapele the following morning. At a small distance, perhaps not more than a hundred yards away, the company's sister ship was riding anchor.

My father stood in the midship aisle.

He lifted his arm in greeting. Then he disappeared into the midship aisle's black hole. He must have other things to do than to stand there waving at me.

And as I have also already said, Eight issued the command for me to come up on the bridge. Then he fell asleep instead of letting me know what he wanted. Strange perhaps, but after all he was mad. I stood before him, thinking most of the things I have related up till now. Whereupon Eight awoke and handed me two packs of cigarettes. Along with them he gave me his blessing and the advice to go and visit my father. Since I did not believe that I at this point would be able to sleep any more than at earlier attempts, I decided to follow his advice. It was quite a while since we had seen each other, my father and I.

For one pack of cigarettes, I was paddled across. I tried to avoid looking down into the water, but I could still imagine how Stockholm would have looked in this kind of close-up.

Arriving at the ship, I asked for my father. He was in the engine room. I felt relieved. The thought of suddenly being face to face with him confused me. I had no idea what to say. I went to his cabin. It wasn't locked. Big as he was, he could probably, quite like the Islander, practice discus throwing with any intruder. Perhaps I should ask him if he had throttled any black ones during the course of the morning. That ought to make him happy.

As a child I had frequently had to listen to his expositions regarding the black population of Africa. According to him there was only one solution to the problem: If all whites left the country and put a fence all around Africa, the natives would soon be climbing the trees again.

What would happen after that, I have never been able to understand. Would they throw us some bananas from time to time?

Cautiously, I sat down on the edge of the berth. His cabin was large, at least four times larger than mine. It was located on the middle deck and had two portholes. Once upon a time the middle deck cabins had been for passengers, but those days were gone. Now the officers had grabbed the luxurious cabins. My father sailed as second machinist. From my perspective, having spent three years sternward among the crew, he lived in another world. At the same time the familiar odor of raw oil streamed over me, the same smell as in my memories. And the different time sequences mingled, as if ebb and flood had strayed from timeworn regulations and schedules and decided to meet in one enormous embrace.

Perhaps we always go forward, bow first, just like ships against the currents that constantly try to drive us back into the past. Since our future is uncertain, we carry along our memories. The idea is probably that our past ought to serve as a lifeline of safety. For me, however, it has always been the other way around. Sometime in the future I would escape my perilous past. I felt faint just thinking of how much work and energy such a feat would demand. And I fell asleep the very second I fell into my father's berth.

I don't want to insist that I dreamed. Since I had become used to sleeping while being awake, perhaps I could state that I lay there thinking about things. I had reasons to do that. I thought of why I had not seen my father for four years. Then I tried to figure out how many years altogether we had spent under the same roof, but I couldn't work out the mathematics. I never do. There's always one year too many or too few. Even as a small child, I would insist with total conviction that I was four when I was only three. I believe that I was thirteen years old when my mother died. I remember that. But I also clearly remember how she always told us children that our behavior would kill her.

Who knows, she may have died the first time I did something naughty, shit in my pants or something equally awful that children always seem to do at the weirdest times.

According to one of my father's favorite jokes, most women do leave their husbands — the problem is that they don't take their bodies along. Perhaps his coarseness contained some truth after all? Perhaps he returned home and was disappointed when his wife took no interest in him? In some ways, he was right. My mother was never really there. There was only a body that read books and became sicker and sicker. When you add it all together you have two absent parents. Because during my first thirteen years on earth, my father may have been at home four years in all. Since I was a little over eighteen when I was lying on his berth in Sapele, Nigeria, West Africa, Africa, the World, and had not laid eyes on him these last four years, one could say that I had seen him only four years of my life. A little less than a fourth of the total time I had been around. I don't know if I figured that absolutely correctly, but why not name him Four, I thought.

"Hi, Four!"

He would not understand.

Already as a child, I was forced to acknowledge that he was more to be pitied than I.

"Christmas presents?" he used to ask mockingly. "Why should you get Christmas presents? I never got any when I was a kid."

With that answer and many others like it, he gave me gifts that lasted all my life.

When my mother died, he was on the other side of the globe. At least that is what I, at thirteen, believed. We postponed the burial. He had a new uniform made. It was elegant, with two stripes on the sleeves. He was handsome. I could imagine him at sea, killing himself with hard, wearing work to save us children from hunger and poverty. I'm sure that is how he saw himself. While I felt like a too tightly stuffed sausage in Småland and had to save myself as best I could.

My wonderful uncle and my fantastic aunt were a great help. I don't understand why I don't mail them postcards now and then from the big, wide world. It might be an inherited trait, something in my blood. My father never wrote to me. Though I tricked him into picking me up in Småland when it was time for my confirmation. Unfortunately, he managed to take off for distant seas as soon as he had me settled in our apartment. In order to take care of oneself, one needs to be fourteen years old and have gone through that confirmation sacrament, in my father's opinion. I doubted that those were enough qualifications. But that's how it was.

I lived alone, worked in a pharmacy, and cleaned the apartment frequently just in case the child-care authorities would come by to check. My cleaning zeal was in vain. No social worker ever came. Autumn went, winter wanted to settle down for good, but spring got angry and threw away all that snow and ice. It was only me it forgot to thaw out.

But how my soul froze and became a spiny, rough block of ice does not make for a good story. What can you tell about a large hole?

One funny thing happened. I decided to become a criminal but I got caught in the first round. The most imbecile policeman in the country cross-examined me. I told him I was waiting for my father, who was supposed to bring me to the South Seas. It was a foolish lie, but one I used to believe when I was little. The policeman let me go without legal proceedings. I found that encouraging. Young as I was, I had managed to talk rings around a cop. He was not exactly Hercule Poirot. Still and all. I learned something: Reality did not resemble the one presented in books. Everything had to do with lying and pretending. Yet the lies and the pretending exercised an astonishing power over reality. Had I not lied my way out of my first police examination in the grandest manner? And did I not remain as parent-free as before? I could continue to stray from the beaten tracks.

Unfortunately my bubbling enthusiasm got icebound in nothingness.

It became lonelier and lonelier around me.

The building we lived in was commonly called the Chinese Wall, since it was elongated and housed so many people. Then someone had the bright idea to put that kind of length vertically. With astonishing speed, they built tall, many-storied apartment buildings right in front of us. It was said that the children who lived in those buildings had a better life. They boasted that they got to travel by elevator. To me, it seemed better to be able to run inside to one's mother in just a few steps, even if I personally could not avail myself of that comfort.

All around the Chinese Wall buzzed seething life, but our apartment could as well have been a snowed-in hut of corrugated iron on the North Pole's white-striped back. Uncaring chance had put me as its guard.

It was definitely the end of the 1950s, that spring when winter burst apart. We were headed for a brilliant future. The generous sun wasted its heat on all of us, but I remained cold and hard. My brumal ground frost was there to stay. Outside the kitchen window, kids of my age flocked together, involved in totally unconscious activities, playing marbles and doing other childish things. Of course they were still in school and believed that a future existed. They could not know that I was in training to destroy the world, using only my thought.

That's how it was. I lived completely alone. Nobody did anything to me or for me. Every day I rode my bike down to my job as errand boy at the pharmacy and manufactured gunpowder to explode the Chinese Wall — just in case I was unsuccessful in annihilating it with just my thought. Every day I stopped at the home of my grandparents, shoveled down some food, and scurried away. They were my father's parents and seemed even further away from me than my father.

Every day when I came home, I ran, as if on an invisibly controlled leash, to the cupboard. There was never anything there to eat. Empty and dusty. Quiet and boring. I was not a huge success as a fourteen-year-old bachelor. If God was supposed to be so damn good and kind to little children, why didn't He ask my mother to swoop down with a few sweet rolls. He could show some common human concern, couldn't He?

That's how things were, that spring. Everything functioned just fine. I was seriously thinking about placing a personal ad. One of the girls at the pharmacy got married thanks to such an ad under "Personal." She looked absolutely frightful. The lenses in her glasses were so thick that it seemed as if all of her had been preserved in a glass jar. If she could find an interested male person, why shouldn't I be able to find a new mother? "Small, nice boy, cleans the house, works and eats out, is looking for healthy mother with strong nerves. Interests: home-cooked meals. Sweet rolls are welcome." Something like that. I was close to actually putting in such an ad, when one day someone rang the doorbell.

A woman blinked in a friendly manner as she looked at what was left of me when I opened the door. She had married my father. She was my new mother. She announced all this to me without batting an eye. I laughed a little nervously. I was so undernourished when it came to mothers that I was hallucinating. Time for personnel care at the pharmacy. A few free medications would not hurt. Not even in my wildest dreams could I imagine that my father, busy sailing the seven seas, would have time to acquire a new wife. A man who did not even find time to see his own children.

But this female stranger stood her ground.

She showed me the shiny new ring.

She was my new mother. She was no mirage, she was the real redheaded kind. Her hair was crimped into tiny curls that made her whole hairdo look like a tinted Persian fur coat. The comparison was close at hand since a black such coat was wrapped snugly around her round and busty body. Indeed, I had acquired a buxom and well-dressed mother. But with my real mother's death fresh in my memory cells, it would be difficult to fall right into the opening of the Persian fur and hug her tightly in a welcoming embrace.

Yet that was exactly what I did.

I hugged her for a long time. I stood inside the fur coat and squeezed her. I suppose I squeezed as much as a parched desert roamer drinks at an oasis, once he has made certain that it's no mirage. My new mother wore a solid corset. As a veteran expert on ladies' lingerie, I acquired the tactile knowledge that it was a couple of sizes too small. She was huffing and groaning a little. The sticky, pungent odor of the fur coat was familiar to me as well. My detective brain drew several quick conclusions. As a confirmation of my suspicions, she pulled an old nylon stocking out of a pocket to blow her nose. She was totally confused. But she was admirable. A totally new mother and the first human being in my life who had dressed up for my sake. The corset a little too small. The fine fur coat even though she had already put it in mothballs. And new stockings obviously bought on her way to see me, probably having discovered a run in her old ones.

To make her relax and feel safer, I walked her around the apartment. It did not take long. We had just three rooms. But those three rooms were so clean and neat that she could not believe her own eyes. As a professional housekeeper, I asked her to do the fingertip test. I knew what dust balls could do to the lungs. But judging from her ample bosom, she had no lung problems. We smiled at each other. We were really making terrific first impressions on each other.

As a child, I was terribly conservative. I wanted to keep my old mother, I would never even have thought of shooting our dog, Sickan, when she was in the way, and had I been given the choice, of course I would have chosen to live permanently in the house of my maternal grandparents — on the upper floor with as many as possible of my relatives present. Now at almost fifteen years of age, I understood that I may be more apt to want to change the way things were as the years went by. As a three-year-old, I could not have accepted a change of mothers, as a thirteen-year-old I experimented with some form of maintained spiritual contact with her, and now, as an almost-adult, I was ready to weed out every trace of memories from our apartment in order for this prosperous stepmother to take my late mother's place.

I opened every cupboard and explained what we could move up to the attic. The bedroom furniture we could burn at the refuse dump — you never know where the lung sickness hangs around. It can bite through a lot, even through corsets. And that would be a pity, I felt, and offered to organize the move of stuff to the attic. In secret, I was working on an alternate plan, of course. The attic was spacious. If I didn't feel comfortable down here, I could move up there myself.

But I didn't have to organize a thing. Ollie, my new mother, took care of it all.

Ollie disposed of our whole apartment in one single day. That was the day I realized that a person ought to move in complete darkness. In the light of day, household goods look painfully decrepit. At least ours did. The dear memory of my brother's avid whittling at the kitchen table was transformed into ugly, deplorable wounds. The furniture looked horribly rickety, loose-limbed, and out of style. Clothes that had been selected with care when bought and worn in gladness disappeared rapidly into big garbage bags. Their destination? The Salvation Army. In a flash I understood that my childhood's building blocks would not follow me through my life's stroll in the direction of the old folks' home. Still, there were traces of narrow-mindedness left in my young heart. There was a painful wrench when I contemplated the scattered remnants of what had been our home.

Much later I found Ollie's singsong dialect beautiful. But right then and there, in view of the whole Chinese Wall's sharply curious eyes, Ollie's voice sounded horrid. It cut right through the unmerciful light of spring. As if involved in a field maneuver, she stood on the sidewalk and proclaimed what should be saved, what would be brought to the auction place, and what must be thrown out.

I was given partial satisfaction when she, as determinedly, pointed to a black, shining, enormous Dodge and declared that it constituted the measure of what could be brought along. Let's face it, Ollie was not beautiful. But she had a fur coat of Persian lamb, permanented frizzy hair, and a black Dodge. I thought of my father with renewed respect. He must indeed be good with women. I slid immediately into the driver's seat. Such a Dodge had never been in the vicinity of the Chinese Wall. I rolled down the window with cool elegance and asked all the gaping little Chinese to be careful with the veneer of the shiny paint. Then I quickly rolled up the window again so as not to let out too much of that sterling smell of leather.

All that was left of our old home was in the car. A few suitcases with clothes, books and papers. All the rest was gone. Yet I felt like a king being with Ollie, carried away by the black Dodge. We forgot to inform the pharmacy. I was supposed to give fourteen days' notice to quit. But I rather believed they could manage without me. If not, there were plenty of nerve pills available. And when they found my various stashed-away basic elements to be used in the manufacture of explosives, they would probably let out a huge sigh of relief. The world was saved. And I with it.

I stole a furtive glance at Ollie and wondered how long she would stay around. She drove very well. While she drove, she told me the story of her life, from where she came, and how she met my father in Oslo.

I believed every syllable she uttered.

For nearly a year I believed her words. And things were generally good. True, Ingemar Johansson lost the match against Floyd Patterson that summer. But other things were happening in the world. I bought myself a moped.

That was not all. I fell marvelously and incredibly madly in love. That is another story, however. There's no room for it here.

I had another reason to take root next to Ollie: I saw neither head nor tail of my father.

But then came the day when my childhood's conservative attitude regarding preserving and keeping both human beings and things as they were was completely expelled. It happened to be the same day that two inquisitive gentlemen visited Ollie and me.

Why was I not attending school?

Ollie became totally confused. She had believed my statements to the letter. Just like my father, she had taken it for granted that my words were true to the fact. Poor Ollie. She had believed me. Luckily, she had no old stocking around to blow her nose in.

Even I had gotten used to the lie. I did not understand why the two gentlemen from the educational authorities refused to believe me when everybody else had done so for more than two years. I was finished with that hateful activity they call school attendance. Was this the time to start proceedings against me? When I was nearly sixteen and had a new mother? Back when I was fourteen, I longed for the welfare people to come. Every day. Oh well. That may be a slight exaggeration. But I certainly wouldn't have objected, had they snuck in and put a few Danish in the cupboard now and then.

Lucky for me, these two had arrived too late. This was the month I turned sixteen and left the compulsory school age. I didn't want to stay with Ollie any longer. I went to sea. To hunt for my father. Somehow, somewhere, we would come face to face.

I wanted to ask him about a very special day.

My uncle's tales also made me want to go to sea and lead a sailor's life. Life ashore wasn't much fun. The funniest person I knew was my uncle. He was both funny and irresponsible, according to my maternal grandmother, who knows everything. To hear her tell it, my uncle always returned bare-assed after a stretch at sea. I wanted to come home bare-assed, too. I wondered what it would look like. I already knew how to wiggle my ears. My uncle had taught me. The childish spirit was alive in him, although he had been drinking and fighting in the big world. I wanted a lot of tattoos like he had.

But I also knew that my father would kill me within minutes if he found me covered with tattoos. He had promised as much. And he was a man who kept that kind of promise. Perhaps I would have time to ask my questions, but I would surely be dead before I received any answers.

*   *   *

My musings in my father's cabin were interrupted when somebody finally entered. My father. He did not look especially surprised, but there was no reason for that either. We had waved to each other a little more than an hour ago.

I jumped up from the berth.

"So you're here," he said.

"Yeah," I said.

We shook hands. When my father shakes hands, he transmits the feeling of being afraid that the other person will get too close to him. Reluctantly, he lets you borrow his hand for a moment. An iron hand on a steel piston, pushing away any vestige of intimacy.

"For how long are you here?" he asked.

"How long are you anchored here?" I asked.

Naturally, he could have said a thousand and one other things. But what was said restored and reestablished the connection with the exchange of words that took place whenever he came through the door after a long absence and greeted us children. The first thing we did was to ask how long he would stay. A rather natural question.

We wanted to adjust our minds in order to balance our other entertainment against the joy of having a father. Would we gulp him down like gluttons with frantic speed, or would we slowly and deliciously savor him piece by piece? Could we continue to build our toy trucks, climb the scaffolds for the new building, steal apples, or sit quietly reading old comic books down in the cellar? Or should we stick close to him and stare at him long enough to have him fixated in our memory, in case he'd be gone the next day?

How long would he stay? Our eager questions poured over him. But he would look hurt, brusquely muttering that we could let him get through the door first. He never understood why we asked, and we never understood why he would feel hurt.

So here we stand again. Father and son. And I have already learned to dislike the very same question.

Perhaps both he and I had wanted to say something else. But our questions were given, written beforehand by our history. We had not been handed any more effective lines of dialogue.

He had already begun to peel off his overalls. A misty breakfast beer was welded into his hand. It did not occur to him to offer me some. I would have liked for him to do that, even if I had declined. But perhaps time stood still inside his head. He had only seen me in glimpses that added up to four years altogether. It might be difficult for him to realize my true age. I tried to stretch myself tall, but he did not seem to notice my impressive height. I was at least half a head taller than he. He was now closer to fifty than to forty. I'm not sure of his exact age.

In our family, we have never paid much attention to birthday celebrations. My maternal grandmother was considered "the gay dog" in the family. On a totally ordinary Monday, she would bake a cake and whip up some cream. She used to defend this by saying that the milk was too rich so she had to skim off some cream. I had no idea when my father's real birthday was. I had even less of an idea of his exact age.

He remained an impressive hunk of a man, almost as broad as he was tall. It would not have mattered if one stood him up vertically or horizontally. When he laughed, it sounded as if someone rolled huge rocks on the floor. Luckily he didn't laugh very often.

To have something to say, I told him about Stockholm.

"We had a guy from Stockholm aboard."

"We have at least five."

"Eight — our captain — said hello. A real tough son of a bitch."

"He's a shit. We have Hansson. He's worse. The scourge of the sea. He even inspects the engines."

I got stuck. If I had said that our man from Stockholm had jumped overboard, he would probably have insisted that their men from Stockholm had tried to imitate the famous Stockholm massacre of 1520.

That is a peculiar trait in my father's personality. If I were to tell him that my feet had grown so that I now take shoe size fourteen, he would counter by saying that his size was twenty-two. I remember that figure — twenty-two — since that was my father's shirt size. They don't carry sizes like that, especially not if the sleeve length has to be thirty-two. But I suppose there are not many adults with his peculiarities either. In a way, I ought to be grateful that he was not around that much when we were little. My brother and I would proudly demonstrate our latest construction, a miniature toy truck that we steered with the help of strings, only to receive the tart information that our father used to have an even fancier toy truck, one with a real steering wheel. He seemed to have had everything, done everything, and known everything.

He lied.

Why did he lie? Why did he always have to cut us down to a very small size?

I got angry. In my head roared a number of answers. "I killed our man from Stockholm. He jumped overboard, but I did it. I ordered him to jump." But out of my mouth escaped only a partly suffocated snuffle. As if I cried saliva instead of tears.

My father did not look surprised. I have always behaved like a half-witted fool in front of him. The overalls formed a ring around his feet. I noticed that his stomach was swelling and pushing forward below his freckled chest muscles. He must have weighed more than two hundred pounds. Half a dozen beers a day had taken their toll.

In his nudity, he radiated clearly the reason for my childhood's poverty. My mother never grasped what was going on, but after her death I did some research in the family documents in Ollie's attic. There were boxes, filled with old papers, Mom's photographs, letters, and documents, including my father's deduction books for each sea journey. Not until later, when I myself had a couple of those blue deduction books and could decipher the different figures, did I understand the real meaning of my father's accounts. He kept half the salary for himself and sent the other half home to take care of the whole family. No wonder we had to scrimp at home while he lived grandly aboard the ships. Considering the cheap price of alcohol at sea, he must have poured a lot of it inside himself in the course of each day.

He had really changed during these four years. His muscles were embedded in fat. He looked like a well-fed pig. It was disgusting — and, unfortunately, I could not step forward and cut a well-earned slice of ham. The only thing I could do was watch him disappear into the shower and hope that he would scald himself.

I left.

During the trip back to the ship, I understood that my state of being tongue-tied in front of this gigantic egotist would remain a permanent one.

The decision never to see him again was simple to make. I erased him from my memory, together with what I had discovered among the papers in Ollie's attic. My father did not exist anymore. Dead and buried — so far as I was concerned.

Alas, Eight did not share this opinion. He stood by the gangway plank and waited for me with his news. Touched all the way to the deepest, darkest corners of his heart by the thought of father and son reunited, he had this bright idea that the two of us should accompany him on an expedition upriver.

See, there were no tree trunks for us to load. Something had gone awry further up the river. The tugboat that pulled down the timber was inoperative and had been left in some godforsaken hole. So we might as well get up there and repair it.

"A hut, two goats, and a Dane who sits and cries. That's what's up there."

He roared with laughter. I did not know if he laughed at the hut, the goats, or the Dane. But I understood enough, namely that most of one's life is ruled by someone higher than oneself. Sternward the jolly boat was already being lowered into the water. A motorman had gone over the engine since Vappu's and my desolate drifting in the river's mouth. I kept listening with half an ear to Eight's conversation with the first mate.

"All we need now are some glass beads to give to those natives," clucked Eight.

Our provision dealer piled up ten cases of beer, a bunch of canned goods, and a spirit stove plus a lot of other stuff, hidden in sacks and boxes, right by my feet. This was obviously no afternoon spin we were planning. As bearer, boy, and jump-ashore whatever, I was a uniquely poor specimen. Cautiously, I pleaded the case for Vappu to replace me but received the answer that the jolly boat would sink with three men of that size aboard.

My father had already been informed over radiotelephone. Eight and I jumped into the jolly boat and picked him up at the gangway plank. We sank a couple of inches deeper when he settled into it with four toolboxes. He looked like an invented character in enormous, flapping shorts and a white, loose shirt. On his head he had placed a dirty straw hat. Under one arm he held on to his rolled-up overalls, tenderly, as if they were a newborn baby. He made room for the toolboxes and carefully placed his overalls between them. The idea was that he would help the Dane to fix the tugboat engine.

Up the Niger we went.

Eight navigated and steered. He was in a splendid, playful mood and splashed in the water with his hands.

"To scare off the crocs!"

He grinned, lifted up his hand in the glittering sun, and waved the finger stumps. It worked, too, because we did not see a single crocodile during the whole river journey. We probably would not have anyhow. But Eight was happy. With his hand trailing in the water, he told quite a few crocodile jokes. Since there were no monkeys around, he was producing the jungle atmosphere. I suspected that his madness had burst out in full bloom under the white visored cap, but I did not want to bother my father with such nonessentials. He seemed to have a hard enough time dealing with his own problems. Rivers of sweat streaked down his closed face. I sat furthest toward the stem; he sat on the box over the engine. We could have held hands. But he was ignoring me. He was closed up inside his own waterfall. Suddenly he stood up, the boat lurched dangerously, and Eight roared that my father should sit down.

"I have to go ashore!"

Surprised, Eight shouted: "Why the hell would you want to do that?"

"You'd like to know, wouldn't you?"

It was clear that my father would not sit down until he got his way. The boat rocked. We had no more than eight inches of freeboard left. Eight sighed and looked around, I pointed toward a dry piece of sand between the thick roots of huge trees and jumped ashore when the bow made contact. What I had taken for sand was a kind of yellowish, corny sludge. I sank down to my knees. Wise from earlier experience, proving that everything always gets worse, I hung on to the boat, unable to take even one step away from it. A jungle marsh like that could swallow a whole freighter, crew and all.

And a small, inexperienced sailor would be gobbled up without leaving a trace.

Then there was this powerful splash beside me. I shut my eyes. Could there be crocodiles in the river?

No, it was my father, who had jumped in. More than two hundred pounds straight down into the sludge and with one toolbox in his hand for a little extra weight as if he had intended to make a hole right through West Africa. He waded along, mud pouring into his pockets, and disappeared behind some big trees. When I peered over the edge of the boat, Eight seemed totally confused. That was unusual. Most of the time, he managed to keep things under control in his rough way. He turned to me with a helpless gesture.

"Where's Johansson going?"

It sounded weird when Eight called my father Johansson. As if my father were a stranger. But then I remembered that my last name was also Johansson. Ingemar Johansson. After this adventure they would have to give me a new name aboard. From Strangler to Jungle Johansson. Anyhow, right now the Johansson Eight referred to was my father.

"Where's Johansson going?"

Eight repeated his question while I crawled aboard.

"To the toilet," I answered.

If you ask my father where he is going and he answers the way he did, he must be headed for the nearest toilet. Simple as that. But Eight couldn't know that. He looked skeptical.

"With the toolbox?"

"Perhaps he carries toilet paper in it," I suggested.

Eight made his way over to Johansson's toolboxes. As commander and supervisor of the crew's alcoholic habits, he knew better. Two of the toolboxes contained beer. The third was filled with actual tools. Now it was not difficult to figure out why Johansson had been holding the fourth toolbox carefully high over his head when he waded away between thick tree roots. Eight snorted like an enraged water buffalo. I understood perfectly well why. With friendly generosity he had loaded ten cases of Tuborg beer in preparation for a pleasant trip with good conversation about the old days. But my father could not fathom such generosity. Johansson knew only himself — and now he stood behind a broad tree trunk and drank beer in secret.

"Perhaps he didn't see the cases with beer." I tried to make my voice cheerful and encouraging. "Maybe he thought the beer was for the Dane."

Eight glared suspiciously and removed one beer cap with his teeth.

"Take one yourself, Johansson."

"Ingemar," I said and tried imitating him in biting off a beer cap.

I could not do it. My teeth wobbled and seemed dangerously close to flying out in the jungle.

"Are you crazy? You and I can't use first names between us," Eight said, grinning. "I'm the captain and you're just an ordinary seaman."

"But we're drinking together —"

"Are we? Are you going to sit there and tell me off? If you do, I'll put you ashore right here. I don't drink with my crew. Especially not in the middle of the jungle. When you're away from civilization, you've got to be more formal. Get it?"

I giggled.

"No. But sir, you may call me Ingemar anyway. Otherwise there are too many Johanssons in a small boat. Johansson the First and Johansson the Second. That's silly. And Johansson Junior only works if you're a millionaire."

It sounded reasonable. Eight asked why I had giggled.

I told my little joke. When I was little and read about civilization for the first time, I took it to be "civil station." For a long time I wondered where that civil station might be.

Things change. If you don't get wiser with the years, at least you get more humble. You become able to laugh at your own stupidity. For example, moments ago I was panic-stricken at the thought that I may become like my father. But while I was telling Eight about my childhood's civil station, I was desperately trying to get the cap off the beer bottle. And then, there I was, big as life, drinking beer from a bottle. I couldn't understand how that had come about.

We were merry as brothers when Johansson came splashing back. His face never showed any expression, but it is entirely possible that at this moment he looked just a tad surprised. All three of us went on as if nothing unusual had happened. At Johansson's suggestion, we cut up a sack and fixed a sunshade. Most of the time we could keep underneath the trees, but at times we had to travel in the middle of the river. There could be a sudden sandbank, a few pieces of timber at a strange angle, an enormous tree that had crashed down. After an eventless hour, Johansson was sweating rivers, the way he had done before. Eight pulled out a beer, bit off the cap, and held it out toward him.

"Do you want one or do you have to go to the toilet?"

Johansson had never acquired the habit of saying "thank you," nor did he ever display exaggerated joy or enthusiasm. But had we killed the engine and listened hard, there might have been a muttered "thanks" deep down in his throat.

I dared ask how far away the tugboat was.

"Thirteen beers," said Eight.

That was straightforward enough. We would have to spend the night on the river then.

"Is there anything else to drink besides beer?" I asked.

"No. But that wouldn't make it go any faster."

Eight laughed wholeheartedly at his own joke. Johansson punctuated with his laughter that could break stone. Soon enough I sat far astern, steering, while the two of them revived old memories. The engine crackled bravely. I wanted to know and hear what the two of them were hollering about, but in the noise it was impossible.

I was left to my own ponderings.

But nobody can think all the time, as my brother used to say. It turns into brooding. I was sleepy from the beer and sank gratefully into an emptiness that matched the monotonous shoreline. Here and there the river forked. We were supposed to stay in the main furrow. Eight threw a bottle of beer in each fork of the river, timing which bottle traveled the quickest. Neither Johansson nor I saw any reason to criticize that method.

As the hours rolled on, all three of us became rather loud. We sang some songs. Our repertoire was rather one-sided. Johansson turned out to have an extremely pleasant baritone voice. Eight was so surprised by it that he stopped the engine. My father was covered with drying mud up over his knees, his now-dry shorts flapped in a gust of wind, the beer belly protruded like an enormous resonant box below his rib cage, the white shirt was drenched with sweat, and the raggedy straw hat was held in his outstretched hand as if he expected monkeys to throw him tributes of bananas. We drifted slowly along the river Niger and his audience of two was listening to his songs. He sang "Indian Love Song" and I could have been struck dead since that happened to be my parents' favorite song.

But I was not.

Eight started up the engine and magically brought out some delicacies from the tightly packed crates. We kept moving straight into Africa, almost like the last survivors of something. But as such, we had full stomachs and were content, even happy.

When twilight hit, we anchored between bulky tree roots. It would have been impossible to get to terra firma, but Eight insisted stubbornly on fixing us something warm to eat. He pumped up the small spirit stove and soon had a cozy flame going. We never put any food in the kettle, however. Too many flying things dashed straight toward the point of light. Soon the pot was filled to the brim. Johansson was of the opinion that the unappetizing mess could be eaten, that is if all those flying insects were boiled in whiskey. He only said that to give himself an excuse to unroll the overalls and bring out a bottle. Eight gave up and was scraping insects out of the pot. He turned off the spirit stove and the jungle startled us with a black wave of hellish shrieks. I, who earlier had been certain that the jungle was silent like an Egyptian mummy, was acutely aware that we were the silence. We carried it with us like an iron ring. What was frightening and unknown was us.

In spite of all the boxes, cases, and sacks, we managed to clear three spaces for sleeping. It was not comfortable, but I was able to fall asleep. And as usual I kept one eye and one ear awake. I was looking out for small black snakes ready to drop from the trees. I thought of Eight's warning. People disappearing in the river. But most of all, my sleep kept being interrupted by Eight and Johansson, who were finishing the whiskey.

They had sailed together at a time when Eight had all his fingers and Johansson could in my imagination still be the father who saved us from all things bad and scary. Whatever I thought and felt about

Johansson, I was intrigued to find out more about him. A part of me was hoping to discover mitigating circumstances. I would never find out anything in a talk between the two of us. He was perhaps a totally different person in the company of men who shared his experiences?

My expectations were not in vain.

Eight and Johansson gulped whiskey and kept talking and spluttering throughout the night, like two old sailors. The alcohol was dissolving their hard protective shells; the velvety black of the night was lifting off the lids. They turned sentimental and cried a little over their wasted lives. They felt immensely sorry for themselves and were soon arguing over which one was most deserving of pity. All the tiny life forms in the jungle fell silent as their voices increased in volume. Suddenly they remembered me.

"Quiet. You'll wake up the boy," said Johansson.

Eight agreed. The small insects resumed their concert, recovering lost territory. A hairy small wing, as from a moth, caressed my cheek. I wanted to slap it away but held myself back. They had finally arrived at a fascinating subject of conversation, namely me.

"Strange boy, by the way," Eight said. "We call him the Strangler. He nearly did strangle a Negro in Monrovia. A thief. Strong as the devil. But sensitive. You can't joke with him the way you do with other guys. He's probably a little mad. He drives me crazy. It's as if he keeps watching you. Like a warden. Like some kind of insect."

"I lost my shoes once in Monrovia," said Johansson, as always unwilling to let me get the better of him.

"So I took up watch by the gangplank. Finally my shoes came walking up, bringing with them a promising young lad. 'Hello, my shoes,' I said and pulled the lad down to the engine room. He learned never to steal shoes from me again."

"Did you cut off his feet?"

"Everybody isn't as crazy as you."

Eight fell silent. But after a few thoughtful drafts from the bottle, he picked up where he had left off without losing a beat.

"Strange guy. I think he has problems. We had an idiot who jumped overboard the other day. Things like that happen. People die. It's as if he can't grasp that."

"Who? The idiot?"

"Your boy. You ought to talk to him. Try to help him."

"How?"

"How the hell would I know? I'm not his father. You're his dad. That's what fathers are for. Aren't they?"

"What?"

Eight sighed. I sympathized with him. He was having the same experience I had. It's difficult to trick sympathy out of a piece of hard rock.

Except for the constant chirping of the jungle, everything was quiet. Obviously Johansson was lying there thinking of Eight's words because suddenly his voice floated through the darkness. He sounded several years younger, almost like a misunderstood child.

"But how do you know?"

"Know what?" Eight asked.

"That you're not his father."

Eight laughed, a dry neigh, like an old horse.

"That's your problem!"

I thought back to my father's worn joke about being nice to all children since you never know which ones are your own. As far back as I can remember, I have heard him say that. A joke that had decomposed like finely ground chalk and fallen flat at our feet. We only coughed, dryly and with effort, when he told the same joke for the thousandth time.

"Yeah, it's true." Johansson chuckled. "It's so sad that one has to laugh."

What?

I wanted to crawl over and shake him. What?! What is it that's so sad?

"The boy has problems. That's true. But imagine if I'm not his father? One never knows."

"What the hell are you saying?" Eight coughed and dropped the whiskey bottle.

I was now more intrigued and started thinking. Why should Johansson not be my father? Sure, he had been largely absent, but still, he was my father. In the tales told of myself as a baby, I hear me cough a lot. I was born with bronchitis and a lot of curls. Everybody except my mother adores me. She is so weak that she has to concentrate mainly on hanging on to the slender thread of life. I bring peace to the world; I bring summer and warmth, although I am conceived in the icy cold of war. My maternal grandmother takes care of me. Sure, I'm coughing like a grown man, but I'm a child and everybody loves me.

That's how it was. At least in the beginning.

One must never joke about such things.

I have proof. I have a witness. My maternal grandmother has told me time and time again about my arrival into the world. Like a wonderful fairy tale to counteract all the misery! That is how she always spoke of my entrance. In the middle of the tale, she will also relate the story of the refugees who came to the school that was turned into a camp. First from Poland, then from Germany and Denmark and the Netherlands and . . . and about little children who cried and clung. And about a small child who had been chloroformed so that the Germans would not take it. And about the mother who was dead. And about how nobody wanted it. And in the middle of all this misery, there I showed up with curly hair and so frail that everybody fought over who would care for me! Everybody loved me. My mother too.

I can hear every word. How Grandma emphasized all that was terrible, how the words almost grew out of her mouth in capital letters.

There wasn't a shadow of doubt in Grandma's eyes, whatever Johansson might imagine here in the jungle. I put my fingers in my ears and decided not to listen. A whole eternity went by. I did not remove my fingers from my ears until dawn.

Could it not have been just a dream?

I rolled right over the edge of the boat and into the water to rinse the uneasy feeling off. When I surfaced, Johansson was looking over the edge. He rolled into the river too, and suddenly there was a snorting hippopotamus beside me. A hundred years ago he swam with me on his back across a lake. The mixture of fear, joy, and pride made me almost suffocate from laughter. Now I was able to swim on my own. I let myself sink into the dark river water and imagined an enormous propeller blade splitting my skull. Then the water flushing in, cleaning out the mass of gelatin that housed my memory. And I did not exist anymore.

Everything was a game. But there are things one simply cannot understand. Death. It is an immovable immensity that nobody is able to describe. You can't just go and pay death a visit and return home to tell about it.

I snorted up to the surface and swallowed a piece of life.

Then it was Eight's turn to plunge in. There he was, paddling around and not a bit afraid of crocodiles. We were again floating peacefully on the Niger's broad back. The nightly conversation seemed to have left no trace.

We were off again.

Our wet clothes dried quickly in the heat. Eight boiled coffee on the spirit stove. There were a few pints of water aboard despite Eight's negative answer to my question of the previous night. Johansson drank his breakfast beer, no doubt to give him courage in case he decided to speak to me about life.

I would have liked to assure him that it wasn't necessary. Both of us were sitting, silent as clouds, while the day was wearing on. The engine sputtered and Eight looked as if he knew where we were going. The magical singing of yesterday was not repeated although Johansson systematically kept swallowing beer.

Toward the afternoon we arrived at our destination. An iron gray sky pressed against the miserable huts, the wounded, scrubby beach, and the rust-spotted tugboat. Except for a few mangy hens pecking down at the river's edge and some small black pigs that took one look at us and ran off squealing, the village looked deserted. Along the riverbank, big pieces of timber were chained together in long rows, ready to be towed down to Sapele.

It looked so dismal that even our engine throttled and remained silent as if out of pure consideration. Who wants to crackle and purr with life in such a valley of tears?

Eight swore at the engine. He saw a week-long return trip looming in front of him if we must depend only on the current. But Johansson promised to examine our engine too as soon as the tugboat was ready.

We moored, stepped up on the rickety wooden bridge, and headed toward the tugboat. In spite of its miserable exterior, it seemed to offer the most inhabitable place for a Dane. Then we heard a sharp crack, like that of a shot being fired, and a splinter of wood flew off right in front of our feet. We stopped. I don't think anyone of us had enough energy to be frightened. Johansson had at least ten bottles of Tuborg beer in his swollen stomach and was feeling immortal. Eight was a captain and as such had become used to people scraping their feet when he moved forward. As for myself, I felt only curiosity. When we left Sapele, the radio had not transmitted any news of a war being declared by the Danes against Sweden. Why would the Dane lie there and practice target shooting at us? We had after all come here to help him.

"Hello?!"

Johansson did the yelling. He held a Tuborg in his hand, still unopened, and he was waving it in the friendliest of gestures. The shot sliced the bottle neck and beer sprayed all over us. Now we knew without doubt that the Dane had to be insane to have shot at Denmark's national symbol. We were rather upset. Johansson sat down on the bridge in amazement and stared at the remnants of the bottle. Eight retreated a bit, and I jumped into the water without further ado. The time had come to take this Dane seriously.

When I emerged, I found myself in the middle of an old Tarzan movie where what seems a deserted village moments ago has, from one minute to the other, spear-carrying and threatening warriors appearing everywhere. There were enough people here crowded around the miserable huts for at least fourteen Tarzan movies. But these didn't seem too threatening. Large and small, old and young, bare chests in every imaginable size and for any taste, beautiful and ugly, toothless and with sparkling big smiles. Some of the smiling ones helped me up at the slippery river edge. They were laughing and yelling. Obviously everybody was happy to see that something finally was happening. From the long and mixed-up palaver, we understood that they felt responsible for the Dane. He had locked himself up in the tugboat several weeks ago. Something was wrong with him and not with the tugboat, consequently there was no guarantee that Johansson's tools were the right thing for what was needing repair.

We unloaded the boat.

Then, like the rest of the village, we sat down to wait. If the Dane had barricaded himself in the tugboat several weeks ago, his provisions had to be running out, Eight reasoned and explained his view of the situation.

"We're dealing with a madman who respects neither life nor death."

A perfect description of Eight himself.

I had to simulate an attack of coughing. I could not afford to laugh and have my ears elongated by Eight's hard stumpy pinches. Johansson had not yet said a word. On his side, we have quite a few Danes in the family, and that a Dane would shoot at him was probably perplexing.

"In either case we can't leave tonight. But we'll overpower him at dawn and get that damn timber hauled down. We have to load it. We have a responsibility. Imagine if Europe's furniture factories came to a stop. Leaving people standing there without furniture. The Dane's going to be conquered, dead or alive. He should be locked up somewhere."

Eight was getting all fired up. In my mind's eye I could see him use those clubs he called hands to smash the Dane beyond recognition.

"Sure," I said. "But where? And how?"

"What?!" bellowed Eight.

"Besides he's a captain. What gives us the right to overpower a captain?" I continued.

I had no desire to sneak up on the bridge and die with the early light of dawn pouring through large gunshot holes in me. I had had my share of adventures in West Africa. The next boat I signed on would be a small barge in an inland lake in Sweden. Sweet water and jolly peasants. It would be the closest thing to a vacation. I agreed with the sailors who declared West Africa as being the world's asshole. It took men like Eight and Johansson to like it here. They were crazy. If they wanted to wage a war with the Dane, they would have to do it without me.

Eight boiled over.

"What did I say?" he shouted. "You're his father! You talk to him!"

"About what?"

For once I was in agreement with Johansson.

"About the difference between a tugboat skipper and a commander aboard an ocean-faring ship, for instance! So he knows his place. We attack at dawn!"

Eight walked off with long strides.

Everything was perfectly clear. The big bullies are always allowed to mistreat those who are smaller. My father did not need to tell me that. He had taught me the same lesson by example much earlier. We sat on a pile of stuff and saw Eight disappear, just as if he were on his way to the post office, right behind the left hut and to the right of two pigs and one emaciated cow.

Soon he was back. He looked down at us, father and son, and obviously found both of us too inactive for his taste.

"We must do something."

"What?" Johansson asked.

Nobody can repeat the same thing over and over and manage to make it sound different each time the way my father can. I was filled with reluctant admiration when we stood on the same side against Eight. All the trip up from Sapele, my father had not said much more than "What?" and "Why?" and "You'd like to know!" Last night, when he was in his merriest mood, he said, "Once I was in the city of Uddevalla twice" and "Do you know that animals are forbidden in the zoo?" Too bad he hadn't asked Eight if he had bats in the attic. Or that he hadn't burped after having his breakfast beer and said, "Good cake. No bones in it." Because that was his whole repertoire. But with what immense richness and variation, wit and intelligence, and wounding precision could he not rule the world with the aid of these meager sentences!

I nodded confidently toward Eight.

What? What in the world are we going to do?

"There's a bar up there," Eight said. He neighed dryly. "A hole in the wall. If there had been a wall."

It was decided that I would guard our belongings while Eight and Johansson waddled off, like two carelessly dressed giant ducks, one in white and one in bleached khaki. Johansson waved his raggedy hat. I expected him to come up with one of his favorite lines, with only a mere adjustment to the present situation.

Such as, "If you've drowned when we come back, I'll give you a thrashing."

But he spared me that.

I was alone. Sitting outside the Dane's shooting range. As long as we did not venture out on the unsteady planks, he seemed to stay calm. To be extra sure, I built a barricade with the cases of beer. There were plenty of them for that.

I lay down, awaiting further orders, and pulled a few bundles on top of me in hope of becoming invisible. I saw my part in all of this as simple: Rest as much as possible while awaiting the commanding officers' whims. Legends are told of sailors who have slept their ways across the seven seas. The only occasions where they are seen are at mealtimes and when the workday is over. Then you find them in their berths, totally exhausted. A sailor knows that it's no good to over-exert yourself, to run around unnecessarily and look willing to knock rust all day long.

I tried to sleep. Now and then voices floated down from the huts. The villagers were probably contemplating the new series of events that had not led to anything except two new customers at the local bar. From where I was, the world fell asleep and I with it. The sky was lead colored with black, broad stripes that wanted to swell and burst out in purple. Far away a few trains were colliding with a herd of elephants. At least that's what it sounded like. It was thundering and booming over the treetops.

In West Africa one can't say that it begins to rain. The violent downpour resembling a raging rapid obviates that understatement. I held my breath so as not to drown and splashed away toward the huts. Darkness had dropped quickly. Under a few tall trees, a roof seemed to lean forward like an enormous dragon. A kerosene lamp glimmered. Inside, seated on some boxes, I saw Eight and Johansson. A ring of spectators was standing at a respectful distance.

When I burst in on them, Eight's face split in his usual friendly grin. I ignored him. Let him be angry. I felt as if the hard rain had already made big holes in my head. Getting a thrashing from my father for having drowned in the rain would be too much.

A crude box wiggled invitingly. I kicked away the goat who stood there butting against it and sat down. They were drinking a rancid, oily mixture from small glasses. That was true jungle juice. When the glass was rotated quickly, the fluid separated and went two different ways. I wondered what it would do to a human being's insides.

Eight asked how much it might cost to buy a mattress.

What a weird question! But as usual Johansson did not hesitate. "Two packs of cigarettes. At the most. Perhaps half a carton."

The heavenly cascade of water stopped as abruptly as it had begun. And the gray day had been colored in with black ink. A naked child clung to its mother, grabbing for a breast. She was helping it along, flashing a sweet smile toward us. Then putting her face close to the child she spoke to it, softly and tenderly, in a language I did not understand. The gestures were understandable, the same way that I slowly grasped what kind of mattress Eight went on about. The jungle juice had totally eroded his judgment and made him forget all about his superior station in life. I stood up and let out a few well-chosen words before I left.

"Don't forget we attack at dawn!"

"What's the matter with Johansson? Johansson, tell Johansson that he can get a mattress, too. My treat!"

I knew it. Eight could not manage to talk to two Johanssons at the same time. The family name was following me with its tail between the legs like a beaten dog through the village. My father was my father even if when drunk he like all men doubted his fatherhood. But that was his problem. Mine was to wish not to be like him and to fill the family name with new substance. Eight and he were free to stagger about in the jungle, supported by their bought women; they could treat them with contempt and call them mattresses, worth no more than half a carton of cigarettes. They could do what they wanted. They could believe that they were free, but actually they themselves were their own prison. It took another kind of life than theirs to break out of oneself.

I repacked our things to get out some dry stuff. The moisture steamed up like tiny white clouds in the heat. Reasonably comfortable, I lay there, staring up at the black night. The only thing you could see was yourself. I wondered if there were a spot on earth where humanity could blossom. Or perhaps goodness only existed as something locked in our chests, a symphony that makes us cry about ourselves and over our lost opportunities?

It was clear to me, once and for all, that I would never get a word out of my father. We would never be able to compare our sorrows. His being the loss of a wife. Mine that of a mother. We had no common language. However I tried, we remained tied in a triangle with him and me in opposite acute angles. And all the less dangerous things in the third one, such as jungle juice . . . mattresses . . . men from Stockholm . . .

How could I have been such a dense idiot? My life at sea was a vain search for my father. When that day of encounter had finally arrived, we had nothing to say to each other.

As a child I imagined my father as a hero, in a tropical helmet and immaculate uniform, sitting in a deck chair and reading a month-old newspaper. The loading of bananas being over and done with for the day. He opens up the paper. But what does he see! YOUNG HERO SENDS SICK MOTHER TO EXCLUSIVE HYDROPATHIC RESORT IN SWITZERLAND! I, young Ingemar Johansson, am the hero. I have found a fortune in gold coins at the city dump. Slowly my father folds the newspaper. He sobs quietly in the African night. His chest is filled with happiness and he knows that tomorrow he will take the first direct flight to Switzerland so that he and the young hero can take turns reading novels aloud to the slowly recovering woman, wife, mother, who bears a rather remarkable likeness to Greta Garbo. . . . Farewell, Africa. Farewell, bananas. I have done my duty. Now my family awaits me.

I blame the goddamned literature. Somerset Maugham has filled my poor brain with bitter and cynical men whose defenses crumble in face of total goodness or who die violently as a direct result of their own evil.

In literature, I would confront my father right now and point at him with an accusing finger. I ought to tell him how I made the terrible discovery in Ollie's attic, how his old pocket calendar almost eerily opened itself to the right page, as if he had been pondering that day, again and again. With a gloomy voice, I ought to make him throw himself to the crocodiles in the river Niger — I mean, if there were any crocodiles in it — or force him to his knees, crying, asking forgiveness for committing gross adultery with Ollie the very day that my mother, his wife, died. He was not in a foreign country the day she died. He was in bed with another woman. Her name was Ollie. Why didn't he make an effort to come home? Why didn't he care enough? Did he fool his brothers, my grandmother, all of our relatives? How did he do that?

But a conversation and such questions lay outside the realm of possibility.

I would never receive any explanations from Johansson, never be given a chance to understand and therefore never be able to forgive. Johansson disappears in a dozen Tuborg beers a day with about twenty standard phrases keeping all real emotion at bay. Johansson is armored, in a bunker, formed by the grim grind of ordinary days. Inside those steel-coated, thick walls, perhaps there once lived a crying child, scratching the walls in vain because it was not allowed to grow up. It had no words. Now it has died. And I have no way of forcing my way inside to see how it once looked.

Life is a far stretch from literature. Or perhaps it's far from how I conceived literature as a child. I am eighteen years old and reality rubs mercilessly away all romantic ideas. Even the wish for revenge. What is the use of killing a person who has already died? My father may simply have forgotten to put his body where it belonged.

Lying there beneath West Africa's firmament, I was pondering these things. Perhaps it was then that for the first time I understood the notion of time for a human being: Time is the body's pulse beats, the body that travels through time and space. The past is ever present. I am not imprisoned in the here and now. I can be found and born at an immeasureable number of moments — and everything happens simultaneously.

My father has attempted to escape his past and therefore remains imprisoned in it. But he has become used to his prison to such a degree he no longer wants to break out of it. To him I am a threat. He knows that I want to make the past come alive inside him.

Still, our meeting was a meeting. I no longer need to search for him.

I tried to derail my thoughts and get going on other subjects. The weird Dane, for instance. Did he also stare at the stars? Maybe he simply had suffered an attack of homesickness?

Nothing but silence emanated from the tugboat. It seemed unsafe to wander about in the dark. I could wait. We would attack at dawn. That's exactly what happened.

Although during the night I constructed a plan less violent than rushing forward against whining bullets. While the morning was still gray, I went to look for Eight and Johansson. They were asleep amid a mess of empty glasses, bottles, and a few rooting swine underneath the stunted roof. I awakened them, rather gently, and introduced my plan — that we would attack the Dane from the inside. How? By softening him up, bringing him out through sentiments expressed in songs.

"Something Danish. Does either of you know any Danish songs?" I asked and tried to look more convincing than the two hung-over and half-asleep individuals I was addressing.

"See what I mean?" said Eight. "He's been studying me for months. He thinks I'm insane. Crazy. Otherwise he wouldn't dare ask his commander to sing in Danish."

"He always looks at people like that. I know. It's damned unpleasant. But d'you know any Danish songs?" asked Johansson.

"What?! Me? Hell no."

"The Dane has shut himself in. He shoots at us. We don't know why, but maybe he's just homesick," I continued.

"So why doesn't he just get going then?" Eight said.

"It's not that simple for a commander. He needs to have a reason."

"He does. He's mad as a hatter," said Johansson.

"And he shoots at us," Eight added.

"Precisely."

They looked as if they were considering the matter, but I could sense that the jungle juice had killed their intellectual abilities for a while yet. Then Johansson brightened. Meaning that one eyelid trembled a hundredth of an inch.

"Hist hvor Vejen slaar en Bugt ligger der et Hus saa smukt. You know — where the road turns, there's a house so sweet or something. It's better in Danish. It's Hans Christian Andersen. My brother-in-law used to sing it. He's a cop in Copenhagen. Half a dozen Tuborgs and he can't stop. Hist hvor Vejen . . . !"

My father cleared his throat with a couple of stanzas, then his voice turned mighty as a howling, brawling water buffalo's.

I had tried to talk some sense into my own head during the long night, telling myself about the futility of longing for one's father — and had almost convinced myself. But the very person I had held in contempt during the night, now singing, was transformed. The straw hat became a tropical helmet, the dirty shirt and the shapeless shorts turned into a dazzling white uniform. My father was a villain but one with overpowering charm. When he sang, a steel spring of vitality burst out of his closed-down features. Perhaps it was those fleeting glimpses of somebody who was open and sensitive that had enchanted my mother? And the other women. They had to have seen something.

I went to fetch a dozen breakfast beers, hoping to create the perfect mood. We sat down and went into rehearsal. The song was strangely beautiful, softly waving as a Danish wheat field and with a pitch suitable for Paul Robeson. It was set so low one could jump over it. All around us stood the village populace, puzzled and all ears. Even the small black pigs had stopped poking about. They might have sensed that we were singing about a country that had built its wealth on the flesh of their brothers.

"If only the Dane had been here!" cried Eight, a tear in his eye and a Tuborg in his hand.

"If it works on a Swede, it'll work like a can opener on a Dane. He'll cry rivers," I promised.

"But if he doesn't?" Johansson asked in the middle of a Danish staccato sound deep in the throat.

I shrugged.

"At least we've tried."

Fortified and well rehearsed we marched down to the bridge. Our audience was following at a cautious distance. Eight had been palavering with the village headman but had been unable to figure out why the Dane had locked himself in.

At the bridge we reconsidered our plan of attack. Yesterday's heavy, leaden sky had been replaced by dazzling sunlight. To walk directly onto the bridge and die with a song on one's lips did not seem an impressively intelligent thing to do. Johansson cleared his throat but had trouble finding the right note. He had experienced the closest encounter with Danish marksmanship as he had been holding the beer bottle when it was shot to pieces.

"Perhaps we could sing from here?" Eight suggested warily.

"It won't be loud enough."

"Or we could get behind some kind of cover," I said brightly. We looked around. The only creatures who would have been able to find something to protect them on this bridge's rickety planks would be three singing pygmies, if they first had been shrunk to the size of about four inches each. But they wouldn't have known those strange, guttural Danish words. We sighed.

Johansson went over to our pile of provisions to get yet another beer. I had arranged the cases of beer as protection during the night. Wouldn't it be possible for each of us to hold a case in front of us?

Eight looked sicker than ever. "And get our legs or our heads shot off!"

In the end, with our combined mental efforts, we solved the problem. Nothing is impossible. We lowered the beer cases into our boat, piled them up at the bow, and felt that this provided a reasonable cover. With the help of the oars, Eight and Johansson would hold the bow against the tugboat when we got closer. No Dane would be crazy enough to shoot up a whole supply of Tuborg, we reasoned, and proceeded to sing cheerily and loudly. "Hist hvor Vejen slaar en Bugt ligger der et Hus saa smukt."

The melody danced across the river. Our voices bounced against the rusty tugboat. Before long we caught a glimpse of the rifle barrel and, unfortunately, could both hear and see our beer bottles breaking in the cases where the bullets hit. I don't know if it was the song or the loss of so much beer that drove tears into Johansson's eyes. Anyhow, he cried while he rowed but kept on singing mightily. Eight and I also did our loudest best.

When we were a couple of yards from the tugboat, the shooting stopped. Our voices took on a timbre of renewed hope. Victory was near. Thanks to Hans Christian Andersen.

"Ahoy!" The word came from the tugboat and vibrated in the air.

Afraid that the Dane would lose the ambiance, Johansson and I kept humming while Eight started negotiations.

"Ahoy!"

"Is that beer that you have there?"

"Not much longer! Not if you keep shooting at it!"

A long silence ensued from the tugboat while we held still against the current and kept singing. Then he called out again.

"Ahoy!"

"Ahoy!"

"What kind of beer is it?"

We all turned pale in the boat. What if the Dane only drank Carlsberg beer!

By now we were close enough that he could take aim above the cases, however deep down into the boat we pressed ourselves. While, as far as I was concerned, Eight was insane, I had to give him credit here for considerable diplomacy.

"Tuberg," he yelled.

The silence from the tugboat was as long as the Niger itself. We could discern the slow swaying back and forth of the gun barrel. Obviously the Dane was deeply touched.

"Ahoy!"

He was beginning to bore us with his constant ahoys. Eight sighed. He evidently was sharing my opinion. But he answered patiently.

"Ahoy!"

"What the devil is that? 'Tuberg'??"

"Do you want Carlsborg? We have Carlsborg!"

The Dane was on the horns of a dilemma. He had initiated a conversation about his country's favorite subject with three dense idiots who couldn't tell the difference between Tuborg and Carlsberg. What should he do? Continue to act crazy — or try to educate the dumb Swedes?

"Which one d'you want? We've both," shouted Eight.

A perfect move on the part of Eight. The Dane would have to answer.

It took time, however.

We stopped singing so as not to disturb his concentration.

Finally he came out on the deck. Behind the reddish blond beard he looked very young and very close to crying.

"A Tuborg!" he hollered.

Everybody in the village let out a cheer that rose toward Africa's vaulted heaven, and giant treetops bowed to this hurricane of voices.

"Tuborg! Tuborg!" The triumphant sound was born in the villagers' happy throats.

We climbed aboard and drank a few Tuborgs with the Dane. He had made it rather cozy aboard. Eight had turned sensitive, and with a commander-to-commander attitude commented that anybody could develop a fit of insanity in West Africa.

I agreed with him.

Everybody was happy except me.

It took us two days to tow the more than half-mile-long dray of enormous timber. Right before we reached Sapele, my father stood astern, pissing. I sat on the engine room's skylight, very close to the big tugboat hook. It would have taken but a moment to remove the pin. Then the cable would have flown like a howling whip sternward and cut Johansson in two, right at his protruding middle. I stared at the hook, at the pin, at the cable, and at my father. For nearly four years, I had fantasized about some kind of revenge. But not until this moment had I understood that a human being's greatest power is goodness. A quality so tenuous and vital that it takes enormous forces to throttle it. My father would spend the rest of his life battling his own goodness, trying to drown it in beer, to wall it up in a bunker, and to suffocate it by silence. But he would never succeed. Not wanting to face the past, he was imprisoned in it.

After a few days of loading timber in Sapele, we weighed anchor. He stood in the midship aisle. He did not lift his arm in greeting. I did. Then he disappeared into the midship aisle's black shadows.

ALGERIA
1976

Erik and I climbed up to the tabular surface, red as bricks, covering several miles and set against mountain ranges, cliffs, and ravines. Every rock shimmered, sated with the day's sun. To the east was the Algerian-Swedish construction. The enormous concrete wall of the dam foundation tied together several cliffs. Walking all over with Erik for about an hour, I slowly began to grasp the scope of the work. To catch and imprison enormous volumes of water behind sufficiently strong armaments, to regulate and control this gigantic reservoir and from it feed irrigation constructions hundreds of miles away in the desert, that was Erik's job as local boss. He directed people and machines with soft-spoken objectivity, fully conscious that things would happen whenever he set pencil to paper and drew a line.

Despite all this, there was something helpless and lost over him. My jealousy was totally forgotten when we stood there, face to face. Despite the constant sun, his skin had remained light and a bit ruddy. Something searching and uncertain showed in the pale eyes. It was incomprehensible why Louise, using a multitude of evasive methods, had maneuvered herself down to Africa for the sake of this man.

When I had arrived at the construction site and asked for her, he had taken my arm with great determination and pulled me away from the noisy camp.

A quarter of an hour later, I began to understand that it was only in my imagination that Erik had been this great magnet drawing Louise here. It turned out that Louise had never laid eyes on him before arriving at this place. She was the one who came to him, asking for his help. Her sudden desire to have a real talk with me had transformed itself into anxiety. She worried over what I would do then. She had begged Erik to prevent me somehow from coming down to the oasis. The only thing he had been able to come up with was to have me thrown out of the country. At the last minute, she changed her mind and decided to meet me anyhow, although in controlled circumstances and in Algiers.

I wondered if Erik translated controlled circumstances to mean cross-examinations by police, imprisonment, and ingeniously fabricated house arrest.

A weak smile glinted in Erik's pale gray eyes as if expanding on the realities of life to the child in front of him was too much of an effort.

"I just said that you were a journalist and would criticize the dam construction in Swedish newspapers. That was enough. Unfortunately the Algerians play only one tune on their pipe. Heavy-handed threat or prison. The country is still suffering the consequences of colonial war. Yesterday's leader and liberator is today's oppressor. There's only one opinion here. That nothing must disturb the mutual relations between the two countries. The Swedish loan guarantees are about something else than money for Algeria. Besides, if it's any consolation to you, I was the one who caught hell in the end. Just for wanting to play the hero and help a damsel in distress. Louise can be most convincing. And she changes her mind quickly, too, since she suddenly conceived the idea to go into Algiers and meet you anyhow. And besides, you don't look too dangerous."

"No more than others," I said. "Is there any material for an exposé here?"

Erik left his weak smile right where it was.

"Possibly human beings' unfaltering belief that they can play the role of God when it comes to nature. But you're looking for Louise."

With confidently drawn lines in the brick red sand, he sketched a map over the activities of the area: the dam, the engineering camp, that of the Swedish concrete workers, the armada of people, machines, and materials plus the network of roads. Further down on the sketch, a few miles west of the dam, he drew a small circle.

"And here you'll find your researchers. They are digging out an oasis. Now and then we give them a hand over there. Mainly to stay in good physical condition."

There was nothing condescending in his tone of voice. And yet — the drawing in the sand was not just a geographical description of the different activities. It was also a study in relations of power between the kind of research that I and other social experts are involved in versus the explosive force of modern technology. In his field the future is shaped. In our field we note history. I expressed my thanks and drove on to the oasis.

I thought back on the last few months. Could anything at all be undone if we backed up in time and geographically returned to Småland, Sweden?

SWEDEN
1975

Once again:

I awaken early and arouse Jonas. We go fishing. Louise sleeps. When I return from our fishing excursion, I lie down beside her. We make love. She cries. Tears well up as from an underground spring. Then she claims that Axel has raped her. The accusation is so absurd I even believe it for a few hours. I contemplate going to Stockholm to shoot him like the wretched cur he is but am stopped by my father-in-law. Instead we finally get rid of the kittens. One shot suffices. Louise is strangely excited and claims that I liked shooting the kittens. I fire a second shot right beside her. Then she is the one who wants me. By that time, both of us are playing on hitherto unknown strings in our inner selves. But when she declares that she wants a divorce, the early hours of this day become understandable. A welding flame starts to burn in my stomach. Whatever she has said and done has only been meant to cover her own panic.

That is all.

Except that I begin to think of Jonas. I immediately see his searching face in front of me. I will lose him. And that loss explodes my reality into chaotic and uncontrollable events. My life's goal was going down the tube: A connected family as a conclusive symbol that I have succeeded in the very thing that I, according to all social laws, ought to have failed to do. I have realized how futile it is to try to understand the guilt feelings in connection with my mother's death, and I have given up the quest for my father's love. In the meantime I made a career out of a happy family life. Transcending my heritage, and getting past my splintered childhood, erasing as well all my foolish experiences at sea and instead building upon what two other role models, my maternal grandparents, showed me of normal relations — that is what I plan as a gift to my son. No crazy quest through West Africa for him, no nagging questions, no paralyzing fear. I would always be there whenever he needed me. Loyalty. Security. And that time will heal all wounds. Those are watchwords I have been hanging on to in vain, convinced that a human being's free choice is actually an iron-hard, disciplined expression of will.

My promises were grand indeed. Only a lonely child could have pronounced them with such arrogance. Having been subjected to betrayal as a child, I could not imagine that as an adult I in turn would be betraying. Of course, twenty years later I should have seen through my arrogance. Instead I have tried to make good my promises, but I have failed and have been forced to feel the self-contempt grow. It overwhelms me all the more when Louise informs me of her definitive decision. She is dead serious, I sense it. My career as family member is ended.

Those are my thoughts when I, as if numb all through, dig in my father-in-law's hole and a piercing pain shoots right through my midriff.

The loss of my son is cutting into me.

I start to hallucinate and see Jonas at the old millpond. He has drowned. I run with him in my arms, screaming to the whole village that he is not dead.

By now I am crawling on the mounds of earth around the dug pit. Louise comes running.

"No! He's not dead!" Louise yells.

I wriggle like a tortured worm on a hook and understand that I have been calling out to Jonas all the time. As if he were dead for real.

It is remarkable. In spite of everything, the pain and the madness, there is nonetheless a focal point of icy observation. I realize that I am trying to wriggle away from the experience of both old and new losses. Still I cannot stop the attacks. I hear and see my surroundings as if from inside a glass jar. My father-in-law goes out and gets the car but suddenly refuses to open the door. The palaver goes on for an eternity. I squirm in pain and try to relieve it by hitting my head on the glass wall. The others are upset. But they're so small. And unbelievably uninteresting.

Why don't they do anything?

Far away I hear my mother-in-law break something. Glass? All of a sudden, my father-in-law lies there, right by my side. An embarrassed expression has taken over his face and the stench of alcohol is strong. I try to speak to him of the disintegrating effects of alcohol and exemplify it by mentioning all the jungle juice that my father and other West African travelers have drunk. It's no good to drink. You forget even your own children. Devote your life to bananas instead. It's so sad one could cry. Or laugh. I try a smile but notice that my father-in-law doesn't understand a word I am saying. How can he when I keep trying to butt him with my head, hitting his nose?

I don't know which one of us is bleeding, and I don't care if it's he or I. I have cramps. It feels as if my intestines are trying to jump out right through the stomach muscles. I want to be a man with a harmonious marriage, small, beautiful, and lovable children, and a little dog to walk and philosophize with.

Finally they get me into the car.

Slivers of glass. Somebody has broken the side window. I keep squirming. Louise holds my head between her knees and hollers that I must not die. In pain, I nod and agree. That would indeed be terrible.

Who is driving?

God in heaven! It's my mother-in-law! I achieve a temporary relief by imagining all three of us as traffic-accident fatalities before we arrive at the hospital.

But you do not always get what you imagine. We survive the trip and I crawl into Emergency. There I have to heave my own aching body onto a stretcher. To my surprise the hospital personnel don't come rushing to my aid. Not even a painkiller is offered in the corridor.

I have only been in a hospital as a patient twice in my life. Once when I was born and once as a small boy when I decided to come down with polio just to scare the wits out of my father and a mean farmer he had placed me with. The farmer boxed my ears because I had been looking at pornographic pictures in a small viewer. I gave up my paralysis strategy quickly since the nurses were too energetic with their shots.

I am therefore amazed when no team of doctors comes running to save me. I have to wait for so long that I almost get tired of my illness. Could it be a conscious saving action? Only a healthy person has the strength to wait for hours to be treated. The rest is sorted out in a natural way.

I want to go to sleep in spite of my stomach pains, but Louise forces me to stay awake and participate in the farce. She is extremely upset when doctors and nurses finally examine me in the corridor. Louise is convinced that I have galloping cancer and demands immediate exploratory stomach surgery. My mother-in-law is rummaging in her handbag. She could be looking for a Bible or perhaps a false beard. Who wants to remain next to a man who is being examined in places nobody would even think of? It is no mitigating circumstance that I am her son-in-law. The situation is indeed distressing. But she must stay there anyhow in order to have something to speak to God about. She has probably read the New Testament's Epistle to the Philippians. "Beware ye of dogs." I understand her. But I do not comprehend why all the nurses have to gather around and shamelessly gawk at the doctor's repulsive and humiliating palpations.

Finally all the experts agree, in spite of my wife's objections. I am going into surgery to have my appendix removed. Louise insists that it could not possibly be anything as trite as appendicitis. The situation demands something grand and dramatic. Why not something that compels her to change her decision about a divorce? Amputation of both legs, for instance.

I can picture Louise in that new role. Pale but collected, fulfilling her mission in life, a true outstanding loner amid her struggling sisters, she stands stiffly erect behind the wheelchair. "She sacrificed her career to take care of her husband." It plays beautifully. I suggest that they saw off the legs. Everybody has heard of mistakes in a hospital. And what do a couple of legs mean when it comes to continued family bliss?

Unfortunately, the doctors stubbornly insist on opening up my stomach. I groan hypocritically toward the congregation and whisper for them to do whatever is needed. The nurses roll me into a preparatory room next to an operating theater. Silence. Only my groans and a metallic noise. The knives are sharpened. I must escape. But how?

The only way out is through the window. I am lucky. The operating rooms are on the first floor. It is difficult to look perfectly normal as I creep away to the taxi station, but people in this part of the country might be used to failed surgery specimens flying out of the surgeon's window. Nobody even lifts an eyebrow when I crawl away from the hospital.

In the cab I am hit by a strong longing for my uncle. Why did we not see each other? I could almost smell the old smoke from his pipe when I was thirteen and traveled by cab with him. Like a stranger, I had arrived alone, by train. My mother was dead. We siblings were separated in the final disintegration, left with the obscure idea that our father was busy loading bananas on the other side of the world. And there in Småland I got entangled in a remarkable tomboy's nets. She could box better than anyone, she was number one when it came to soccer, and she grew so fast one could hear it. Fate or luck or indifferent circumstances put Louise in my path. She was flat-chested at the time and excitingly dangerous with her inky, straight eyebrows under the blond bangs. I remember her as a farmer's daughter, but she was the daughter of the man who owned the country store. All of that lives inside me.

"So it goes sometimes," my father-in-law commented, seemingly unperturbed by my return.

We sit in the cellar and drink from his bottle of schnapps. My father-in-law is a first-class enigma. He is the prototype in my essay meant for the prime minister's eyes. He is the man who simply tries to live and survive, but everybody keeps taking big bites out of him. He is the loser, whatever happens. My father-in-law is the unknown quantity in Swedish politics. He is a man without hope, really, but he votes with the conservative party. Why?

The stomach pain is toning down, becoming a trembling echo, and I ask where my son is.

"He's with your uncle. You know. The one who's so great with kids but otherwise is an irresponsible sort."

I nod and drink. When all is said and done, perhaps it is that simple. I have never been allowed to be an irresponsible sort, even when it would be normal to be such a person.

ALGERIA
1976

Last time I saw Louise, which was in Bordj El Kiffan, she was radiant. Now she looked like a rejected ball of dust, pale and resigned.

What had happened?

I perceived my visit to be some kind of test I had to take and decided to nod in a friendly way, like a wise old monk, whatever happened. As ill luck would have it, I managed a fiasco straight away. I was completely caught off guard by a sudden insight regarding Erik. When I encountered Louise, I knew what was wrong with him.

"But he's an alcoholic!"

Even though I tried to bite my tongue the moment the words escaped my mouth, they were clear enough. But the regular Louise of old was not there anymore. The new one dug into the sand with her thin feet, smiled, and kissed me tenderly.

"I know. I'm going to save him."

"Does he know that?"

"No."

"Couldn't you save me instead?"

I tried to laugh but it sounded as if I had a cough. Behind her the rest of the camp's inhabitants approached, the usual academic gang. All of them managed to look as if they were seriously considering counting the grains of sand in the Sahara.

"That's no fun. You're always saving yourself."

"What do you mean?"

I received no answer. Her colleagues were descending upon us, polite but also a little embarrassed as if we had caught each other playing some inappropriate game in the sandbox. They commiserated with me on my illness. I wondered how much they knew but did not dare ask them to be more specific. Oh yes. I had been ill for several months. You do vegetate and waste away in the hospital. It felt good to move around a bit before sober and serious reality set in.

I did not listen attentively to Mattson's explanations during the guided tour. He was a small, fat man with an eager bounce. Sweat poured out of him. He reminded me of close-ups in poorly made pornographic movies. You are supposed to participate in the general excitement but boredom sets in. When Mattson spoke about his life's greatest research project, I felt exhausted.

"Five million!"

I smiled. "An impressive sum."

"Yes. Isn't it?"

It was impossible to stop him. The idea was that the desert inhabitants should build up an oasis the traditional way. More springs must be discovered for a steady flow of water. Wells had to be dug, twenty yards straight down in the sand, and the water guided for miles by ancient methods to the largest vein, where it would be divided by a simple but ingenious measuring system. A "comb" of wood was lowered into the water groove to split up the water in several flows. Every family's water ration, depending on family size, number of camels and date palms, was regulated by the holes in the "comb." The researchers were as enamored of this thousands-of-years-old system as they were disdainful toward Erik's computers, machines, and concrete walls.

But Mattson was deeply concerned about the natives' delaying-action attitude toward the venture. He had come to realize that the desert inhabitants had been collected by an official in the Algerian state machinery. The few genuine desert people were rebels. The majority around here were in fact city folks. One might assume them to be political undesirables.

Mattson's frantic optimism was a smoke screen to hide his fear. He did not dare formulate the simple truth: He was the unwilling chief warden of a prison camp. One of the few in the group who knew several Arabic dialects, he was far from stupid but perhaps blinded by the size of his research grant. Now his allotted desert people had demanded a regular water pipe with a faucet from the dam construction, while they kept digging for water in the correct, ancient way in the hostile desert. Erik had granted Mattson's desperate plea. He even let a truck dump sand over the mile-long pipe, rendering it invisible, charging the cost of labor to the researchers.

Then some friendly soul had pointed out that the date palms in the hopelessly dried-out old oasis had been dead for a long time and would never bear any fruit. It was only thanks to Erik's pipes that anything green grew. In pure desperation, Mattson had set half of his desert inhabitants cutting down the dead palm trees, thereby destroying the protection from the northern wind. The sand moved in over the oasis in huge drifts. A few stiff-jointed camels had been chained to the tree stumps in the hope that they would take over the role of windbreak. The camels kept complaining with stubborn, hoarse voices. Some of the Swedish researchers were not used to hearing the nightly crying of such large animals and were becoming "increasingly nervous," Mattson said.

He was solidly enthusiastic on the surface but on the brink of collapse underneath. I'm used to it. I have a special kind of magnetism that attracts madmen and nervous breakdowns. No crying camels are needed around me to make people jittery.

It started with my mother. She fell ill the moment she saw me. So Mattson talked and talked, all the time looking ready to run away.

We were sitting in his trailer, a combination of office, living quarters, and a place to shower. Lately it had become an outlet for feverish union activity among the other researchers. They elected a representative who made demands, and formal negotiations were carried out. Again the sociologists had to turn to the dam construction engineers. Erik could deliver especially developed housing units by air from Sweden. All this meant that Mattson had spent millions on his research project before even one drop of water had been brought to the oasis according to plan.

In spite of his problems, he poured whiskey for us and was extremely friendly. A frightening individual. Quite like me a few months ago, wrapped up in artful self-betrayal and going through with something unbelievably idiotic. After a few glasses, his flattery regarding my field of research was forming dry sand around my feet and threatening to suffocate me. Did he think I still received invitations to the prime minister's informal get-togethers? Though scandals in academic circles have a tendency to spread quickly, my mistakes might have been less important than I had thought. Unless Louise had spilled the beans, the news of my self-inflicted fall from grace could not have reached the desert.

I was beginning to understand why Louise had felt this unexpected need of me. Even camels cried in this false oasis.

Her inserted asides during Mattson's verbal enthusiasm slowly lent a satirical glow to the whole thing. Though it could be said that I was throwing rocks while in a glass house, I could not refrain from criticizing Mattson.

"But what's the use?" I asked quietly.

Below the mountain range, the white desert sand shimmered. The window of the trailer was open. Raggedy clouds presented a shadow play on the sandy surface.

"Acquisition of knowledge," Mattson said as if this fashionable pseudo-scientific phrase fully explained the need to set a number of millions rolling.

"So you can tell the people of the desert that they really know what they already know?"

Mattson, not quite as friendly now, pointed at me with a plump finger.

"You question everything and everyone. But that large dam construction over there will make the hidden knowledge of the people disappear! It will erode and disintegrate in proportion to the number of water pipes and faucets. Soon no human being alive will know how to care for camels. We're going to build a factory here soon. Camel cheese. Have you heard of it?"

"Oh yes," I said. "When I was at sea. As a joke. The Arabs have known for thousands of years that you can't make cheese out of camel's milk. That kind of knowledge doesn't disappear. You call their knowledge hidden only because you can't grasp it. It's the sociological researcher's usual trick. Nothing exists until we have formulated it."

He got so mad that he literally threw me out of the trailer. A few of the false desert inhabitants flapped by in their djellabas and disappeared.

"That was fun! In the old days I'd have felt responsible for your behavior. Now I don't care," said Louise, who had followed me out of the trailer.

Whereupon she disappeared, only to reappear between a couple of dead date palms. She turned and walked away on the white sand. I followed her, humming to myself. I knew my Louise. Her downcast and tragic figure was partly due to her feeling increasingly ill at ease in this oasis of self-delusions. She had needed me for affirmation. My task was to blow the whistle when she left the ship. Her thanks would be my reward.

To make love in the Sahara below the moon's jolly old man's face was a perfect illustration of our reunion, I thought cheerfully and trotted on in her footsteps.

Less than a mile away was a halfway demolished pile of rocks. Louise explained what a marabout's living quarters had looked like. The remains of the construction, hardly tall enough for a man, revealed that it could have been both a burial place and a temple in memory of a holy man.

"Splendid," I said.

I lifted her up a little against the dismantled rocks. The old man in the moon was grinning down at us. And she let me slide inside her. Her legs pressed like iron bands against the small of my back, and it was over before we had even grasped what we were doing. I sank down on the ground, leaning against the warm stone wall. For a brief moment, the different time and space concepts were uncovered and clear. The world with Louise and Jonas came together in the palm of my hand. The other hand amused itself by drawing abstractedly in the sand. As always it turned out to be a floor plan of a house. I keep drawing ideal abodes for my family. My life having been a constant move, the floor plans are some kind of contemplative pitching of a tent. I am drawing that which will never be a reality.

When I met Louise, my philosophy was simple: It is difficult to give up a chest of drawers that you have never had. Exactly! From early childhood, the idea that my clothes would forever and ever be in the one and same place seemed an illustration of complete security. To Louise, such a desire was a petty bourgeois contamination. The institution of family was the true center of the plague, the enemy, when we examined our lack of freedom. The paradox was that she wanted to get married anyhow. Consequently both she and I are paradoxes. What I struggle to reach, she struggles to give up. Our backgrounds guide us. Mine is the autodidact's mental fox trap, where a kind of double vision develops. To conquer the world means to conquer or be conquered by the bourgeois culture. The harsh criticism of oneself flourishes. What have I really done other than travel as far from my background as possible? I belong to orderliness. And the orderliness reigns.

Just as in the Sahara. At least within my field of vision.

I fumbled lazily for Louise to show her the plan for the house, but she was gone. On the other side of the pile of rocks rose an enormous sand dune. Her footprints seemed to lead toward the end of the world. I hurried after her. She was standing a small distance away on the other side. Her body was arched in ecstasy against her own hand, hidden underneath the thin dress. Her face was closed, contracted and concentrated. It wouldn't have surprised me had fangs suddenly glinted between the pulled-back lips. It was such a total and sensuous pleasure in its complete, closed-off loneliness that neither I nor any other man could possibly gain entrance into her kind of inner world. The light of the moon was soiled by quickly passing clouds. It turned black and then again sparklingly white. She had fallen, her body bent around her own arm.

I slid back into the running sand.

An image of my mother flashed, as if superimposed with that of Louise and then as a dull sorrow about which one can do nothing.

I had snuck into my maternal grandmother's huge pantry, where my mother used to rinse herself with salt water from the ocean that we children carried home in bottles. Most of the other time, she was lying very still, very sick. I was perhaps six years old, and it was the first and only time I saw my mother nude. Her pleasure was intense below the sprinkling sun-warmed ocean water. She played and enjoyed herself, liberated from us. From me. I could never give her what a simple bottle of seawater could. I and my siblings, the whole world — everything was rinsed away and obliterated.

Back at the ruins of the marabout's holy place, I erased my ideal family house floor plan in the sand. Our meeting had not been an affirmation but a farewell.

When she came sauntering down after what seemed an eternity, everything was over between us.

"Good," she said and kissed my cheek lightly.

"Can't we remember something that was fun?" I wondered. "You remember our wedding — that was fun!"

"Sure. I had a miscarriage a few weeks ago. I was pretty far gone. That was fun, too. Everything is fun to you."

"Where did it happen?"

Louise told me how Erik had personally driven her to the nearest hospital and then taken her to the construction camp and forced her to rest. She had not wanted to disturb me since I was preoccupied with a chewed-up turtle and a mad dog. Slowly she and Erik had come to like each other. They had decided to live together as soon as he had finished his contract. He was divorced and had a daughter the same age as Jonas.

"How perfect. My son in an alcoholic family."

"Erik's changing. And I'm going to start working as a family counselor."

"Isn't that putting the wolf as shepherd?" I asked.

The thought appealed to me, however. After our seven years, Louise must have enormous funds of knowledge. After seven years of marital rounds, Ingemar Johansson throws in the towel. I have always said that Louise ought to be a cartoon. She always comes up with the utterly unexpected. She is ahead in time before it can look back and reflect upon itself. I myself was a totally lost cause, stuck in the past and longing for a perfect future. As a small child, I wanted to be old. The whole idea of life scared me. If only one somehow could skip it without dying.

"What did you mean when you said that I always save myself?"

"You've never been loved. So you've spent all your years loving yourself. That's the whole thing."

"Help yourself and God will help the others, as my father used to say."

"Like father, like son."

"The last time I went to sea, my father and his father drove me to

Stockholm. Somewhere along the road, the three of us found ourselves standing there, pissing, in a grove. Yes, indeed, here stand three generations pissing, I thought.

"My father started it, illustrating the male Swedes' fear of using sentimental or highfalutin adjectives.

" 'And the fucking sparrows squeak,' my father commented.

" 'And the goddamn sun shines,' I said.

"I thought he'd notice the irony. But then my grandfather muttered, 'Hell, it looks as if the damn summer is coming this year, too.'

"Every time I drive past that grove, I see it as a monument to three generations' inability to express their emotions. Have I told you about my meeting with my father in West Africa? He stood aboard a ship in Sapele when we dropped anchor."

Louise smiled and lay down in the sand.

"Oh yes. Many times. But tell me once more. Do that instead of asking who was the father of my baby. Or how I feel. I asked you to come here in a moment of weakness because I thought you were the father. You could have been. But we'll never know now. It's too late. Tell me about your father instead. He's a wonderful excuse for you being what you are. Which version will you choose? Do you kill him dead or not?"

Louise was calm and strangely distant. Normally she would have thrown heavy candle holders, urns, or books at me while supplying me with her opinions. I grabbed the chance and told once more the story of the meeting with my father. It couldn't hurt. I thought I did it rather well. Had I been Louise, I would have decided on the spot to give me all the love I had missed.

"The only emotion you're familiar with is a feeling of loss," Louise said and stood up. "And that loss you have indeed recouped. I suppose that's why you've been unfaithful in such a tremendously predictable way. How many women have you really slept with since we got married? If you at least had enjoyed it, I'd have said nothing. But now I'm tired of it. Go home to Jonas. Go home and take care of our son."

Never had Louise been more beautiful than at that moment. She disappeared over the dunes. Perhaps she would walk all the way to Erik. I leaned against the holy man's burial place and wondered how things had been between him and his women. Perhaps he had as much fun at his wedding as I had.

HOW IT ALL ENDED
or
The Marriage to Louise

Our wedding had indeed been a remarkable affair. We were two children getting married, two children who had fooled each other completely. The first meeting aboard the train cemented our relation. We became fixated in parts neither of us could play. Completely dumbstruck, I had listened to Louise, a wonderfully amoral love priestess telling about her sexual debaucheries. I suddenly became repressed and shy — cold sweat was breaking out all over — just thinking of myself once making my first entrance to the world between the legs of a woman and now topping it off by having to go back in there.

I think the meeting with Louise was about sudden and complete love. Everything that I had been was demolished. I disappeared, as if in a black hole, before I even touched her. The problem with me, as my brother used to explain when we were children, was that I tend to think too much. Already then, I saw love as an eternal birth struggle. What if one got stuck and couldn't get away?

Ever since I was thirteen, I had been struggling with my infatuations. Before long, I was a very tired and disillusioned man, who, at the age of twenty-three, met Louise.

What was it really that took place?

Total blindness? Small brain hemorrhages in both of us? How could we get so excited about the parts we chose to play? Louise presented herself as a totally instinctive volcano, happily rolling around in sin and sensuous pleasures. I fell willingly into the part of the frail piece of wood, accidentally falling into the volcano and burning up.

We got engaged, became pregnant, and married, all at a speed that would have broken a tabloid writer's fingers on the typewriter keys. It was a civil ceremony. Louise had a grandiose stomach, I a chalk-striped suit, and my in-laws nervous tics in their benevolent smiles. I sympathized with their difficulty in accepting that Louise, a girl from a good family, was marrying a simple sailor. That's how they were seeing me. I didn't even have golden stripes on a handsome uniform. Such a comparison was close at hand since Louise had a cousin who had married a sea captain. It was the presence of this handsome idiot that made Louise begin to talk, extremely loudly, about my moral excellence.

"He's been at sea for seven years and never been with a whore! Isn't it fabulous! I mean, we've all heard about sailors and bordellos and whores!"

The timing was perfect for the orchestra to stop playing dance music. Louise has a peculiar way of formulating words that deal with the sphere of sexuality. The words shape themselves as huge capital letters in her gap and roll smoothly out over her lips. No mumbling at all for her. With her strict religious upbringing as the bouncing mat for everything that the rest of us try to hide, things fly out of her with orgiastic factualness.

My mother-in-law dropped ice cream on her dress. I tried discreetly to signal the astonished musicians to resume playing. But they were much too interested in what would follow. My just lawfully wedded wife's voice thundered across the dance floor. Her interpretation of my small confidences had grown to unbelievable dimensions.

"He couldn't fuck a whore if you paid him. Because he's a man of moral standing. Isn't it wonderful? He can't even be unfaithful. That's why I'm marrying him. He's so moral that I wonder what will happen to him if we get divorced."

Everyone in the restaurant including the musicians and the personnel was listening with rapt attention.

Louise fell silent and looked around. A normal human being would at this point have melted into the carpet. Not so Louise. Instead she stood up, stretched to her full height, and stared back at everyone.

"The rest of you motherfuckers here have of course no idea what I'm talking about. I'm talking about a morally erect man, upstanding to such a degree that you'd never even get close to it!"

I nodded in agreement. It sounded good. But I understood nothing.

I felt a vague discomfort. Even in the middle of misery, one can feel flattered to be the star of the event. The cousin's sea captain stared, probably fantasizing putting me in the stocks. My father was not present. He had no time. He was loading bananas for the Swedish populace. But my brother was there, representing the family. He looked stunned.

Louise was asked to leave by the maître d', who had rushed over to our table.

My in-laws, pretending that nothing had happened, were pulling Louise between them. The rest of the group disappeared, and I was left at the table with fourteen half-eaten ice cream dishes with cloudberry jam. The dance orchestra was launching into their next dreary number, and I was taking a walk around the table drinking all the leftover cordials. Why not?

In a dimly lit corner, I was trying to be philosophical about what had happened. Things could be worse. The wedding night had been celebrated in advance. There was clear evidence of my manhood.

My friend the sea captain zeroed in on me. He was as aroused as Louise, with one difference — he was deeply insulted. Either I had been at sea for seven years and done my share of rolling or else I had falsified my seagoing papers. He knew too well how things stood at sea.

What should I do?

We began to fight halfheartedly in the poorly lit restaurant. He tore my suit and I managed to pummel his head right into a big platter with elk meat.

We kept on fighting without much conviction.

My brother managed to separate us. Being an expert on women, he said that I had planted my last oat.

"What did you tell her? That you only held hands with girls before you met her? You better go home and lie instead!"

"About what?" I asked.

I didn't get it.

So it went. Our wedding celebration was only a mild prelude, the first and not the last time I would be the victim of my wife's outspoken nature. She loved to discuss sex with total strangers, provided I was the illustration. I remember one adventure she managed to turn into one of her showpieces. The problem with Louise was that she kept mixing up intimacy and publicity. She relished my little story as an example of my "moral rectitude" and it could roll over her lips in the most unexpected circumstances.

The story takes place at the time our son, Jonas, was born. Unable to apply for student loans, according to Louise, if we wished to remain independent, we moved to the city of Norrköping and looked for work. I was happy. Louise got a job at the clinic for sexual disease and I worked on a tugboat in the harbor. While we walked around town pushing the baby carriage, Louise enjoyed nodding discreetly to the right and to the left describing to me the various venereal diseases of the passersby.

It seemed as if the whole city found reasons to come to her desk. I had nightmares about a gigantic germ swallowing our little family. Of course, sometimes I had other fantasies.

It was winter and bitingly cold. I had found an old fur cap at the Salvation Army store. We no longer used the surname Johansson — it had changed to Rutger — and I was in the process of shedding my skin, turning from sailor to adult student. In the bus, wearing the fur cap this piercingly cold winter day in question, I was suddenly overtaken by an erotic feeling so powerful that I began sweating profusely. I was seeing myself as one enormous penis rocking in and out of the fur cap. I wanted desperately to disappear from the bus. In a few seconds, the fontanel would split open and spray gallons of sperm into the furry head covering. I would look like a cupcake, covered with icing. What if somebody noticed? I thought. At the same time, to my amazement, I was rocking in a rhythm that had nothing to do with that of the bus.

The bus was filled to the last standing room. I was sitting on the bench that runs along the side of the bus, and a woman, a good deal older than I, her fur coat open, was rubbing her genitals against my knee. We found ourselves promptly inside a dense and inconsiderate desire for satisfaction. Shortly both of us would be reaching a climax. There was nothing we could do to stop now. Helpfully I pressed my knee against her circular movements, at the same time as she was holding me in a pumping, squeezing grip. We never looked at each other, both of us pretending that nothing at all was happening.

Two stops before mine she tore herself away. There were about ten people left in the bus. It did seem rather strange for her to be standing between my legs. I slithered up on the seat, blinded by the sweat running down my forehead. She turned around, smiling. Would I come? Images ran wildly beneath the fur cap. She was walking ten yards ahead of me, we were walking through the front door, up the staircase, she was opening her apartment door, and in the hallway we were throwing ourselves at each other, like wild animals. The sky turned red as a passion flower. The dreary suburb was a hot, pulsating jungle. There would be no need for us to walk in the usual, boring way to her door. I understood then the meaning of erotic fantasy.

But what did I do?

I froze. I could not even lift my hand to press the stop button. At the end of the line, gasping for air, I managed to collect myself and stumbled out of the bus, whereupon I began walking home.

Light glimmered in our apartment windows. As I came closer, my steps grew lighter. I ran the last bit. I tore open the door and stormed in to my family, feeling like the hero who had undergone a wearing and extremely trying test. There I was, having relinquished an anonymous and immensely thrilling, orgiastic love tryst.

Louise, to my disappointment, showed no admiration for me. Her cousin with the sea captain had arrived without warning and without her captain. The two of them were about to go out: The cousin needed a man. And they were planning to collect such a specimen at a nearby bar. The air was thick with their emancipation, and Louise's words to me were crushing.

"You'll suffocate from all your morality! Why didn't you take advantage of the situation? If we were to get divorced — what the hell would become of you?!"

This is the point where Louise usually ends her story, when told in public, by condescendingly patting my head as if I were a stupid dog, not knowing any better.

It was then that I decided that next time I would definitely grab any offered opportunities. The rumor spread. Mostly thanks to my dear wife's advertisements. While she was telling her girlfriends how my "morality" was preventing me from doing anything, I was offering them discreet but practical opportunities to test her statements. An excellent exercise. As if being born a little each time or divorcing Louise step by step.

The seven years with Louise turned into seven incomprehensible and painful ones and we discovered much too late that she had never meant a single word she had pronounced with such gusto. It was all pure verbal bravura and phony emancipation. Mere words to cover her own fear of being left alone. She would speak constantly about unfaithfulness, divorce, sex, and the disintegration of family in order to keep the ghosts out. She was speaking away her fear while I was acting out mine. We were equally stupid and childish, the two of us.

Eventually I had to admit to her the extent of my training program. By that time, my unfaithfulness had taken on considerable proportions. It dawned on me finally that it was I who was betraying myself.

Louise's self-esteem needed a sparring partner. She chose Axel. A stupid choice since he was my father figure in the hierarchies of the academic world. The mathematics of love were simple to her. Revenge. An eye for an eye. She would have to work hard to catch up with me.

ALGERIA
1976

Secret police agent Omar became uniquely nice and useful the moment my person was declared uninteresting. Almost magically my Volvo was repaired. Omar's friends produced miracles. My maternal grandfather would have applauded such craftsmanship and ingenuity. His last years were filled with tremendous pain. Wherever he turned, people had been transformed from artisans to machine servants. He felt contempt for this one-sided development. Nobody could repair anything anymore, he kept lamenting, only replace parts.

Now the Volvo purrs through the Sahara like a contented cat as I drive back toward Algiers and Bordj El Kiffan, leaving the oasis behind. The trip takes one day and one night.

Each time I drive through the desert it reminds me of all the years, days, and hours I have spent staring out over oceans. The Sahara's stiff sand waves in the cold moonlight give me the same feeling of smallness or greatness — I don't know which — that I experienced when my eyes met with the unbroken horizons of the sea. Along the road, the car's shadow sails across the sand as a giant ray fish, silent and untiring. I feel exactly the same, suspended in air, moving forward. I have left Louise. We are no longer intertwined. Her pain is no longer mine and mine is no longer hers.

In Bordj El Kiffan nothing looked the same.

It's one thing to read in a cheap detective novel about what a place looks like following a thorough search and quite another to stand in the middle of the devastation. My hospitable Frenchman's model train setup was totally demolished. Not one thing remained as it had been. Furniture, dinnerware, all his Wagner records . . . everything was crushed and trampled and lay broken on the floor. It must have taken hours of intense work to pulverize everything so methodically, every large and small part of the Frenchman's unique home. My few possessions were all destroyed. Even the already broken tape recorder with my French-language course had been stomped upon. The course book had been turned into confetti. I had only been a guest and never had a chance really to get to know the owner of the house, but I felt robbed, undressed, and invaded.

What could have happened?

Murder? History catching up with a lonely former French soldier?

I sat down on the overturned bed, swallowing with effort. I felt like crying and as if I had been beaten all over. And I had no idea why. I wanted revenge.

Omar entered into the hall from the garden, pushing the door open. In his arms he was cradling the old dog, and over his shoulder he carried the Frenchman's most prized possession, the MAT 49 machine gun.

The dog looked dead. His saliva was dripping on the stone floor.

"It's not dead. But almost," Omar said in perfect Swedish.

If you ever run into someone called Omar in North Africa, brace yourself. As for me, I have met too many Omars. This was one too many. I sighed. Both of us knew what needed to be done.

While we walked down to the long, deserted, sandy beach, Omar told me of Monsieur Verdurin's hasty escape from the country. Monsieur Verdurin was an old *pied noir*. He had apparently been working for all those fanatical organizations in France that dream of the return of the colonial empire, with full restitution both of the important families and of French honor.

"But how could you let him stay here?" I asked.

We were standing on the beach with the Mediterranean night breathing softly. The sound of the wind and the ocean seemed annoyingly eternal. Algiers's lights made an arch toward the heights a few miles away. How many times haven't I seen the city at a distance, when I was at sea? How many times haven't I slowly approached other cities? Heaven and ocean becoming one black entity, a few words of command from the bridge, our ship gliding closer to an alien coast. I was only sixteen years old, the first time I arrived in Algiers. The night was as inky, the breeze as faint, and the ocean breathing as indifferently as now.

Omar put the poor dog on the ground. It whined and rattled. I put the spade into the sand and began digging.

Standing in the pit, I swallowed and suddenly felt as if I were back in the same hole, being sixteen years old. Omar took the MAT 49 from his shoulder and handed it to me when I had crawled out of the grave.

"Monsieur Verdurin told me how good you were with it."

"Really?" I said. "I'm a stupid Swede who lives in a country filled with unrealities, but I can take apart and put together that machine gun blindfolded. Strange, isn't it?"

Omar walked off a few yards, leaving me with the faintly whining dog. I checked the MAT 49. Most likely, Omar was a clever tool in a game I did not understand. But he was a fool anyway. He had carried the machine gun over his shoulder with the safety off. I held out my arm and put the muzzle of the gun to the dog's forehead. I wondered who had kicked apart his innards. The beast stared back at me, showing his teeth. It looked like a smile. I pressed the trigger.

The sound was sucked up by the night and the gasps of the swells. Omar returned. We heaved the dog's body into the hole and Omar took over the spade work. I stood beside him.

"What happened? Did you destroy Monsieur Verdurin as painstakingly as you did his home?" I asked Omar when he had filled the sandy pit. He shook his head.

"It was the family. I managed to get him away in time."

"The family?"

"The family, the relatives, and the religion. If you have any idea what such concepts really mean. Our French friend managed to seduce the girl who cleaned the house. That's his version. Hers is that he forced himself on her. Remember how angry the women around here were when they discovered that you were alone in the house? That was just a mild breeze compared to the hurricane that occurred here today. Religion and morality are not as easy to control as one may believe."

"There are parts of us that can't be ruled, that can't be reached," I mumbled. "I remember another night," I said. "Last time I dug a hole in Algiers, we put something quite different into it."

We began walking along the beach, away from Bordj El Kiffan's lights. And I told him about my first encounter with Algiers.

ALGERIA
1961

The road to Algiers begins in an attic in Sweden. Ollie's attic.

Another year of my life had rolled by. I was ready to celebrate my sixteenth birthday and nobody remembered my mother's death anymore. People threw their thoughts forward. You had to hang in there. Otherwise I could miss my next mother, too. I never understood why Ollie had married my father, since he was never at home. But that was not my problem.

It was a cozy year. Ollie had her own business, being the widow of a greenhouse grower of cucumbers and flowers. She had no ovaries and therefore, according to her, a better hand than most with children. Ollie was a modern woman. Her educational method was simple. As long as I tried it out at home first, I could do whatever I pleased. It was the same method I myself had developed during my parent-free spell in the Chinese Wall.

However, I was no longer the only one at Ollie's. After a week my sister arrived. As for my brother, he stayed with our maternal grandmother. He had definite opinions about Ollie. But he could afford to have them since a maternal grandmother is even better than a real mother. Our maternal grandmother would have won the title of National Grandmother of the whole of Sweden — had she opened her home to me and my sister. That didn't pan out and we learned to make the best of it.

It was a strange feeling to have siblings again in the home of a total stranger. From her old family, Ollie had already a stepson. His name was Kurt and he never said more than one single word: "Michelin." As I understood, it meant that he went around longing for French tires. But I could be wrong. He was married to a handsome woman, Elsa. They lived downstairs, we lived upstairs.

Kurt would stare at me suspiciously and mumble "Michelin." He was the brooding type and almost turned me into one. I wondered what that one word of his really meant.

But who am I to complain? My new family could look and act any way they wanted. As long as you have your health, as my grandmother used to say. Not everybody has the luck of getting a new mother, work, and even a fun leisure time. I worked in a store as errand boy. As such I was picking up cucumbers from our greenhouse. It was always Elsa who handed over the crates. She was wearing only a shirt tucked into some blue jeans. And sweat was pouring out of her armpits. She was tanned and very blond. Her breasts would have made my uncle rave about heated cantaloupes.

MY FATHER, HIS SON

As for me, I walked around wishing I were a cucumber. I couldn't help it. As soon as she touched a cucumber, I would get an erection. It was aching and throbbing. I would make some clumsy excuse and rush up to the attic above the garage. That's where I spent my free time, indulging in erotic fantasies.

One year is a pretty long time, after all. And much of what happened is another story, faring perhaps best by being stored away, like my mother's pictures and books that had been packed in that attic. The attic is where I read through my father's old diary. Upon reading it, I drew the conclusion that he and Ollie had met each other long before my mother died. And that was why my brother had refused to move in with her. He was always a step ahead of me, but then he had for a long time been totally clear in understanding where a man's propelling power lies. I kept fighting it. An impossible task. It was horrendous. Every time Elsa grabbed hold of a cucumber, I turned blind with desire. After reaching the attic, I would throw on some old clothes, struggling to lessen the pressure and become normal again.

"Whatever you do, do it at home," Ollie was always fond of saying.

It was on such a day in the attic, one year later, that I heard her voice outside. If she had guessed what I was doing, she had decided to leave me alone in the attic. Peering through the small window, I saw two men standing beside her. They were inquiring why I had not been attending school. Poor Ollie, she was in despair. I suggested that she falsify my father's signature and offered to get my sailor's papers and go to sea rather than dishonor her. It seemed meaningless to go to school in order to become something. Better I went to sea to acquire a somewhat childish nature, like my uncle. A couple of years of being rocked by ocean waves would make me a new and better human being.

Remembering my cooking classes at school as being fun, I decided to sign on a ship as a cook's apprentice. It gave one a feeling of security to know how to cook one's own food, prepare the sauces, and take care of oneself.

It seemed acceptable at the seamen's agency. Ollie decided to help in my new life, and we bought half a dozen checkered cook's pants.

I paraded proudly around the house in my new pants until my assignment arrived.

Ollie insisted on driving me. She went as far as to follow me aboard the ship, introducing herself, asking questions about cleanliness and hidden dangers, telling everyone that she knew the lay of the land at sea. She was married to a seasoned deep-sea sailor, and I was the son and heir to that wonder of a man. The whole thing was terribly embarrassing. Such motherly concern was new to me. With mixed feelings, I waved good-bye to Ollie. I would deal with the suppressed laughter aboard later.

A storm of raw laughter greeted me as I stepped out on deck in my checkered cook's pants, asking the whereabouts of the cook's domains. I had been signed on as unseasoned seaman and not as cook's boy, because such a position did not exist at all, I was told, except on passenger ships.

The crew would probably have laughed me over the railing and down into the North Sea, on which we were already rocking, had the boatswain not taken me under his wing.

"Leave the lad alone," Bengtsson said.

Boatswain Bengtsson was from the Swedish west coast. He had been at sea so long that he walked like a crab. Walking behind him made me dizzy. He grabbed a paint bucket and brushes and scurried back and forth with me at his heels across the ship all the way to the capstan.

"Red lead," he said and put a brush into my hand.

I stared at the colossal iron heap. Wheels and levers, winches and chain cables. Which was front and which was back? And why did boatswain Bengtsson want the gray-painted capstan red?

But those were questions a mere deck boy could not bring forth. I peered into the bucket with red paint and went to work.

I was alone up front by the capstan. I stayed there painting for hours, experiencing my first feeling of intoxicating delight in hard, physical work. Before long, a flaming red monument towered before me. Bengtsson had a real shock upon seeing the capstan. He was so utterly amazed that he dropped his left eye. It rolled down toward the cable hold, and I threw myself after it before it disappeared into the sea. I picked up the small hard porcelain ball and held it in my hand.

It had happened so fast I acted on pure reflex. Bengtsson hastily put the eye back in his face and began scolding me very loudly as if a demon had possessed him. The idea had of course been for me to find bare rust spots and cover them with the red lead.

I began to cry. It wasn't fair. I wanted to go back home. But then I remembered that I had left home forever. That made me cry a little more. Bengtsson came close to dropping his eye again. He had never seen a sixteen-year-old cry before. I told him it was probably an old case of nerves.

We chatted for a while, standing by the fire red capstan, while the North Sea's green waves were growing taller and taller, leaving Sweden behind. I swore to Bengtsson that I would not tell a soul about the porcelain eye.

"I can't see well enough with the other one," he explained. "It would mean packing my bag and walking down that gangway plank, should anybody ever find out about it. You can't have visual aids if you're going to work on deck."

It was difficult to understand the logic in Bengtsson's reasoning. How could a porcelain eye be a visual aid?

"Where there's a will, there's a way," Bengtsson said with conviction. "A strong will — and you can do anything."

His initial surprise at my tears was quickly transforming itself into a strong paternal feeling. But before going on about my new dad, I must describe how I became a real sailor during my first journey out.

On our way down through the Bay of Biscay, on a summer day sated with blue when the water looked like oil, we were given the order to open the fifth hatch. The third mate had been down there and noted moisture damage to the dynamite, which, according to the bill of lading, required a completely dry storage space.

Never had I seen such weather before. Our ship crawled forward between two enormous blue planes. Heaven and ocean melted together and it was difficult to know if we were right-side up. The horizon was endless. In this wide expanse, with enormous quantities of nature and water, everyone was becoming spiritualized, as if walking in some glorious light. Everyone except me.

I was lost in erotic fantasies.

Right on top of the fifth hatch, a girl was sunning herself. She seemed to have come out of the sea itself. She did not look to be older than I. There I was, struggling with the enormous bolts of the lid, screwing and screwing, switching to another bolt, and, during half an hour's intense work, I had seen her from every one of the three hundred and sixty degrees. Now and then she changed position. The hatch was in line with my chest, so it was as if she were lying on a gigantic table, squirming and moving. I tightened my muscles. I too kept changing positions in order to look professional while I was screwing and unscrewing with the large T-shaped lever. Sometimes I had to bend and pull. Sweat dripped into my eyes. I slipped and dropped the lever. I could hardly breathe. I don't know where love takes root in others but in me it gets stuck a little everywhere. First a big frog lodges in my throat so I can neither swallow nor speak normally. Then I get some weird, burning spots along my back. My legs turn numb. I trip over things. The blood boils. There is a buzz in my head and my body becomes seemingly fragile. I have given these symptoms quite a bit of thought. Perhaps love is nothing but reflexes, memories of the totally defenseless child's experiences of panic and pleasure.

Bengtsson came hurrying along with his crablike walk, wondering what the hell I was doing. He shooed the girl away as if she were a fly, and she disappeared without even a glance at my bulging muscles. A few hours later, I stretched my ears as a gigantic tent all over the ship and managed to pick up her faint laughter and snatches of conversations she was having with an older woman. She was the daughter of the chief engineer and it was her mother who was with her. What could I do to get close to her?

I went to Bengtsson for advice. He was doing some calculations in a small black book and on the shelf next to him were some well-worn math textbooks. He was grateful for the interruption, scratched his head, inspected my clean ears, and was clearly pleased that I had come to him to learn. A discussion on the art of seducing women was a welcome distraction from mathematics. I kept my questions as general as possible, hoping he would not guess who it was that had so turned my head.

"Women," Bengtsson said and closed his real eye. "Women are drawn to that which is male."

"One would hope so," I mumbled, careful not to disturb his train of thought.

I was disappointed.

"Then the question is: What is truly male?" Bengtsson continued and removed the porcelain eye in order to scratch. "I'll give you an example."

He replaced the porcelain eye and squeezed the good one tightly shut while asking me to hold up in the air any number of fingers I chose.

"Two," Bengtsson said.

That was correct. I held up one finger.

"One," Bengtsson said.

This went on for a while. He could see with his artificial eye! I had to keep my hand in front of his other eye to make absolutely certain.

"We have here an example of the total power of the imagination. I make myself believe that I can see with my porcelain eye and consequently I can," Bengtsson explained to me.

"Why can't you learn mathematics the same way?" I asked, trying to break the magic.

"I probably don't really want to. But let's leave the math on the shelf and go back to women. You're wondering what to do, what the art of seduction really is, and I'm going to tell you. It's as simple as learning to see with an artificial eye. It has to do with will, total concentration, and complete conviction, that's all. They become a power greater than you. If we have time one day, I'll teach you. But practice on that chick for now."

Bengtsson brought out needle and thread to fix a pair of worn jeans. The séance was over. I shivered in spite of the heat. He had understood everything. And the rest? I hadn't the faintest idea what he was talking about. He winked at me and smiled. With his good eye closed, he held up the needle and threaded it without any trouble.

"You see? It's all a question of willpower."

I ran out of there and up on deck. Bengtsson's laughter echoed behind me. It was evening and the moon was out full. I sauntered around the fifth hatch and tried to concentrate. If my will was strong and I believed in my ability hard enough, the girl with long, blond hair would suddenly lie there in her scanty swimsuit.

I concentrated until my scalp ached. Nothing happened.

Bengtsson's power wasn't working. To count fingers and thread a needle with a glass eye seemed like minor accomplishments. I was less sure that the power he was touting could be transferred to something as mysterious as girls.

My head hanging low with disappointment, I walked up to the bridge. I had the eight-to-twelve watch, and it was time to take my turn. The seaman standing on the bridge wing grinned, mumbled something that I did not understand, and disappeared down the steps. He was a Spaniard, and I had not yet learned the common mixture of Spanish, Italian, English, and a smattering of French. The ship had collected a mixed crew during many years of journeys between the Mediterranean ports.

I just nodded. I was in a terrible state. I could hardly breathe. I was not even sure I still possessed legs. When I walked, it felt as if I were grazing the deck with the trunk of my body. I couldn't get the chief engineer's daughter out of my mind. To use me as watch and lookout was putting the whole crew in peril. The only thing my retina retained were endlessly varying images of the sunbathing girl.

Boatswain Bengtsson was wrong. It was not a question of concentrating on the object of my infatuation but rather of my inability to concentrate on anything else. What was her name? How old was she? What if she were all of seventeen? That would be horrible since I was sixteen. We'd never be able to communicate across such an age gap. She was probably going to school, preparing for one degree or another. That would also be an insurmountable barrier. I would never be able to write her a letter. I couldn't spell! Imagine me writing "my beautiful lady" and have it come out as "my beautyfull laydee." Her friends would all giggle about it.

On the other hand, all I would have to do was to leave out words I could not spell. "Hi!" I could spell that. When we were married, I might cautiously go as far as to "Hi! Hi!" and later to a "Bye!"

But would that be enough if I were at sea and she at home caring for the children? Perhaps so if I added the date of my return? My father had managed with only a postcard communication, so why not me?

The picture was clear. Instead of sky and ocean, I was seeing our cozy little cottage. We were sitting in armchairs reading poetry during the evenings, quoting an especially delightful line to each other. At night, we first kissed our rosy little children on their cheeks, then folded our clothes neatly and crawled into bed, turned off the light, and made love to some exquisite, surging music.

I smiled to myself and hummed a little in the soft, warm night. The Bay of Biscay looked like molded tinplate under the friendly face of the moon.

It would be a perfect marriage.

All I needed was to meet her and learn to spell.

"Are you standing there singing to yourself?!"

It was the second mate. The second mate was retired from the marine corps. Always dressed with careless elegance, he looked as if he had stepped off the cover of a book about English Second World War flying aces. He smelled of after-shave from his graying mustache and mints from his mouth. Unfortunately he couldn't see more than ten yards ahead of him. He more than anyone would have needed Bengtsson's ability. This good old guy's surname was Hawk. I have no idea what had driven him to enroll in the merchant navy or how he had managed to get to sail as second mate. But as such he was dangerous to one's life, charming, and well versed in deceit.

Already when I had my first watch he declared his intention to impart to me the mysterious knowledge of navigation. Rules for yielding, the different ship lights, and other essential pieces of information. After just a few days I had become his infallible hawk eyes. My pride knew no boundaries. I thanked my lucky star for not having been born a hundred years earlier, when chief mates whipped their unseasoned deck boys with cat-o'-nine-tails.

"Listen you," Hawk said. "If you can tear yourself away from your operatic practice, Katrin would like to learn how to steer the ship."

I had just put my body back in working order. The legs reached down to the deck of the bridge wing and my breathing was generally normal. But now I was losing it all over again.

"Help!"

"What is it?"

Hawk let out a cloud of breath mints and after-shave over my head.

"I can't walk."

"Sure you can," Hawk said. "She isn't dangerous. She's only fifteen years old."

He tore away my fingers that clung firmly to the railing, and I tottered over to the steering wheel.

It was so dark that I could hardly see my intended wife. But that didn't matter. Every line of hers was etched in my head. At age thirteen I had learned a lot from an artist in Småland. He and I could matter-of-factly catch the constantly changing play of lines in the female body. At sixteen, there was no question in my mind but that I was an expert on a woman's body. I had spent years studying it intensely at a distance.

Katrin stood by the steering wheel. I swallowed and said "Hi." She might as well get used to my intended form of letter writing right from the start. Second mate Hawk could have married us on the spot, had we not been underage. A wedding at sea has a certain romantic flair.

In the faint glow of the compass light, both of us were hardly visible. While I explained the principles of steering, someone installed tiny sprinklers in my armpits. Soon I was wet as the sea from sweat. Katrin had absolutely no idea in the world about manual steering or the compass. She was simply wonderful. When she was lying on top of the fifth hatch, I had had plenty of time to estimate her weight to be around one hundred and five pounds. Now I found it remarkable that so little could be so much. All the time she kept saying lots of fascinating things.

"Gee . . . I can't . . ."

I consoled her.

"You can."

"No! Look at this!"

We were growing closer. A couple of more tension-relieving lines of dialogue and I would fall to my knees and propose marriage. I had to touch her hand lightly to correct obvious mistakes. At one point, she put her hand on top of mine as I was demonstrating how little really one had to do to make the huge ship move forward straight as a thought.

The high point of the evening came when she ran off.

"Gee . . . I'll never learn that!"

A few days later we were unloading the dynamite at the roadstead outside Lisbon, and I was given the task of counting the wooden crates. All of me was afire. The reason was of course Katrin. Secretly, we had stolen a few interesting minutes up on deck, protected by the darkness, and had agreed to do the White City together. All she had to do was to try getting away from her parents.

As soon as the dynamite was off the ship and put onto barges, our ship was allowed to put in at the wharf. It was Sunday and the rest of the cargo could wait. A few cautious questions had supplied us with important advance information. You could take a bus out of the city to some not too remote beaches perfect for swimming. The knowledge had been forwarded to Katrin's parents. They were horrified at the thought of taking a bus in the sweltering heat. That was when I, Ingemar Johansson, came into the picture. Simple conclusive arithmetic proved to her parents that I was the most suitable escort.

After inspection, detailed instructions, and a few thoughtful ear pinches, courtesy of Bengtsson, we were able to walk down the gangway, continue across the quay, and then have Lisbon, Portugal, Europe, the World all to ourselves. I had entered the ship with checkered pants but was going ashore with the chief engineer's daughter.

The ecstasy of the shimmering afternoon was like a double-exposed photo. When Katrin laughed, I imagined the crew, lined up along the railing, staring at us as we disappeared side by side.

Under the influence of Ollie's liberal child-raising methods and my earlier rather parent-free condition, I was clearly on my way to becoming a rather boring type. I had nothing to rebel against. Ollie could have been the road to an interesting teenage life, but it was no fun sitting at her kitchen table drinking, swearing, and smoking.

With Katrin it was different. The beach and the swimming could wait. She pulled me along to the nearest pub, drank poison green cordial and chain-smoked while she animatedly asked me about my favorite places. She had a much more fun teenage life ahead of her than I. Katrin was really prepared to do everything, drink, swear, and perhaps even to go all the way to leave her childhood and its ironclad rules.

To my disappointment I understood that I would never be as

childish as my uncle. Of course he always returned home bare-assed since he had a mother who made him new pants. Being both mother and father to myself, I had become prematurely old. As gently as I could, I put forward my opinions to Katrin. I was not going to indulge in any sinful activities with her before we were married. We could instead acquire a few memories for our old age. For instance, it would be nice for our grandchildren to hear about the Jesus statue at the inlet to Lisbon's port. A Swedish connection existed, too. Jesus was made out of concrete from the Swedish city of Limhamn, which is why we sailors used the term "Limhamn Jesus" for him.

"Try to look at it like this," I suggested. "Three minutes ago, when you gulped down your fourth glass of cordial, I happened to notice Lisbon's most well known abductor of women. Sundays are their best days. That's when the girls tell their parents that they're going to church and instead hang around bars and drink sticky liquors. Right now you'd probably be chloroformed, had you not been with me. They do it with a tiny needle. When you wake up, you're already sold and delivered to a bordello in Tangier. It's lucky that I'm here with you. I can tell immediately if a person is honest or not."

"Oh no," said Katrin, spitting the liquor back into her glass. "Is that true?"

I was not drinking at all. I was so excited I wouldn't have been able to hold a glass. Quietly I suggested that we disappear through the exit in back. Katrin wondered how I knew that there was a back door.

"There's always one," I said. "But since every villain counts on it, we'll take the regular one."

Katrin was filled with admiration. It's the details that make all the difference between truth and lie. We agreed on a secret signal. If I wiggled my ears, she should just take my hand, look straight forward, and follow me.

I wiggled my ears, she took my hand obediently, and we went into the city to find the concrete Jesus. It took plenty of time. First we took a bus and then a ferry. But once there, while Jesus radiated peace toward us, the sun had fallen straight down and the red sky over the ocean had become a deep black.

"Why do you want to stand there and stare at something as silly as a statue?" Katrin asked.

"Because," I answered. "Because I know a guy who helped build it."

"How interesting!"

I heard the irony. Katrin was sulking and I was tired. I had no more to offer in the way of adventures. I suggested we go swimming.

We walked down to the beach. A boy our age offered to guard our clothes for a few escudos, and we waded in our underwear into the lukewarm water before it became too dark.

"How do we know he won't steal our clothes?" Katrin asked when she had swam out a bit.

I coughed, stopped, and remained standing on the bottom. Swimming has never been my strong point. As a sailor I rather believe in a quick death.

"But of course you could see right away if he was an honest person or not," Katrin said and kept on swimming.

I quickly splashed back and ran up to the beach. The clothes were gone.

"It was too dark," I explained to Katrin. "Hard to see."

"Should we spend the night?" Katrin asked. "We could bury ourselves in the sand. If you do that, you don't get cold."

"Then it would be as well if we didn't get up again."

"But if I help to bury you, there's nobody to bury me," Katrin said.

We did not manage to solve the problem. It's always like that. I want desperately to do my best, but something goes wrong.

We walked over to the ferry station and after a few hours of begging managed to get enough for the fare across. We returned to the ship toward midnight. We weren't cold at all. It was a warm night. And we did have fun. Our little mishap would be something to tell the grandchildren. But once aboard, all my dreams of the future were crushed. Katrin was snatched out of my hand. Her parents were worse than my made-up women abductors. However much I wiggled my ears, I didn't get Katrin's hand back in mine.

It was at this very moment that I became a real sailor.

"I know all about you sailors!" Katrin's mother screamed.

"You should," I said. "You're married to one."

The chief engineer promised to wring my neck, but Bengtsson saved the day by offering himself as neck wringer. He quickly pulled me astern and planted his enormous right hand in front of my nose while he delivered a sermon.

"You don't treat a girl from a good family that way. You're a sailor now. Better stick to your own."

Bengtsson did not need to hit me with his enormous fist. He still managed to nail the caste mark effectively to my forehead. I was another kind. And he promised to show me what kind that was. Unfortunately, a few days later, he insisted that my innocence needed some protection against the raw life of a sailor. A real Ollie. She used to tell everyone about the first time she met me when I lived alone in the apartment.

"Clean as a doll's house. Ingemar is a regular little housewife."

She nodded proudly. What she didn't know was that all along inside me boiled a desire to dirty everything, to clump around with muddy boots on expensive rugs, wipe sticky fingers on the tablecloth, and blow my nose in the curtains. I never had the strength to disappoint her, however.

And now I had Bengtsson on my back. He behaved like a father and in no time we became a fused-together couple through Lisbon, Valencia, Barcelona, and other ports on the map. The next thing I knew, I was sitting in a bordello in Casablanca, waiting for him.

I waited a long time for him in that run-down institution. There was a bar and a blackboard on the wall that factually announced the available possibilities and their prices. Women of every age, size, and color rubbed willingly against my legs. I thought of Elsa and her cucumbers. It was high time to do something about this. But, according to Bengtsson, I was not ready yet. He was still remembering my tears.

"You don't find such innocence every day. We'll sell you to the Arabs instead and make money."

Every time we came to Casablanca and went to a suitable sidewalk café, soon enough there would come a drooling old coot asking whether I was for sale. Bengtsson negotiated. I followed the geek into the first back alley, where Bengtsson stood ready to take me back.

Sometimes we would run into a bit of trouble, but mostly the sale was annulled quickly and quietly with Bengtsson keeping the money. He could be very persuasive, an ability located in his hard right fist. The success was then celebrated at the same old bordello every time.

Whenever I demanded my part of the profit, Bengtsson responded by pinching my earlobe. I had to be content drinking Coca-Cola and waiting for him. While I appreciated his warnings and hard pinches, it was no fun sitting totally sober in a bordello. The stench, the sweat, the misery, the monotonous jukebox music, and the eternal slurred questions about prices, positions, and variations tore any further thoughts I had about love out of my mind and heart.

So he drank and went to bordellos while I waited to lead him back aboard. At the end of one rambling nightly expedition, we ended up standing on the pier, gazing up at the ship's iron side that seemed to continue all the way up to the Spanish sky. We were in Cartagena. Katrin had long ago gone home with her mother, and I couldn't visualize her chief engineer father as the bearer of my one-syllable love letters. It was lonely in Cartagena. Bengtsson was drunk as a skunk. He was standing there pressing his weight against the side of the ship, undecided as to whether or not he would let me carry him up the gangway. He had perhaps noticed my depressed mood and decided to give me a treat. I don't know.

A sturdy wind was blowing in through the inlet toward the port straight against the outer side of our ship, which was anchored close to the quay. Bengtsson pointed to the limp mooring lines.

"Now we're going to move this heap of metal," said Bengtsson.

He asked me to put my back against the ship's side and apply all the pressure I could against it.

"More than six thousand tons," I said. "You can't move more than six thousand tons of metal."

"Oh yes. If you really want to."

Bengtsson's face turned an interesting shade of purple. The porcelain eye nearly popped out of the eye socket as he pressed his back against the hard metal. The ship slowly moved away from the quay! I don't know how long we stood there in the sweetly balmy night. Bengtsson was pressing and pressing against the ship while I was staring at the impossible undertaking. Finally he hung about a yard out over the edge of the quay, against the ship's side. Afraid of his falling in, I pulled him back.

"Thanks," he said and collapsed, panting heavily.

I had to almost carry him aboard.

All the while, he was urging me to help out with his mathematical calculations. We would soon be in Marseilles. He had a fiancée there, and it was time for him to settle down.

"I got money when I lost the eye. But the French keep changing things around. A zero here, a zero there."

"Tell me about the eye," I said.

"None of your business. See how much money's left. Madame Lajard and I thought of expanding. It takes capital, and she's getting impatient."

I leafed through his black accounting book. The pages were filled with remarkable equations.

"This'll take some time."

"Just concentrate."

"When will we be heading home?" I asked. "Home to Sweden?"

"It'll be a while. Haven't you heard? We're going to work charter for the French. Marseilles–Algiers. And then some vegetables from Casablanca so it will look honest and aboveboard."

"Aboveboard?"

"Yeah, aboveboard. Honest. We Swedes are honest folks. Aren't we?"

He was already stretching out on the berth. He had put his eye in a glass of water. I tiptoed out of the cabin. But just as I was closing the door, I heard his hoarse voice.

"Don't be sad. Get used to the fact that a sailor never goes home. Some try. But they're an unhappy lot."

I don't know how Bengtsson could guess that I was homesick. I went down to my cabin and threw myself on the lower berth. In the ship's innards, the auxiliary engine buzzed like a merry bumblebee. I existed in a no-man's-land. I was a sailor and consequently classified as some kind of ruffian with no morals. But judging from Bengtsson's hard pinches, I still passed as an innocent child who could be saved. Despite his example. If he were engaged to a Madame Lajard in Marseilles, why did he spend so much time with the other ladies?

But he was far from the only enigmatic person aboard. Right above me, on the upper berth, there was a seasoned and true sailor from the north of Sweden. He was seventeen years old and was already losing his hair. Every day he washed it carefully, hoping to make it thick and healthy. He was fixated on the idea of finding a miracle shampoo in each foreign port.

As for me, I was slowly discovering that paradise didn't exist. Not in Lisbon, not in Valencia or Barcelona. Casablanca, Tangier, and Ceuta were frightful holes. Savona, Genoa, and Naples were cold and harsh. Tile. Neon lights. Endless rain. Jukebox music and garishly painted, grotesquely grinning faces. Smoke and noise. All of us are trying to communicate something, but most of us don't know how. Sorrow and loneliness are so enormous they provoke loud voices, laughter, music, and boisterous joy.

Playing along on false strings requires a special kind of talent, one I did not have. Bengtsson was right about that. Still, I resolved to study the various possibilities of entertainment a bit further. Chances were I would one day become a seasoned man myself. I too would then acquire a girl in each and every port.

Bengtsson demanded reports about my proficiency when it came to washing socks, darning holes, and keeping my ears clean. In many areas, he was fulfilling a father's functions. In turn, I was able to help him with the problematic computations in the black book. Bengtsson had saved his money since shortly after the Second World War. He did not tell me where he kept it. But he had realized that it had undergone a huge devaluation, and that the French since 1959 had reduced their bills by one zero. The question in his mind was — how much was left? Bengtsson was only familiar with plus and minus. To deal with percentages and unknown factors was outside his ability. I was the first one he trusted enough to let look in the black book.

Bengtsson had spent more than twenty years of his life calculating back and forth on its pages. He had manipulated zeros and decimal points so many times that it took me weeks to untangle the mess and find the original figures. Finally the facts stared me in the face: Bengtsson was a multimillionaire in worthless French paper money. It wouldn't even buy a bus ticket along La Canebiere in Marseilles.

I could have cold-bloodedly looked into his porcelain eye and told him the naked truth. Instead I helped him save money. I had a vested interest in guarding his funds with such zeal. I very much wanted to become a member of the family from the moment I had laid eyes on Madame Lajard's daughter.

The first time we arrived in Marseilles, I had long since figured out that Bengtsson's French money was worthless. But he invited anyone in the sternward crew who wanted to come along to Madame Lajard's. She picked us up in her small Fiat.

Driving along a winding road through the black area of the city, we finally arrived at her bar. Despite its seedy looks it seemed to be a cozy place. Nobody wanted to leave. That was the house in which Bengtsson planned to spend his old age. If anyone had tried painting the warped walls, they would probably have crumbled at the touch of the brush.

The bar itself was just a few sizes larger than the Fiat. At the furthest wall hung a curtain with indescribable intertwined flowers. That piece of cotton separated the bar from a sleeping alcove with an iron bed where Madame Lajard and her daughter slept.

The daughter's name was Julie.

Madame herself was the sort of woman who seemed to know how to behave at all times. Julie was not Katrin's one hundred and four pounds of Swedish standard weight but a well-rounded one hundred and forty pounds of Mediterranean dynamite, polished with olive oil and honed by the whistling mistral.

I was beginning to understand why Madame Lajard wanted to know about Bengtsson's financial status.

The bar was so crowded that the supporting beams on the sidewalk shook from the effort of holding the wall in place. But the day Julie took off with some bloke, the rickety building would empty out. No sane person would seek the way to Madame Lajard's shack, were it not for her daughter.

As for me, I began to think of cucumbers right away.

Bengtsson introduced me. Unfortunately I dared not move away from the gimcrack bar. I had to press my lower body as hard as possible against the planks. Julie came over and smiled. We could not speak with each other. As do all French citizens, she nourished the opinion that there existed no other real language in the world than the French one. It didn't matter. We did not need to speak to each other. It was obvious that she was immensely intelligent and had a terrific sense of humor.

And I was undeservedly lucky.

When Madame Lajard finally threw out the customers, Bengtsson asked me to stay. It would be risky for any one person to go back to the ship alone. While the dangers of the city were discussed in Bengtsson's remarkable Mediterranean language, Julie wiped the bar with long, sweeping movements. Everything she did was miraculous. Had it been up to me, I could have sat there for hours, watching her tidy up the place.

It was decided that I should stay. Madame Lajard and Bengtsson retired to the alcove behind the curtain, leaving Julie and me with each other. The jukebox sparkled suddenly, and Julie selected a record. Edith Piaf sang about something that probably had to do with love. Soon a faint rhythmic squeak, emanating from the iron bed, meandered all over her melancholy voice and made the room cheerier.

I regretted not being French. I could picture a Frenchman with an elegant gesture and a relaxed joke leading Julie out onto the floor in a passionate tango. As usual, I was unable to move a limb. But Julie came over and lifted me up into her arms. A ball of soft clay, I was born to be shaped to her challenging body. We rocked to and fro. The available floor space was no more than a few square yards. Behind the curtain Madame Lajard moaned. The iron bed squeaked. Edith Piaf sang. I tried to think of root canal work without Novocain, outdoor bathing in winter, and the dog Laika who once upon a time rotated in a space capsule and died. I thought of the Ingemar Johansson who had been beaten by Floyd Patterson and of more and deeper root canals. Nothing helped.

I have read of men who dribble their sperms a little everywhere. Such things happen and, according to books written by experts, are nothing to be ashamed of. I agree with that.

I thanked her as discreetly as I could and waddled over to the nearest chair in a dark corner.

I later got used to dancing with Julie and was able to control myself.

We sailed between the five ports — Marseilles, Algiers, Ceuta, Tangier, and Casablanca — just like a regular bus service. A set schedule. Quick loading and unloading. No hesitation. Every now and then schedules were upset or distorted. Human beings or machines broke. Bengtsson had his rhythm and I had mine. After a few quick hours in Marseilles and the nearly two-day-long trip to Algiers, he felt it was time for me to get him a bottle of wine. The port was fenced off with heavy barbed wire and sandbags. We unloaded our machine parts. A few crew members insisted that those were weapons for the French Army, but most did not care one way or another. Personally, I was mainly worried about the many inspections along my way as I was getting Bengtsson his bottle of wine.

I was worried about Bengtsson's economy but could never bring myself to tell him the hard truth about his lost fortune. Anyhow, he was intensely involved with other things. Madame Lajard took her time, the whores in Casablanca took theirs, and in between he needed a rest. He taught me no more about women. I practiced with total concentration on Julie what little information he had imparted.

While Madame Lajard and Bengtsson made love on the shaky iron bed behind the curtain, Julie and I danced to old records. As time went on, we learned to exchange a word here and there. I wondered who her father was. It could not be Bengtsson, who didn't have one good word to say about her.

"As soon as that whorish kid gets married, we'll close shop and renovate the house. But we'll keep the jukebox. It's nice to have music."

After those words I was not sure that I liked Bengtsson anymore. But he was my passport to visiting Madame Lajard.

When we came back down to the harbor, I used to practice moving the ship away from the quay, just using my hands. It was hard. But occasionally I had a feeling that it did move.

It was after such an exercise that I found my cabin mate in a sorry state. The sailor from the north of Sweden had shaved his head. It was ineptly and sloppily done. Blood dripped from his face and neck. If he had no hair, he said, it couldn't fall out. We discussed the pros and cons of the method for a while. I had read that natural baldness was a sign of intelligence. The brain is able to grow larger since all the hair that is to grow out is being stored in the skull, like a ball of yarn. When the supply runs out and there is no more to grow, there is more brain space.

I was joking of course.

The sailor was in no mood for my philosophical nonsense. He ran off with the idea of throwing himself overboard. Several of us were able to subdue him.

He was sent home. We got a Dane in his place. He was one year older than I, a strong, flaxen-haired type with a handsome and thoroughly false face. All he had to do was stick his head out of a porthole to make the whole quay look like a rallying point for lovesick idiots. Of both sexes. But he never seemed to notice anything. The crew had told me in various details about the Mediterraneans' attitude about affairs of love. Everyone talked about their sexual freedom. As long as each one kept within their own territory. The warnings were clear and written in stone — it was important not to stick your ass out in North African ports. Even Bengtsson with his porcelain eye and iron fists would now and then sniff the air like a frightened dog. Love between men lay threateningly and obvious all around us.

I had heard so many tales about the North African ports that I often jumped high in the air in pure terror as soon as I saw more than two Arabs at the same time. There were excellent reasons to stay close to Bengtsson's enormous fists.

The Dane on the other hand seemed to sail on a totally different ocean. He felt that the two of us should go out and find our own adventures. He had already accompanied us to Madame Lajard and met Julie when he suggested that we find some fun of our own elsewhere. If I entertained any hope of conquering Julie, it was time for a little on-the-job training.

I did not require a lot of convincing.

We snuck ashore in Algiers and wove through the barricades in the harbor. If the general situation in Algeria was tense, it nonetheless appeared to be under control.

We arrived at a bar. The Dane ordered some beer and we began discussing the evening's strategy. That took considerable time. We kept on drinking beer. The evening passed in tingling anticipation.

When it was time for the next move, we became painfully aware of our ignorance. We knew of no good addresses. We agreed to ask some guys next to us at the bar. They were dressed in civilian clothes. But their crew cuts and shaved necks were as telling as field uniforms. Nice guys. Probably officers, since they were allowed to be out of uniform. We struggled through with sign language and the most essential words from our meager vocabulary. Soon a brotherhood sprang up between us and the three Frenchmen who, as luck would have it, shared our exact intentions.

More beer was ordered. Glasses were raised. Laughter floated in the air and everything was perfectly clear. I suppose I was the only one who was nervous. To become a seasoned sailor was a major turning point in one's life, after all.

A little later we drove through the city in the Frenchmen's car. Algiers is not a large city. You could miss most of it if you are full of beer and dozing off. Large parts of the city were in darkness. We laughed and toasted each other. The three French guys tried doggedly to teach us a children's song. But that was hopeless. The Dane sat in the back with two of the guys and I sat up front beside the driver. That was my good luck — and rotten luck for the Dane. When the car stopped with screeching brakes, he cried out that we should run. But it was too late.

The two in the back dragged the kicking Dane across the sand. Through the side window of the car I could see the ocean and the black horizon. I sat as motionless as my buddy in the front seat wanted me to. The machine gun between his hands was no joke. He grinned and pushed me out. I fell and crawled under the car. From above me I heard the Frenchman's clucking laughter. I understood him. Trying to hide underneath the car was futile. As soon as they were through with the Dane, I was next on their agenda. Could I possibly bury myself in the sand?

I had to face this whole situation soberly. I was stuck, I was unbelievably and unforgivably stupid, and I would never again in my life associate with Danes.

I crawled out from under the car.

The kind of love the soldier intended to force upon me was giving me cold sweat. I fabricated a huge smile for him. He put the machine gun on the hood of the car, and we walked into the black night.

As soon as we were out of the cones of light created by the car's headlights, I started to run in a wide circle to lure him as far as possible away from the car in order for me to get back to it first.

It worked. But the machine gun was no longer on the hood.

Had it fallen off?

I clawed frantically in the sand for the bluish weapon. I can see every detail of that night in front of me with horrible clarity. It's like a dance macabre.

A hand grabs hold of my leg. The Dane stands a small distance away. The car's headlights illuminate his face, swollen from crying. The machine gun doesn't sound real. Just a faint pop. The soldier who had pulled at my leg stares in frozen astonishment toward his stomach area and falls headlong into the sand. The other two come rushing forward with crooked smiles and outstretched hands. The Dane whirls around. It looks as if the two soldiers had been slashed right through the middle. They fold up and fall. I crawl forward and reach into the car. When the headlights go off, we are able for a moment to believe that nothing at all has happened.

The Dane's sobs sounded as if his lungs were trying to force their way out through his mouth. Slowly, everything fell silent. Both of us were waiting for some kind of reaction from somewhere. For us the last few seconds had been hours of noise and roar.

Nobody arrived. The beach remained quiet and empty. The Mediterranean kept heaving, as indifferent as before. And the Dane did exactly what I did. We crawled on the ground and touched the three soldiers. They were dead. We began to giggle hysterically at our impulse to crawl, as if the ground itself would split open if we stood up. Finally we sat there, leaning against the car. What should we do?

Having talked it over for a while, we arrived at our conclusion.

We would bury the three corpses in the sand and drive the car to Algiers. If we left the bodies where they were, questions would be asked quicker and somebody might recall seeing us together in the bar. The Dane's flaxen bangs were not easy to forget. Neither one of us had any desire to explain matters to the French military police. We had had more than our fill of French soldiers.

The trunk space in the car was filled to the brim with equipment. Weapons, boxes with explosives and wires — things that any comic book–reading child would recognize even in faint moonlight. Among the tools, we picked out a collapsible spade.

The Dane got the shivers. He shook like a leaf and did not want to dig. He finally came over to the pit and we both started digging.

After a little more than an hour, the surface of the beach was as smooth as before. We started back. I drove. Ollie's black Dodge used to have a magical attraction for me. She would let me drive, as long as I drove the car at home in the yard. That training came in handy now.

We parked the car in a dark alley and found our way down to the harbor. I'll never understand how the Dane managed to get the machine gun aboard the ship. We sat and worked with it in our cabin, taking it apart with complete concentration. Neither one of us was ready to admit what was going on inside us, but we were both terrified and had trouble sleeping.

During the night, the Dane was sobbing loudly in his upper berth.

I decided to forget the whole event. If Bengtsson could concentrate hard enough to see with an artificial eye, I ought to be able to erase what had happened.

It worked rather well. The problem was the Dane. He had far bigger a problem than I. On the way down to Casablanca, he drank more and more and wanted to jump overboard. It's no easy task to speak seriously about life with a Dane, but I tried as best I could. He kept on crying, declaring that he no longer believed in life. As I was consoling him, I soon began to sound like my confirmation pastor back in Småland. Centuries of hollow clichés popped into my head, as if they had always been there, waiting for the fitting occasion.

I finally managed to put him to bed.

He was crying and I kept holding his hand.

While I thought he would be grateful to me, to my astonishment, he arose the next day out of his berth like a demonic killer. It was my scalp he was after. He hated me. I had witnessed his fear and his humiliation. He could not stand that.

In Casablanca we waited in the roadstead to get to the quay. Again the Dane loaded himself up with beer, following my every move with black glances. After a few hours he was so heated and unstrung that he grabbed the first weapon he saw and started chasing me all around the ship. We had happened to stand in the mess room so he grabbed a bread knife.

"Help!" I cried, running for my life.

On the bridge stood Hawk smelling of breath mints and after-shave. I ran right past him and out on the other bridge wing with the Dane in close pursuit. You get the strangest impulses when you run for your life. It wasn't until I ran down to the deck again that it hit me that Hawk probably had reasons for smelling deliciously all the time. I turned, running up again to check it out. I was right. The cloud of after-shave and mint also contained a faint smell of alcohol. Oh well, he had been nice and had taught me to navigate. What a pity that I would never be a third, second, or first mate myself. Meanwhile, the Dane was gaining on me. He was both broader and taller than I. The tip of the bread knife tickled the back of my neck. It was at that precise moment that I swore never again to save anyone insisting on jumping overboard. That was it for me and brotherly love.

The weirdest thing of all was that the crew seemed to take the Dane chasing after me with a knife high in the air as some kind of entertainment. I had to save myself as best I could.

In the end, Bengtsson intervened. Putting himself right in front of the Dane, he stared him down with his porcelain eye. The whole thing was cleared up for the moment. The Dane promised to stop drinking beer. One more knife fight and he would be put ashore.

But I was left sharing the cabin with him and having to spend the nights with him on the upper berth. Mostly I lay awake, waiting for the Dane to jump down and strangle me.

After a series of tense and sleepless nights, the Dane finally asked for forgiveness and we became friends again. As time and the ship went on, the episode with the three French soldiers paled. We never spoke of it. Now the Dane wanted to come along with me and the bosun to Madame Lajard's place.

Blond and handsome as he was, I had early on felt that he couldn't be trusted. He made both women's and men's heads turn. And he had a blind spot in the middle of his skull. Once he got hold of an idea, he could neither hear nor see.

My love for Julie had manifested itself in a few quick touches. But most of the time I sat dreaming by the jukebox, waiting for the bar to close, the customers to be thrown out, and Madame Lajard and Bengtsson to retire. I had become used to this routine and had gotten into the habit of nodding off in order to have strength later for what might develop. The truth was that I only slept a few hours each night and welcomed that short catch-up nap. My salary was the lowest aboard and my hours of overtime were the highest in number. About an average of fourteen hours most days. This said, it was a mistake, I know, to fall asleep in front of Julie.

That evening, I woke up as usual. The bar was closed. Madame Lajard and Bengtsson had already retired behind the curtain. The jukebox was glimmering and the loud sound of music covered the creaking of the iron bed as well as Madame Lajard's cooing and moaning. Julie, meanwhile, was nowhere to be seen. I was debating at the bar on what to drink to restore my vitality.

I then heard noise coming through the open window. The shutters were closed. Peering out through the slitted openings between the slats, I spotted Julie lying across one of the rough beams that supported the building. The Dane was standing behind her.

Stumbling out alone over railroad tracks and past dark shacks, I was making my way back to the ship. Bengtsson could use the Dane as guide and support if he wanted. And sure enough, at dawn they arrived unsteadily, arm in arm, singing. I took the machine gun and let it fall between the ship and the edge of the quay. Hearing the splash, the two of them hobbled over to the edge to look down.

Bengtsson, taking an unsteady step, tilted his head far back in order to be able to see me.

"Right. You're learning. But you're slow."

The Dane confided much later that he had paid Julie. But I understood that because I had witnessed the Dane's humiliation, he wanted to see mine. And not just this time, but again and again. Julie would not be enough. I waited, refusing to go ashore, even with Bengtsson.

"You're poor," I told Bengtsson. "You might as well burn those pieces of paper."

"I know that," he answered. "I just wanted to teach you a little math. It'll come in handy."

Here I had spent many and fruitless hours going through the figures in his black book and all he had in mind was to teach me math. I no longer understood people. How many kinds did actually exist in the world?

The fate of the Dane was turning sad. He became wilder and wilder. He could not erase from his mind as easily as I our Algerian episode. He continued to chase me with knives, iron bars, or what other loose object he could find. It was tiring. So much so that one evening I stopped and just stood there, offering him my throat. Swinging the knife he slashed my pullover. Discovering that there was a human being beneath so stunned him he lost his balance, dropped the knife, and disappeared.

That same evening — we were in Marseilles — we heard a tremendous bang against the ship's outer side. Along with the rest of the crew, I ran up on deck and peered out over the deserted quay. What had happened? The only one who could not be found was the Dane. After a while we grew tired of speculation and returned to our berths.

Morning arrived with some commotion on the quay. A forklift had disappeared during the night. We stared at the distance between the quay and the ship. Not more than half a yard, and yet the forklift and the Dane had managed to fall through it. Only I understood what he had attempted to do. While I kept struggling trying to move the ship Bengtsson's way, by concentrating my own strength, he had to get some help. Cheating as usual. A diver confirmed the suspicions and brought up the Dane, from whose long, blond hair Bengtsson picked off some slimy seaweed. The consulate negotiated for transportation home. A few plastic bags were wrapped around him and the Dane was put in cold storage.

Of all places on this earth, I signed off the ship in the small town of Köping, Sweden. We arrived with desert sand, wriggled into the sweet water of the lake Mälaren through the sluice in Södertälje, and ended up smack in the middle of Sweden. Nobody found that especially remarkable. I was the only one who had not yet learned my lesson.

Boatswain Bengtsson stood by the railing and waved good luck. I would need it. The mess boy and I had bought a few turtle babies in Casablanca. They were hid under my sweater and chafed against my stomach as I was squirming through a hole in the fence to avoid going through customs. That hole had been made by others smuggling alcohol and cigarettes.

Just a few yards on the other side of the hole the customs officers drove up in their black car. Starting to run, I stumbled and fell on my stomach. The customs officers looked pleased. They had finally caught a live one. I pulled out the flattened turtles from under my sweater. Disappointed, the customs officers drove off. They would have a funny story to tell. It's not every day somebody tries to smuggle in something that is perfectly legal to bring into the country.

Bengtsson was still standing by the railing, looking at me as I was throwing the dead turtles in a ditch, and walked away. I decided there would be no more ships and no more sea for me, not ever. It took me seven years to live up to that decision. There have been many times since then when I thought of Bengtsson, trying to re-create his ability to concentrate.

SWEDEN
1976

I drive from Marseilles to Sweden through the affluence of Europe in amazement. What I had taken for granted before my stay in Algiers now appears abnormal. I look upon the isolated opulence of Sweden with shame and even guilt.

While the pictures of my teens fade, bit by bit, they have helped me understand how much I have missed my father and how often I had been trying to find him in other older men. Now, after the breakup with Louise, I am on my way home to my son. What am I going to do for him?

A year ago, Jonas and I had gone fishing together. We had collected enough worms and were walking along the pebbly lane. I was ahead, carrying the thick end of the fishing rod of bamboo. Jonas was following, holding on to the thin end. I would sneak a look back at Jonas's damp and expectant face.

I was aware of looking at my own childhood in his questioning eyes. Combined with my memories, he was now an evaluating center that was weighing me down with guilt. Was his future being destroyed by his parents' selfish and unreasonable demands?

He was looking at me as I once had looked at my father, and I found it difficult to sustain.

Anyway, that was the beginning of the end between Louise and me. After that we just tried to live on, as if we were still a family, as if we were able to forget; trying to be adults. For the sake of Jonas.

The week after our violent argument, we manage to create a miracle of harmony. My mother-in-law tends to my needs.

Jonas is unusually quiet while his parents busy themselves with illogical mental exercises. Now and then he asks if we can go fishing.

Louise is busy carrying on long and agitated telephone conversations with her girlfriends. As usual she questions why all the professors at the university are men who do not approve her new and fantastic combinations of subjects and wonders when a divorce is most suitable, taking the age of a child into consideration.

The whole point of her telephone monologues is of course to show the importance of her life compared to mine.

In order to have access to an available telephone line, I register at a hotel where, along with a few other researchers, I set up an opposition camp. We act as a sort of support group behind the union in the usual game play between labor and management. An economist with party book in his pocket turns out to be a real nice guy. The world consists simply of "we" and "they" to him.

While the economist insists that everything can be looked upon objectively, we live well. All I have to do is sign my name and I have both a hotel room and a per diem. My uncle comes over one day and asks how things are going.

I never thought my uncle would pose that question. I am able to calm him.

"People will always want to drink from exquisite crystal, right?"

"I mean with you. How are things going with you?"

My uncle has to leave without an answer. I don't know how things are going with me.

Fall rushes like a train right into our black winter. Jonas and Louise return to Stockholm. We are commuting as usual. But the chaos is not comfortable. To escape I try falling in love with a waitress at the hotel. But it doesn't work. I have neither the conviction nor the ability to concentrate. The economist enters the stage and comes up the winner. He perhaps asked her to come to his room and look at his party book?

There are moments when I feel desperate and wish I could return to the sea. But how can I do that when the country no longer has a merchant marine? Besides I need glasses nowadays. It's no good. I will never learn to see like old boatswain Bengtsson. I wonder if he ended his days in Marseilles?

My day looks as if it needed the whole week. Everything is normal. A meeting with Axel in Stockholm is set up. This is our first meeting after the business with Louise. I have spent great energy to avoid seeing him, but now it is unavoidable. With a faint smile, I drag myself through the familiar old corridors, while acquaintances hug each other, turn away, or just hurry past.

As expected, Axel could not have been friendlier. And I have no double-barreled shotgun along. We converse as if nothing at all had happened and get right down to the business at hand.

Louise has had an offer to write about the male versus the female world of imagery in some kind of oasis in Algeria.

Axel is good at convincing people. He has no trouble selling a bewildered student on the idea of doing a three-unit essay on the practical problems of shoe brushing for left-handed individuals.

I nod. And understand that Louise has swallowed it all tooth and nail. How does he see my future?

We are getting there.

"I have a feeling that you have isolated yourself," Axel says, sounding like a concerned and troubled physician.

Obviously Axel has been contaminated by the modern catchwords. I play along.

"I feel the same way."

"Good."

"My father-in-law is going to buy that advertising sign in the center of Stockholm," I say. "Isn't it weird? He'll probably use it to urge the Swedish people to vote conservatively. That's his dream. Isn't he strange? An impossible man to understand. What does he get out of it?"

"You're always full of little anecdotes," Axel says, a discontented wrinkle in his forehead. "I read your proposed contribution to our next conference. It has no more meat in it than what you said right now. Why don't you grow up?"

Axel is obviously fixated on the image of me as an immature child. In order not to disappoint him, I jump him and try to strangle him. If he insists on playing the part of my father, he has to take the consequences.

He is surprisingly strong. We tumble around among piles of papers that illuminate the thoughts of the Swedish people with merciless academic astuteness. It is embarrassing and improperly intimate to fight the man who has been like a father to me during a few dizzying years of hunger for knowledge. And who has had the bad taste to be seduced by my wife. I keep hitting him as best I can but get as much of a thrashing back. Rumors travel like wildfire within the walls of the university. Before we are through with each other, the corridor is filled with people. Somebody has opened the door to get a better view. But nobody tries to stop the fight.

When we have had enough and go to wash up, I have managed to split Axel's upper lip. He might need stitches. On the left side of my face, he has given me a throbbing black eye. We push our way back through to Axel's office. He closes the door firmly.

"We have work to do."

We clean up the office in silence. I am already behind schedule in my day and feel nauseous when Axel suggests we both take the day off. Nobody is even going to notice our absence, he insists.

The fight seems to have put him in an excellent mood. For quite some time he has wanted to go and take a look at the French Impressionists. I must have read about the exhibition? If we go right now before lunch, we don't have to deal with big crowds.

Silently and staring stubbornly at the ground, I accompany Axel. In the museum's echoing hall we are the first visitors. I can only see with my right eye. Axel grabs a light hold of my arm and guides me to a small painting that from afar looks to be the least interesting of the lot. It is murky and dark and not at all what you would expect from the French Impressionists.

"I'm going to show you something."

I look at the painting and read: "Claude Monet. *Coin d'appartement, 1875.*"

"Yes?"

What does he want?

"Tell me what you see."

It's part of Axel's pedagogic splendidness never to mention his own conclusions. He is of the opinion that a continuous dialogue is the goal.

"A boy," I say. "He stands a small distance inside the door with . . . is it climbing plants or drapes? There is a woman dressed in black. . . . I didn't know you were teaching art history too."

Axel sighs and picks at the scab on his swollen lip. It gives me pleasure to note that his speech is slurred.

"I don't wish you ill. You take care of that very well yourself. Perhaps you aren't any more than what you usually reduce yourself to be — an emotional idiot, caught in your own pain. You'll never see other people or the rest of the world if you don't make an effort."

"Thanks, Dad," I said. "That was nicely put. Really decent of you to fuck my wife, too."

Axel shakes me. His voice echoes in the empty exhibition hall.

"Louise wanted you. She wanted you as a man. Not as a small boy who never dares step out of that goddamned door. For a moment she needed someone who could see her. It happened to be me. Think about it. I have to go."

He is in a rage and storms out through the swinging glass doors, leaving me to do exactly as he bade me. I stand in front of the painting and think. Unfortunately I can't think of anything impressively intelligent. Other people seem capable of spouting judgments and opinions the moment they see a splash of oil on a canvas. It has the opposite effect on me.

All of a sudden, I feel Louise rustling by my side. Axel had dragged me here by order of Louise. She had obviously just accompanied

Jonas to Småland and turned right back around. Wasn't that decent of Axel? Such a helpful type. First he helps Louise, then me, and now both of us.

"Do you see it?" Louise asks. "The oil lamp there in the darkness? It's placed at the exact same point as the woman's clitoris. And the clinging vines cover the hard doorjambs. And far inside sits the most dangerous one of them all. Mommy. Monet probably didn't know what he did. Perhaps he himself never became more than a boy who never took that step outside. Otherwise why would he paint so many women? Look around. Women and children. Idyllic outdoor scenes. But they are being observed. Perhaps by that little boy who never became a man. We were here last Sunday, Axel and I. I thought that you and I could talk to each other?"

Louise is rather amusing at times. She ought to be a comic book. Perhaps both of us belong in one?

"Jonas?" I ask.

"With my mother."

"OK then. Go ahead and talk."

With sadness and logic, Louise suggests a trial separation. She speaks of Africa and describes Algeria as if I had never been there. I let her ramble on. I should settle down in Småland, she says, and become a father.

We were extremely reasonable and I am still nauseous from it.

It's early afternoon, and we walk, arm in arm like an old retired couple, home to the apartment. When all is over for a couple, there are still plenty of details to see to.

We go to bed early and undress quickly, like a couple of siblings competing to see who gets into bed first. I negotiate a bit of love-making for old times' sake. It is as if I wanted to drag her out into my own white desert.

During the night I awaken with the same piercing stomachache as once before. I scream and hit my head against the wall. In some strange way, it helps the stomach pain if I create pain elsewhere. Louise is bewildered. I refuse to go to the hospital. They might put me straight into surgery.

I have always wanted to meet our neighbors on the same floor. Now I do. Only a few years ago, Clara Larsson was our country's foremost porno film star. Then all of a sudden she disappeared. Many speculated that she may have taken the big step across Øresund and fused with the jolly porno gang in Denmark. But in fact, there she is, reborn as an adult student, wife of a doctor, and next-door neighbor to us. Her husband is friendly and firm. She herself is lithe and strong as a female hunter in the field. I haven't a chance. There are four of them, wrapping me in blankets and carrying me to the elevator. Clara Larsson is unresponsive to my questions having to do with how a porno movie is made.

"Perhaps I could give you a call sometime?"

"You do that," she says.

"What's your number?"

"It's unlisted."

Her husband is a doctor. As such he has seen everything and he understands. He brings out his car. They stow me away inside and unload me at Emergency.

With a choked voice and shivering with cramps, I maintain firmly that I am perfectly healthy. Clara Larsson walks off. She has done her bit. Louise confers with the doctors and, finally, I am left lying there, all alone.

"I'm not in pain," I say. "I mean, it was when I was a kid that I had this pain. You mustn't cut into me. Promise!"

"We promise," says a man of my own age, nodding.

I shiver. What if he thinks of Clara Larsson instead of me when he puts the knife to me. But strangely enough, he keeps his promise. Sometime toward dawn, the pains fade away. We agree that I should stay for observation.

"But not on this floor," says yet another doctor. "Guess which one?"

He reads my chart and continues, "You may walk on your own. Then we'll bring you down and take a little look inside you. We'll make a complete inventory before we even think of cutting. OK?"

I am the man they must not make holes in. I wander off, completely beside myself with happiness, to the floor for the insane.

The psychologist has wonderfully brown eyes and looks like Rita Hayworth. We establish perfect rapport right away, and I decide to stay for good. She thinks it is every human being's duty to understand herself or himself. Sometimes I believe what she says.

I never take any of the medicine, however. I get the pills from the nurse and stuff them into the end post of the iron bed, having unscrewed the small plastic lid. After a day or so, I have to pour water into the post for the pills to dissolve and make room for new ones. One night a strange hissing sound awakens me and I discover that the bed has tipped over. The hollow iron leg has eroded away. In spite of my repeated statements that I am certifiably mad, I stand accused of vandalizing county property when the damage is discovered. Nobody considers what could have happened inside me had I swallowed the medicine. But things could be worse. I have a voluntary nervous breakdown and can decide by myself when to go home.

And when Louise sends a telegram, asking me to come and see her, I throw myself into the Volvo and turn its nose toward Algeria. As if I had not learned one single thing. That was the beginning of the story. Or the end.

But I believe the nonstop drive through Europe is the end. I gain a new understanding of Sweden, where everything is clean, quiet, and, most of all, empty. Black fields with spots of spring snow. Pine forests stretching toward the iron sky. No visible human beings in the village I drive through. The windows in the Pentecostal revival church are illuminated. A lone caretaker sweeps the stairs. There is probably a prayer meeting inside. The railroad station is silent and dark. It has been turned into an emigrant museum. Two refugees from Chile stand beside the hot dog stand. Dressed in thick, padded overalls, they can hardly move. We nod to each other and chew on our hot dogs. They smile warily, and I get on the road again. It's as lonely as in the Sahara. Until a small boy walks along, happily swinging his schoolbag with books. His future erases the desolation.

I am home and yet not at home. The oil company has removed the gas pump in front of my father-in-law's place. People prefer to drive forty miles to a larger town to buy gas.

I am disappointed that Jonas is not at home. He is visiting my uncle. I am uncertain whether or not I should join him there. But when the kitchen clock has ticked loud and long enough between each word my in-laws and I find to say to each other, I decide to walk over to my uncle's house. It's cold and black outside. Light spills out from the houses, revealing dirty snowdrifts.

My maternal grandmother had one of those glass balls with a motif from Rio de Janeiro inside. The ball was the size of a fist, and when turned upside down it was snowing over Rio de Janeiro. Grandma was always wondering if it really did snow in Rio de Janeiro. Once I offered to investigate the matter for her. She looked at me, and her eyes were disapproving and astonished.

"It's more fun not to know."

That's what she said.

I think of her words as I am standing outside my uncle's house, looking through the window straight into the kitchen. My uncle is a wonderful, fun person. My son, Jonas, sits in front of him at the kitchen table. He is trying hard to concentrate. I don't have to guess what he is doing. He is trying to wiggle his ears. One day I will tell him the story of how I ended up in this part of the country. I have to tell about the past in order to break out of it. I know exactly how I will begin:

The snowflakes had a hypnotic effect on me. I was getting more and more drowsy, but I needed to keep my eyes open. What if I missed my station and got off at the wrong one, rushed out into the white arctic tundra, totally dazed, only to be met by wolves who were ready to tear me to pieces! Now, that would be unforgivable and unworthy of a true Trapper.

(From *My Life as a Dog*)